Out of the Dark
Book One

By
USA Today & Bestselling British Horror Author

Claire C. Riley

Out of the Dark
Book One

Copyright © 2016

Written by Claire C. Riley
Edited by Amy Jackson Editing
Cover Design by Eli Constant of Wilde Book Designs

This book is licensed for your personal enjoyment only. This book may not be re-sold or given away to other people. If you would like to share this book with another person, please purchase an additional copy for each reader. If you're reading this book and did not purchase it, or it was not purchased for your use only, then please return and purchase your own copy.

This is a work of fiction. Names, characters, businesses, places, events, and incidents are either the products of the author's imagination or used in a fictitious manner. Any resemblance to actual persons, living or dead, or actual events is purely coincidental.

Thank you for respecting the hard work of the author, she thinks that you are totally badass for purchasing this from a reputable place and not stealing it!

Out of the Dark Synopsis.

We are temporary. Finite.
The choices we've made, the people we have loved. Who we used to be no longer matters. Because now it is all about the ending. And the ending always comes too soon.

There's fear in the dark. And behind every drop of light, the shadows creep and the darkness comes in the form of clawing, red-eyed monsters. They hunt us—stalk us…they are desperate to destroy us.

But I have a reason to fight the darkness and everything in it. A small glimpse of light that lives within my golden-haired daughter, Lilly. She is my strength. She is my everything.

Every life is an untold story, each scene unfolding until the final act. But our ending has yet to be written, and I will continue to protect us, until I cannot.

Dedication.

For my daughters, know this…
You are my hope when it seems there is none.
You are the light when the world seems bleak.
You are everything, when it feels that there is nothing.
I will always love you.
I will always fight for you.
I will always suffer for you.
And I will always be with you, even when you can not see me.

Love Mummy x

Out of the Dark

Book one

By
*USA T*oday and Bestselling British Horror Writer

Claire C. Riley

Chapter One.

#1 Appreciate what you have.

There are times when I wish for the old days. For bills, and jobs, and too much TV. For fast food, sports cars, and thoughts about the ozone layer and how we can repair it.

Now we know that there was never any way to repair it. That it didn't matter how high your cholesterol was in the end, because you were always destined to die a slow and agonizing death. Or maybe you would be one of the lucky ones, maybe you would go quickly. Regardless, you would still die and you wouldn't be around to see the ice caps melt.

So what would I say if I could go back in time and speak to the old me? Or even the old you?

I'd say this: Get fat—eat the food you love, because soon enough it will be gone. Love freely, but trust no one. Always hate with regret, because hate is such a waste. Drive fast, but be mindful of others on the road because one day, in the not-so-distant future, you might need one of those people that you overtake and undercut, to save you.

I would tell you not to waste too much of your time pondering what to do with your life, and just enjoy the here and now as much as you can. Because before you know it, it will all be much too late. Doctor, lawyer, farmer, computer technician, police officer, delivery driver—in this world that I now live in, none of that matters. Who you *were* isn't important anymore; it's who you *are* that now holds the greatest significance. And most of us, those that are still alive, are not good people at all.

I look out across the calm ocean with a sigh. The waves gently caressing the pebbled beach remind me of happier times, when I would go crabbing with my mother and father. I never killed those little crabs; I just liked to catch them and watch them scuttle around in my blue plastic bucket. Perhaps that was a hint as to the sort of woman I would become.

"Mama?"

I turn to look at Lilly through the cracked windshield of the car and offer her a small smile. Her little hands, as usual, are clasping her dirty brown teddy bear with all their might. Her wide brown eyes stare back at me in confusion until at last recognition flickers across her face and she seems satisfied with who I am, and that I am not far from her side. She knows that in this bleak world, I am all that she has left. Just me and her teddy bear.

She closes those brown pools of innocence again and snuggles back down into her car seat, a thumb pushing between her rosebud lips to help soothe her. She should know by now that I am never far from her side. She is mine, and I am hers. It has been this way since we found each other in flowers and light. I will never leave her—not until I have to.

I slide off the hood of my car, my jeans making a

strange screech and scratch sound on the dented red metal. I take one last drag of my cigarette and stub it out into the dusty ground with a shake of my head. I swore I'd never smoke again. That's another thing to add to the list: if you want to smoke, do it. But be aware that when they run out—the cigarettes—there's no running to the store to get more. You get little in this world.

I walk to the edge of the cliff to get a better view of down below. The sun is just setting over the ocean, creating a myriad of color before my eyes. It finally dips, and like a snap of the fingers the light is snuffed out. The night embraces us with its cold, treacherous fingers. It is easy to believe that everything is okay when I am up here. I can pretend there's nothing to be afraid of—no boogeyman hiding under the bed. No evil in the world. Just me, Lilly, and the sound of the ocean.

The waves pound against one another, the froth building and crashing against the sandy beach cove below. The saltiness of the ocean leaves its presence on my dry lips, making my thirst even greater.

I startle when Lilly's small hand clasps mine. Looking down into her melancholy little face, I try to force a smile for her, but it comes out as little more than a contorted grimace. Still, I tried at least. I always try.

"You should be sleeping, Honeybee," I say as I gently squeeze her warm hand. Her skin is still smooth like silk, not rough and calloused like mine, and I rub my thumb across the back of her hand over and over, my smile coming easier now. She always soothes me without even having to try.

Lilly continues to stare blankly up at me until I reach down and pull her into my arms. She doesn't resist, but clings to me like a little koala bear, her arms and legs gripping me tightly around my waist and neck. That thought makes me sadder still. She will never know what a koala bear is. In this morbid world, they are all gone now, along with almost every other beautiful thing that once existed.

I stare up at the stars, tiny pinpricks of hope in the darkened night sky. My heart feels heavier than usual tonight. Lilly's hand tips my chin down so that I am looking at her again.

"Where are they?" she asks in a whisper.

"Down there," I say, pointing to over the top of the cliff that we are on.

She peers over as much as she dares, her tiny fingers digging painfully into my skin as she watches the abominations moving below. They are awake now. They came alive with the snuffing of the sun. I feel her fragile little body shiver and tense in my arms and I grip her tighter, more for her comfort than anything else. Because I wouldn't drop her for all the world. My grip on her is as fierce as my heartbeat, relentless and unforgiving. It knows no bounds, and would only surrender when those monsters ripped my still-beating heart from my cold, dead body.

"It's okay. We are up here, and they are down

there. We're safe," I reassure her, pressing a kiss to the top of her head. "We have our light still." With a gentle smile, I point to the streetlight, which inexplicably is still lit after all this time. It makes no sense, but I've given up trying to figure it out. I'm just grateful that it is here, blanketing us with its protection.

"For now," she whispers back solemnly. Her words cut into my heart, carving a piece of it out and sending it away. I nod, because I cannot lie to her; she sees through to the truth every time.

"Yes. For now, for tonight. And that is what matters. Tonight we can dance under the stars." I smile and twirl her around in circles, and she giggles and buries her face in the crook of my neck, her warm breath washing over me with each gentle laugh.

It is the sweetest sound I have heard in a long time—her laugh. It's quite possibly the most beautiful sound that is left in this world. Better than the time we found the little gray kitten with its one white paw hiding under the burnt-out car, crying for its mother. The sound was so inexplicable to me. It was something I hadn't heard in so long that I had forgotten that it even existed. A small meow—a cry for help, from a kitten of all things! Of course, it died a week later from starvation. There wasn't enough food to feed ourselves, never mind a kitten. Lilly had lost the will to speak for almost two weeks after that. I thought she was gone, lost, absorbed back into herself forever. But she came back, eventually.

Lilly laughs again, harder this time, the sound breaking free from her heart-shaped mouth, and I twirl her faster, making us both dizzy and breathless. Her laugh is even better than the sound of the breeze moving through the long grasses and flowers in the field that I had found her hiding in—though that is a very close second. My clever little Honeybee, hiding in amongst those sunflowers. I thought it was the most beautiful thing I had ever seen, that field of sun; as if God had shone His light upon that particular place, bringing her to me and me to her. In the middle of a world filled with so much loss—so much death— a gray world full of sorrow and pain and misery, how could there possibly be so much brilliant yellow beauty? I had wandered among the flowers in awe, my jaw slack and my eyes wide and brimming with tears. My hands skimmed along the tops of the flowers, the petals soft beneath my palms.

It had felt like a sign.

I had wanted to give up that day; I was ready to let go and move on to the next world, and then I saw her: my Honeybee. Her little scrunched-up face peering up at me, surrounded by the yellows, oranges, and greens of the sunflowers. She was like a gift. I was so close to losing it, and then she—Lilly—was there, her face a more beautiful canvas than any sunflower could ever be.

We wept in each other's arms that day, so happy to have found one another. A mother without a child and a child without a mother. Both lost and broken. Both dying with no hope. But together, things seemed more possible, and I have hope now. I think she does too.

Lilly and I dance until the sky darkens further and the stars seem to multiply, though she does not ever let me put her down. She grows heavy in my arms, and her eyelids begin to flutter closed again. I take her back to the car and place her in the little seat, and I clip her back into it safely, being careful not to wake her up.

I learned my lesson the hard way of not buckling her in when she sleeps. Having to make a hasty retreat with a small child screaming and rolling around on the floor—blood pumping from the small cut to her head she just received because she had fallen out of her safety chair—is a journey I don't want to have to make ever again. She suffered a serious bump to her head that day, and I still feel guilty about it when the sunlight shines on that white sliver of a scar on her forehead.

I light up another cigarette after I shut the door on her sleeping form, and I go to stand at the edge of the cliff again, looking down at *them*.

They gurgle and hiss, their red eyes staring back up at me. The sound of their jagged nails scrambling for placement on the side of the cliff worries me, but they cannot climb, I know this. So we are safe. For tonight, at least, thank God, we are safe.

*

Light peeks over the top of the hillside, glaring in at me through the windshield—a soft orange glow turning to a brilliant yellow as the sun rises higher. I rub my eyes and slouch further down in my seat, wanting more sleep, but the sun retaliates and rises further, making me groan and fully awaken.

"All right, all right," I mumble to myself. I shouldn't complain—the sunlight is our friend, our savior. But some days, I am so very tired.

I turn in my seat and see Lilly still sleeping, her little thumb still tucked into her pink mouth. My mouth twitches into what could possibly be considered a smile, but then I surrender myself to my misery again as my stomach aches and I crease over in pain. I open the door and get out, taking my smokes out of my back pocket and lighting one up before I've even shut the door behind me.

The first wave of nicotine hits me and I relish the pleasure it brings. There are only four things that bring me pleasure these days: Lilly, my cigarettes, food, and light. I walk to the edge and look down the cliff face, knowing that the monsters won't be there now—they are never there during the day. The night is their only friend.

However, their previous night's antics are there to be seen, unfortunately, in the form of a bloodied pebbled beach and mutilated carcasses. I don't look close enough to see if the bones are human or animal, or even their own brethren, I never do. It doesn't matter anymore—dead is dead, no matter what it once was. I gave up worrying about other living things long ago. I can't do anything about it, so I prefer to blot it out. I would prefer to blot the entire world out if I could, but I can't because I have Lilly.

I finish my cigarette, feeling the hunger pangs subside a little, and I go to the trunk of the car and open it to check our supplies. I know we are running low on everything, and if we don't find food soon, we will run out and eventually starve. I can survive without food longer than Lilly can, but it's been days and I can feel myself growing weaker. The cigarettes were a great find to curb the hunger pangs, but I'm going to need real food soon. There's only so long I can do this without food, without sustenance, without the energy it gives me to keep on going.

I pull out the last of the canned food: a small can of pinto beans. She hates pinto beans, and I hate the effort of having to make a fire to cook them on. I was so pleased the day we found the stash of cans in the deserted gas station. So pleased. The people inside were long since gone. But now, as I stare at the last can, I think the beans were a curse, because we haven't found food since that day. I throw the can to the ground in anger and slam the lid down on the trunk with a small sob. When I look up through the window, Lilly has awoken and climbed out of her seat, her pale face staring back at me through the window. Her wide brown eyes blink rapidly, looking frightened, and I immediately turn my sad face into a happy one for her. I beckon her out of the car to stretch her legs.

I pick her up as she climbs out, giving her a quick

squeeze and a kiss on her dirty forehead before pushing the soft curls back from her pretty face.

"Morning, Honeybee."

"Morning."

"Did you sleep well?"

She bobs her head, her eyes going wide as she looks into my face. "I need to pee—bad." She bites on her bottom lip, a small frown crossing her face.

"Okay, let's go pee together," I say with a smile and put her down. I take her hand and we walk away from the car and toward some small green bushes at the side of the road.

She stops as we near it, her sneakered feet skidding to a stop, and I turn to look at her.

"Check it," she pleads.

It's my turn to nod as I pull out my small knife from the sheath at my side, release her hand, and walk the rest of the way to the bush on my own. I know there is nothing in there. She knows it too, because the monsters only come out at night, and they hide in the darkness of buildings, mostly. This bush isn't dense enough for them to hide in—light pierces through the scratchy branches—but I play along anyway. I always play along if it makes her feel better. Because I strive for her happiness, though at times it seems like an impossible task—to keep this little girl alive and happy. But I try.

I slash into the bush with my knife. "Better come out, monsters. Lilly has to pee, real bad." I turn and watch as her sweet features soften into a smile. "If there's any of you in here, you better move along or you're gonna get it." I slash and stab one more time for effect and hear Lilly giggle loudly behind me, the sound almost taking my breath away. "All clear," I say as I stand and turn to her.

She runs over to me, promptly pulls down her dirty pants and white cotton briefs, and squats next to me as I do the same.

We finish up and make our way back to the car, Lilly doing a little skip as we go, and me retrieving the discarded pinto beans. She climbs in the back of the car and retrieves her teddy and then comes to stand by my side. Mr. Bear has been with us for several weeks now. I don't like her getting attached to things, but he makes her happy. He has at least stopped some of her nightmares.

"I'm real hungry," she whispers up to me.

"I know, Lilly. I'm working on it."

I open the trunk back up and pull out the last bottle of water, and I take a long swallow before handing it over to her. She gulps it down greedily. I want to tell her to slow down and to ration it, but then I eye the last can of pinto beans and decide to allow her this small satisfaction, since she's going to be eating her least favorite food today. And tomorrow...who knows what she'll be eating?

I gather some small sticks and then use my almost empty lighter to start a fire. I slowly add more sticks and some dry grass to the fire until it is big enough to cook on. I found the lighter—and the cigarettes—a week or so back. Which was lucky, because my hands were covered in so many blisters from making fires using two sticks that I could barely hold Lilly's hand without it hurting. The lighter makes things much easier. Eventually the fire is burning well enough for me to heat the beans for her, and soon enough she's tucking into them with enough gusto to make me laugh.

"I thought you hated them," I say between drags of my cigarette.

"I do." She smiles and fills her cheeks, chewing greedily. "But I'm hungry."

My stomach grumbles loudly, and heat rises in my cheeks. I'm glad that I'm sitting down as a dizzy spell passes through me, making my empty stomach twist in on itself. The headache that has been building all morning eventually breaks free, and I feel momentarily blinded by the pulsing pain behind my eyes. The urge to squeeze them shut and moan in agony is heavy and ripe, but I contain it because I don't want to frighten her.

I stare off into the distance, controlling my breathing until the pain subsides. My cigarette burns down between my fingers until it singes the tips and I drop it with a yelp. When I look down, I see Lilly is staring at me sadly, fork poised before her open mouth.

"You should eat," she whispers.

"I'm okay, I ate earlier," I lie easily. I suck on my finger to ease the burn, but it does little to help.

Satisfied with my answer, she continues to eat, and I stand and sift through the first aid kit until I find the last painkiller. I pop it in my mouth and grab the water bottle before realizing it is empty. I drop the empty bottle back into the trunk of my car and force the dry, powdery tablet down my equally dry throat. I feel it wedge there and I continue to swallow until it starts to dissolve, leaving a vile, bitter taste in my mouth. *At least it's down* is all I can think.

I pinch the bridge of my nose to ease the pain of my headache. Both frustration and anger burn through me. Tears build behind my lids, but I press them away with the heel of my hand and I turn to Lilly as she finishes the beans and lets out a small burp.

"All better now?" I ask.

She nods and smiles before picking up a stick and drawing in the dirt on the ground. Everything is dirty these days—dirty and ruined. And dying.

Chapter Two.

#2 Trust your instincts.

It's early afternoon before the headache subsides enough for me to think clearly, and I approach Lilly with thoughts of a scavenger trip. As usual she instantly says no, but I press the matter with her. We have no water and now no food. If we don't go today, we'll need to go tomorrow, and if not tomorrow, then the day after. Each day that passes, I warn her, I grow weaker and less able. We have no other choices; it's only a matter of time. She doesn't reply to me. Instead she climbs into her chair without further words and refuses to look at me.

I pack our things back into the beat-up car, and as I back out of our parking space I pray that we have a safe trip and make it back up here before nightfall. I glance at Lilly in my rearview mirror. She's sulking, her hands wrapped tightly around Mr. Bear and her bottom lip poking out in a pout. She still refuses to look at me, but she'll be happier when we have food and water. Perhaps I can find her a coloring book, or maybe a toy—anything would do at this point, though I know I'm grasping at crumbling straws.

My stomach gurgles in pain and anxiety as we drive away from our hilltop encampment. I climb out and pull the large gate back behind us, snapping the lock into place, and continue down the ruined road, dodging burnt-out cars and dried-out bones. Our car leaves tracks in the dust, showing just how long we've been up here, and I'm satisfied that no one found this path. No monsters, no humans—no one. We are still safe. For now, at least.

It's an hour or so before we are back in any form of civilization—if you can call it that now. Everything here has been picked clean—I should know, I've tried almost every house in the little seafront town. I know that I'm going to have to go further afield this time, and that's even more worrying. At least here, I know more or less what to expect. I know where the nests of these things are, and I know most of the places to avoid. I roll down my window, letting the sea air into the car to help clear my thoughts. Stress eats away at my empty gut but I ignore the pain as best I can and grasp at memories of playing by the sea, the water washing between my toes.

I drive out of town with a worried sigh, and Lilly's voice whispers to me from the back seat.

"Where are we going?"

"There's nothing here anymore—nothing we can eat or drink. We need to drive to a different town. One that will have food." I watch her in my mirror. Again, she doesn't argue with me on the matter, but looks away with another pout and begins to cry softly against Mr. Bear's brown, matted fur. I think I'd prefer her to argue with me than cry. At least then I wouldn't feel so guilty at making her sad, or so full of self-doubt that we are doing the right thing by leaving. I wish there were another way, but there's not. Food and water are our goals. And of course a coloring book. *She'll be happy then*, I reason as I continue to drive, trying to ignore her soft whimpers from behind me.

Another hour of driving passes with nothing but ruined houses, collapsed buildings, and abandoned cars. We pass down a tree-lined road and I see a small sign pointing to a turnoff on the left. I stop the car and look around before I get out. I examine the road carefully, seeing no recent tracks of any sort—no telltale wheel marks from other cars or footprints, and even more thankfully, no claw marks from the monsters. The road is almost invisible, blocked by debris and bushes.

Satisfied, I get back in behind the wheel, take the turn, and follow the ruined road upward between the trees, panicking when they become so tightly packed that they momentarily block out some of the daylight. Lilly has fallen asleep, and for that I'm glad. I don't think she would be happy about our current situation at all, and I'm not sure my gut could take any more guilt.

The road eventually opens up onto a long driveway, and right at the end is a circular island with bright green grass in its center. Behind the circular, green-grassed island there is a huge mansion with enough windows to put a glass company to shame.

"Jesus," I murmur to myself. My stomach does a little flip, but my heart is excited. *This could be the mother lode*, I think as I drive faster toward the house, sending dust billowing up behind us.

I drive the car around the circular island in front of the house, pulling to a stop outside the large, heavy-looking wooden front door. Lilly is still sleeping soundly, her small snores sounding peaceful. I wonder whether to wake her or leave her be, thinking that the rest might do her good. I step out and look to the sky. The sun is still high, indicating that there is plenty of daylight left. The sky is bright and clear, not even the sprinkling of a cloud to be seen.

I think she'll be okay here, I decide. I haven't seen signs of the monsters or another human. In fact, it's been months since we've seen another human. It's probably safer in the sun than inside the danger of the shadows from the house, so I decide to leave Lilly sleeping until I know it's safe. I make my way to the front steps and peer in through a bottom window beside the wooden door. Nothing moves inside. The place is covered in a thin layer of dust, and again my heart flips in excitement. The front foyer of the home is like a greenhouse—more expensive glass lets in sunlight from every angle.

I walk around the perimeter of the house, checking in as many windows as I can, and find the same thing: dust-covered furniture and nothing more. Around the back of the house is a large barn area, and my head tells me that it's a prime monster hideout. I clench my knife tighter and head over to it as quietly as I can, stepping through the overgrown lawn and dried up flowerbeds. I should leave it be, but I'd rather know than not know. I don't like to be surprised.

I peer up at the barn, seeing gaps in the slats of wood where the sun can seep in. *Sunlight means no monsters*, I think as I brush my filthy hair away from my sweaty forehead. My hand tentatively touches the latch on the barn door. It's rusty and stiff, and will take both hands to push it up, meaning that I have to slip my knife into a back pocket so I can have the use of both hands—something I don't want to do, not even for a minute. If something is inside there, I need both hands free to fight. Indecision twists my gut, and with a heavy heart I put my knife away. Because if we are to stay here tonight—if we are to be safe—I need to know that this place is definitely free of *them*.

With shaking hands, I pull the door open wide, putting all my strength behind it. I could leave whatever might be in here to its own devices, but really, when night falls, if we're still here, the monsters will hunt us down and slaughter us like pigs. So I have to check everywhere—for Lilly's sake as well as my own.

Sunlight explodes into the dark barn as I yank open the heavy door, a creak and a groan sounding as the hinges stiffly move. I wait for the noises of hissing and screaming, for the burning and toasting of graying flesh, but nothing happens. Dust motes floating in the thick, stagnant air are the only signs of movement within. A bubble of laughter tickles the back of my throat as my heart races wildly in my chest, rocketing at a hundred miles an hour. I look inside the barn, safe in my place in the sun at the open doorway. I see nothing of use: rusted old tools, horse saddles, engine parts. I shut the door—latch it, too, just to be sure—and then I pull my knife back out and continue my perimeter search with a more confident step.

Arriving back at the front of the house, I feel the trace of a smile grace my lips. From every window I looked through, the place seemed untouched by anything human or monster. No one and nothing has resided here for a very long time, it seems. This means a couple of things: food could still be inside, and perhaps even a place to rest for the night. I squeeze away tears, which threaten to fall at the thought of that. Perhaps this place could be safe for a while. It seems almost too good to be true, and I swallow back my happiness, not daring to trust in it yet.

My eyes fall on our car and fear ignites like a spark from a match: the back passenger door is wide open—Lilly's door. I run to it and look inside, my heart ravaging my chest cavity. Both Lilly and Mr. Bear are missing. I climb inside and check under the seats, scrambling out the other side of the car.

"Lilly?" I whisper shout. Panic ripens in my chest like a balloon being overfilled. I want to scream her name from the rooftops, but I can't. The balloon of panic is filling and filling and threatening to explode.

I take a steadying breath and look around, trying to calm my raging emotions, panic threatening to overflow from me at any moment. I look at the ground, seeing little footprints at the side of the car. Without a doubt, they are her footprints. They head toward the house, and without a second thought, that's where I head too. I need to find my little Honeybee. My Lilly.

Chapter Three.

#3. Stay close to your loved ones.

I follow her tiny footprints, trailing them toward the back of the house, and I realize that she had been following my steps. My eyes flit to the barn, seeing the heavy door still closed like I left it. I lose her footsteps somewhere in the overgrown grass, and I blink back furious tears—furious at myself for ever leaving her, furious at my stupidity. She must have been so frightened when she woke, seeing that I wasn't there by her side—the place I always promised to be—and went looking for me.

I choke on a sob as I hear her voice calling my name, and I turn and run toward the sound. My leg muscles pump, pushing foot ahead of foot in my eagerness to get to her. I see her small frame by the back door, her little curls glistening in the sunshine as if spun from gold. She turns and sees me and begins to sob quietly as she hugs Mr. Bear.

I reach her in seconds, my arms wrapping around her in a blanket of warm protectiveness, dragging her up into my arms. I crush her small frame to mine and kiss her head over and over as I blink back tears.

"I'm sorry. I'm so sorry, Lilly," I whisper into her hair. "I'm so, so sorry."

Her body shakes in my arms. "You left me," she whispers against my neck. "I was all alone."

I shake my head. "No, never! I was just checking that everywhere was safe, and you were sleeping, and…" I hug her fiercely. "I'd never leave you. Never ever. I'm so sorry."

I pull out of the embrace and look into her face. Wetness covers her cheeks and I wipe it away with the palms of my hands, smearing the dirt there. She reaches out with her little porcelain fingers and wipes away mine, and I kiss her damp fingertips and continue to beg for forgiveness.

"I'm sorry. I promise not to leave you again. Next time I'll wake you."

She nods, happy with my apology, though I can still see her face tinged with panic and sadness, and my heart is still beating furiously.

"Promise?"

"I promise. Cross my heart and hope to—" I don't finish the sentence.

"Can we go now?" she whispers, her eyes sad but her words even sadder.

"I think there may be food inside. I want to go in and look."

She shakes her head furiously. I know what she is thinking: the last time I went into a house, I nearly didn't make it out—but we need food and water and other basic things, and this place seems so empty.

My stomach gurgles loudly and amusement flashes in her eyes for the briefest of moments before flickering out again.

"See? Even my belly thinks it's safe to go inside,"

I say with a smile.

She takes a deep, shuddering breath and finally nods, sniffling as she does. I can tell that she is trying to be brave for me, and I'm grateful. I'm scared too, so I can only imagine how she must feel. I balance her on my hip and go to the back door, and I wipe away the dirt on the window and peer inside. I lean Lilly over so she can see in too.

"See? The dust is settled—nothing has been in here for a long time," I say, turning to look into her large brown eyes, trying to offer her some form of reassurance.

She peers in again and then looks back at me. "No monsters?"

"I don't think so," I reply.

"No people?"

My heart pains for her. "I don't think so." People have been so cruel. "We have to try, Lilly."

She juts out her bottom lip but nods all the same, clutching Mr. Bear tighter to her chest.

"I need to put you down for a minute. I need to break the lock." She shakes her head, her fingers digging into me.

"I have to." I gently pry her white-knuckled grip away from me; her chin quivers, but she relents and slowly slides down my body and to the ground.

I dig the tip of my knife into the keyhole and jiggle it around, hoping that it will magically unlock, but nothing happens. I look through the window again and huff until I feel Lilly tug on my jeans leg and I look down to her.

She points to the small cat flap at the bottom of the door. "I can't fit through there, honey."

She continues to stare at me, eyes wide, frightened, and glossy as she points again. I look from the flap to her and get her meaning.

"I want to help." She whispers it so quietly that I barely hear her.

I shake my head. "No, no way. Anything could be in there."

Her brow scrunches up in confusion. "You said that there were no monsters."

"I don't *think* there are any monsters."

"You said there were no people."

I rub my forehead, my headache coming back with a vengeance. "I said I don't think there is anyone in there. I can't say for certain on anything."

Dizziness overcomes me and I know I need to sit down. The heat beating down on me, the worry, and the lack of food and water in my system have all built up to such a level that I feel faint again. I sit, lowering my head between my knees, and take slow, deep breaths. I'd do anything for a drink of water right now. I close my eyes, feeling Lilly's little hand on my shoulder, patting me in an attempt to comfort. Her head rests a second later near the same spot. She knows that I'm getting sick; I was a fool to think I could hide it from her. She's so smart for her age.

"I'll be okay." I mumble.

I keep my eyes closed as I concentrate on my

breathing, listening to the steady thrum of my heartbeat and the birds chirping in the sky. Time stands still, or perhaps it waits for me to catch up. I know something is wrong when my head feels heavy and it drops suddenly between my knees as I nod off and wake myself up all in the same fraction of a second.

I jump and grab for my knife as my eyes spring open. I stand quickly when I find Lilly to be missing again.

"Lilly?" I spin on the spot looking for her, my eyes landing on the cat flap as I step up to the window and look inside.

She's on the other side of the door, reaching up from her tiptoes to snag the lock open, but she's too small and can't reach. Her wide eyes find me at the window and she gives a little shrug. I look past her into the room behind, hoping to find something she can stand on, but see nothing but coats and shoes. I crouch down to the ground and push the cat flap up as I peer inside. Lilly's face comes nose to nose with me a moment later, her cheeks flushed.

"I can't reach."

"I know, Lilly. Don't worry. Come out now."

"I could go look for a chair."

"No. I want you to come out now." Pain flashes behind my eyes, rocking my body and making me gasp. "Come out right now," I say between clenched teeth. I sit back on my haunches to catch my breath as hunger pangs run tight across my abdomen. I pull out my cigarettes with shaking hands and light one immediately in the hopes that it will again alleviate some of the pains, which are becoming more and more frequent. I watch the little door for Lilly, frowning when she doesn't come straight out, and I poke the door upwards with my hand while exhaling smoke out of the side of my mouth. "Lilly?" I see her little feet tiptoeing away. "Get back out here now!" I whisper urgently, my voice tinged with desperation.

She looks back over her shoulder, at least pausing to consider my request, but she eventually ignores my urgent whispers and keeps going until she's out of view from my vantage point.

I stand quickly, throw my cigarette away, and stare through the glass. I curse in hushed whispers when I still can't see her, and run to the next one along to try and find her. Nothing but a very heavy-looking leather armchair and some crowded bookcases fill this room—no Lilly, no monsters, and no danger. I move to the next window, catching a glimpse of her back as she passes the open doorway.

I quickly move along the building to the next window, watching as she peeks around the doorway, her curls catching the sunlight shining through the window. She looks out at me with a shy smile. I smile back and point to the corner where a small wooden chair rests, covered with yellow, aging paperwork. Lilly totters over, pulls everything off it, and attempts to pick up the chair. It's only a small chair, but she's so little herself and she can't wrap her arms around it.

She looks to me and then back to the chair, stubbornness etched across her sweet features as she clasps its wooden back in her fingers and begins to tug it behind her.

She drags the chair out of the room and down the long hallway. I cringe at the sound of the wood scraping along the wooden floor, feeling helpless standing outside. I look behind me and then up, seeing that the clouds have begun to gather for a storm, effectively blocking out the sun's protective rays.

Panic burns my chest. We need to get going soon or we won't make it back in time. Our light is waiting for us up at the top of the cliff, its safety mocking us from this distance. I look away from the darkening sky and back in the window, the shadow of something passing the doorway a split second later. It's so quick I'm unsure if I actually saw it or if it was just my imagination. I blink and stare into the house, praying it was just my imagination.

Seconds later, Lilly's piercing scream cuts the air, breathing life into my nightmare, and I feel my heart freeze in my chest.

Chapter Four.

#4. Remember, you're stronger than you think.

I run along the side of the building to the stupid little cat flap, peering through it on my hands and knees. Lilly is holding the chair in front of her, its legs pointing at the monster hissing at her. It stays back, away from the light shining in from the window, keeping to the shadows of the doorway.

"Lilly!" I yell. "Open the door, Lilly!"

The monster looks at me, its eyes glowing a deeper red as it bares its mouthful of sharp teeth at me. Its nails *click-clack* against the wooden floor as it steps forward, but the sun touches its skin and sends it squealing like a pig and scooting backwards into the shadows again.

Lilly continues to cower behind the chair, her body racked with sobs.

"Open the door, Lilly. Use the chair," I plead.

She never takes her eyes from the monster, her fingers clasped tightly to the wooden slats of the chair as her body shakes and fat tears fall freely down her cherub cheeks.

I clamber to my feet and look to the sky as clouds overhead continue to build, the light dimming. *Please, no,* I silently beg. The sunlight is our only protection. I look in through the window again. The monster continues to stare at Lilly. Only once do its eyes stray to me, almost as if it can sense that she is the meal and there is nothing I can do about it. I bang my fist on the glass in frustration, making Lilly jump and the thing hiss. I look back to the sky again; clouds continue to fill it, threatening rain and thunder. Panic fills me to the brim, ready to overflow from me at any moment.

"Damn it." I pull down the sleeve on my sweater, covering the end of my hand as I slam it against the glass. After my first attempt doesn't break the glass, I hit it again until it finally smashes through, sending splinters raining down to the floor.

I scramble up and begin to climb through the small window, catching myself on several shards of glass and feeling my blood ooze from me, my knife gripped tightly in the palm of my hand all the while. I fall to the floor clumsily, straying into the shadows for a split second before scooting backwards and putting myself between Lilly and the monster.

"You're okay now. I'm here," I whisper to her through my ragged breaths.

She continues to sob quietly behind me.

"I'll protect you, I'll always protect you," I say with more conviction than I truly believe.

A shadow falls across the room and the monster sidles closer, a look of almost glee on its distorted face. I want to sob and cry and stamp my foot at the unfairness of it all. There's food here, I know there is. We're so close.

The shadows deepen, making the thing almost at touching distance. It stalks backwards and forwards, watching us, waiting, and biding its time. Its fingers and toes curl and uncurl, teeth constantly bared and hungry as it snaps at the air. I glance to the window, seeing the last of the sun finally covered by darkened clouds heavy with rainfall as the monster pounces with a sound almost like a cackle. My knife quickly comes up from my side, catching it off guard, and slashes it deeply in the stomach. I twist and pull, feeling leathery flesh tearing. It continues to snap at me, screeching into my face as it pushes me backwards. It hovers above me, its teeth snapping to find purchase even as its eyes widen in pain when I twist and pull on my blade. I hold it back, one hand gripping tightly to its throat, and plunge my knife deeper into its gut with my other. It can't have my Lilly. I hear the telltale slop of insides tumbling to the floor and kick out at it. It falls backwards, its legs and arms stilling.

 My breath is ragged in my throat, and Lilly is still crying, almost wailing uncontrollably behind me. I turn and scoop her up into my bloodied arms and I squeeze her trembling body close to me as we both gasp for air. This isn't the first of these that I've killed, but it was the easiest kill, and considering that I'm so undernourished and weak, I struggle to work out how that is possible. Is it conceivable that they could be weakening too? That after gorging on the human race and purging us to near extinction, they are now slowly starving? The thought both saddens me and makes me rejoice—to think that they could be weakening—

dying, even—just as we too are about to die out.

Both species, wiped out. It all seems so pointless.

I climb over its destroyed body with Lilly clinging to my side, her face buried in the crook of my neck. I don't look at the monster. I know that it is now dead. I step into the dim hallway, clicking the door firmly shut behind me, fear driving me forward when I should probably be running to my car—but for what? For how long? Sooner or later I'll be too weak to protect her, too weak to get her anywhere safe, and then my little Lilly will be all alone in the world with no one to look after her. Better I find us food now and stay alive for a little longer.

The house is huge—huge and quiet. Dark shadows play against every wall, our steps echoing all around us. The thunder starts outside, the pitter-patter of heavy raindrops against the windows of the many rooms. Lilly stops crying; only the occasional snivel comes from her still form against my hip. She's getting heavy, or I'm getting more tired. The adrenaline is wearing off, but fear is still running rampant. The two things collide in my head, making me feel dizzy and unsteady on my feet. I sway into the wall, feeling Lilly stiffen.

"I'm okay, Honeybee, I'm okay." I kiss the top of her head and push off from the wall with blurring vision, terror filling me. I'm so close. I continue to walk until the narrow hallway opens up to an entrance hall. A large glass window in the circular ceiling makes the space bright and welcoming—more so than the rest of the house, anyway. Lightning flashes, causing our shadows to move and make me jump. Lilly begins to sob again. I can feel her warm tears trickling down my neck. I don't blame her; I want to cry too.

I head to the front door and look out the windows, seeing our car there, seeing freedom so close. But again, I know I can't leave here without food. Hell, we probably can't leave here at all tonight. Not with this storm, and the darkness it brings. The streets will be swarming with the monsters. They love the rain and the darkness.

I move away from the window and head down a different hallway, finding room after empty room. The house is covered in a thick layer of dust and I can't fathom where the hell the thing had been hiding, or if there are any more. Every room has a huge window in it—no place for a monster hiding from the light to be in. There are no footsteps or claw marks or piles of bones. Nothing. I want to ask Lilly if she saw where it had come from, but I don't want to frighten her any more than she already is. I somehow, mercifully, stumble upon the kitchen, my heart jittering in my chest as I make my way to one of the large cupboards and look inside. Disappointment rings in my ears at the sight of plates and bowls. I try the next one and find something similar. Despair pummels my body, and I know that I won't be able to hold it together for much longer; I can feel my emotions breaking away, giving in to the misery.

A sob clogs my airway as I open a third cupboard, and my eyes bulge as I finally see what we so desperately need—can after can of food—and I release the sob with a loud splutter.

"Lilly," I whisper.

She doesn't move, and I whisper her name again until she pulls her face free from the space between my neck and my shoulder. I twist her on my hip so she can see the food and I let out a small laugh of manic glee as I let my tears explode and I sag back against the kitchen Island.

We made it.

She blinks away her tears and stares in awe at the food before finally turning to me with a wide smile. She lifts a pointing finger to the food and I nod and step closer for her. She plucks a can free from the shelf with her chubby hands: fruit. She smiles again and bounces on my hip, and I quietly laugh again.

We're going to be okay. For now, we're going to be okay.

Chapter Five.

#5. ... But we're not as strong as them...

A new morning has come and gone, and early afternoon welcomed us with a sunny smile—yesterday's storm has disappeared like a bad dream. We wake almost simultaneously, the glare from the sun a happy sight upon our faces. Lilly hugs me closer and I squeeze an arm around her little body, feeling bones jutting out. But it's okay now—there's food here, lots and lots of it. We ate like pigs last night, and today we'll do the same. And the day after too. We'll fill our stomachs, put meat on our bones, and live for a little longer. I sigh almost contentedly.

We root through the dusty, overfilled closets and find clean clothes, piling our old, tatty ones into a heap in the corner. I roll the sleeves up for Lilly, and do the same with the pant legs. It makes me sad, when we find a child's bedroom, to think that once there had been someone only a little older than my Lilly living here. I can't help but wonder what happened to them. Did they make it out alive? I hope so. God, I hope so.

When the world went to hell, the planet rocked, reeling from the realization that such evil could live among us in plain sight. We were nearly destroyed, but as confusion and fear gave way to anger, we came back. When the second wave attacked, we were prepared and we fought. God, how we fought. But for every monster killed, two more would replace it, until the human race fled and hid. But you can't hide from what you are.

It has been one year, six months, three weeks, and nineteen days, and Lilly and I have only ever stumbled across a handful of living people. They were not good people. They were desperate and afraid, and with that desperation and fear came violence. There is now more to fear in this world than the monsters. Man is now its own enemy.

They hurt us. My body still holds the scars, and Lilly's dreams are haunted. But I put an end to both their torment and our own. I freed us, and now we are much more careful.

I shake my head to dislodge those thoughts and memories. I don't want to think about those people now. We're here, and they are not, and we have everything we need for now: food, water, some smokes—I even found a coloring book for Lilly. This place won't be safe forever, but it is for now—for today, at least. And in this world, this cruel life that we lead, you live for today.

My head feels a little better today, but the low throb of starvation still burns in my gut and makes my head and body ache, so I take two of the painkillers that we found in the medicine cabinet and swallow them down with flat orange pop from the pantry in the kitchen. *Flat pop never tasted so good,* I muse.

Lilly sits happily at the kitchen counter, a bowl of dried cereal on one side of her and a coloring book in front. Some of the pictures are already colored in, and again, it makes me sad, but Lilly says that it makes her happy, that a piece of the child that lived here still goes on in this world. That makes me happy again. She's so smart.

Lilly feels safe here, in a house with walls and beds and toys to play with. I can't deny that the feeling of carpet between my toes isn't something to appreciate. That this home, with all its homey things, doesn't make my world seem somewhat normal—at least for now.

I finish my breakfast of canned fruit, and leave Lilly in the sunny entrance hall; it seems the safest place for her, given all the windows and the glare coming in from the sun. I've checked every inch of this house and found nothing and no one else here. A small, downstairs, windowless bathroom is where I find dried blood and bones—the place where the monster had been sleeping. Like it had gone into some sort of stasis after a while, trapped between the sunlight from one room and the shade of the bathroom—the only room with no windows. Hope blossoms in my heart that maybe the world could come back from this. There must be people somewhere working on a cure, a way to kill these things off, or turn them back to what they used to be.

I step up to the back door, unlatch it, and swing it open wide, letting in sunlight and fresh air. I reach down for the monster's ankles and begin to drag it outside, wondering why it doesn't burn up when the sunlight touches it now that it's dead. I had dragged it in here last night, trapping its body within this room. It was dead, I knew that, but I didn't want Lilly to have to see its body again—not so soon after it had tried to kill her in this peaceful house.

Its head bumps harshly against the doorframe and leaves a dark black stain. I continue to drag it out onto the lawn, away from the house, before grabbing some of the old newspapers I have brought with me and laying them across the body of the man. I tuck some inside the jacket of his torn suit and stuff some up his sleeves and up his pant legs, being careful not to touch too much of his scaly skin or sharp nails.

I guess this was the father—before he became the monster within. I shake my head sadly and stand back up, pulling the matches from my back pocket. I strike one, and with hesitance I throw it onto the body. I watch him burn, his skin crackling and popping, melting back from his distorted face, his bones altered beyond comparison, his lips stretching back to reveal the tiny pointed teeth caked in black. As his hair fizzes and pops, the smell reminds me to step back, the scent getting too strong. I look toward the back door, seeing Lilly standing there watching. I gesture for her to come over and she does, and I pick her up automatically.

We watch as the monster burns, revealing a more primitive form: that of a man. The man he once was, before all of this happened. Before the infection set in and changed him into something indescribable. A monster. To something more animal than human. It kills me to think that he was once like me, yet somehow he turned into this thing, this monster. From the bones I found, he killed his own family: a wife and two children. The raw, animalistic instinct taking him over must have been agonizing, and I have to believe that he fought against it with everything he had.

"Will I become like that one day?" Lilly asks quietly.

"Not if I can help it," I reply without hesitation.

"But that's what happens, isn't it?"

I don't reply, but look her in the eye with a soft smile. "You'll never be one of them. I promise you." Of course, I can't promise her. There are no promises in this world anymore.

"But I have the lines." She points to her tummy, where we both know the lines of infection have begun. "And you have the lines," she says innocently.

"I know," I reply, breathing through the ache in my gut.

"I don't want to be a monster." She hugs me, squeezing me tightly, her other arm clutched around Mr. Bear.

"I know. And I won't let you. We have food and water, and we'll be okay for a little while now." I rub the hair back from her face, seeing the dark trail of poisoned black blood, faint in her veins, reaching up like paths on a map from her back. I know I have them too, but mine are darker. Everyone has them, or will get them eventually.

"Everyone is going to die, aren't they?" she whispers.

"We'll be okay," I lie. "You'll always be my Honeybee. Okay?"

She nods. "Okay." She looks toward the burning corpse and then back to me. "Can we go color some more?"

I smile. "Of course."

We walk back toward the house, and I swallow down the tears that threaten to flow. How long do we have left? A week? A month? A year? I have no idea. But at least we have food and water now. For now, there is hope of a tomorrow, and the promise of life.

We'll be okay for now, me and my Honeybee.

Chapter Six.

#6. Don't forget the little things.

The days are long, but the nights are always longer. Though the monsters don't find us, we hear them. Each night, their cries and screams echo into the darkness. Each night we fear that they will discover where we are. But they don't. We stay inside as much as possible during the day so as not to let our scent get into the air. I don't even know if they can smell us that way, but it seems feasible—at least as feasible as anything else these days.

Lilly plays with the toys in the little girl's bedroom. Dolls and teddies, jigsaws, and more books than we've seen in a long time. She seems content here, happy to be in a home environment rather than living and sleeping in a car. Not that I can blame her, of course, though I am yet to sleep in any of the beds, choosing to spend most of my nights wandering the halls of the large house, keeping vigilant for the monsters.

I watch Lilly playing in the child's bedroom, leaning against the doorway with a mug of coffee in my hand. It all feels so normal. A mug of coffee, Lilly playing on the bedroom floor, Mr. Bear by her side. So normal and yet so surreal. In many ways more unreal than the world we live in now. Her little face lights up as the dolls talk back and forth, her voice changing for each new character she acts out. Lilly's hands direct their plastic limbs into strange directions and I frown as the game gets more and more heated, one doll hitting another doll over and over.

"And then you'll die, you'll die and die and die," Lilly says loudly, and throws the dolls away.

She looks up suddenly as if she had forgotten I was there, and her face pales. She crosses her skinny arms over her chest, her eyes never leaving mine, her chin quivering.

"Are you okay?" I ask. But really, what kind of question is that to ask a child under the circumstances? Is she okay? Of course she's not. How could she ever be okay? So I rephrase the question in a way she might understand better: "What did the dolly do wrong?"

She finally looks down at her hands. "She was very very bad. She went outside when she wasn't allowed."

I bite on my bottom lip and move further into the room, placing my mug on one of the many shelves. I walk across to her place on the floor, and I kneel down on the colorful rug.

"Was it dark outside?" I ask and she nods. Lilly has never talked about what happened to her, and I have never asked. I open my arms, and she immediately climbs onto my lap and presses her face against the soft fabric of my blouse. "It's okay. I'm here now." I kiss her hair.

Lilly isn't my daughter, but she may as well have been. I love her with all my heart, and it pains me to see her in so much distress. I wish nothing but a happy, normal upbringing for her. And yet, that's the one thing I will never be able to give her. I can give her everything I am, but I can't give her a normal, safe existence. And I can't bring her real family back.

"I want to say sorry," she whispers. "You should always say sorry when you're bad."

"You should," I say with a small nod. "But you weren't bad, you were frightened."

"I was," she agrees quietly. "I was very frightened. How do you say sorry to someone that isn't here anymore?"

I pause, thinking of her words and what they could really mean before landing on the real reason for her distress today.

"You mean if they are in…" I want to say heaven, but it seems like such a bitter word on my lips right now.

"Dead," Lilly says bluntly. "If they are dead." She looks back up at me, her wide eyes full of so many emotions that I struggle to find the right words to help her, to ease her pain in some way.

Because she has never been this forthcoming with me. We found one another, and from that moment on we were each other's. We had never questioned each other's past, who we were prior to the monsters coming. It never seemed important. Yet now as I stare into her eyes, I feel it might be the most important thing in the world to her. She's five, or maybe six, I think. Though she's never confirmed any age to me.

Inside, though, she's so much older.

"I used to be a teacher," I say, though that is a lie. But hearing that I worked in a supermarket stocking the shelves would be much less important to a child of six. So I lie. Teachers are superheroes to six year olds, and Lilly needs a superhero right now. "I used to tell my children that you could talk to people that weren't there."

She leans away from my chest to get a better look at me, and she cocks her head to one side as she tries to gather some understanding to my words. "How?" she finally whispers.

"You just close your eyes and think of the person that you want to apologize to, see their face, and then think the words."

"Like a prayer?"

I nod, though I hadn't really considered the act as a prayer. But I guess that's what it is, really: a prayer, a wish to God—though I gave up praying to God long ago. Lilly looks away from me, her gaze going soft as she considers this. When she looks back up to me, her pale face is much calmer. "I can say sorry to someone that is dead?" she asks, and I nod again.

Lilly seems happy with that, and she climbs from my lap and kneels by the side of her bed, her hands clasped in front of her in prayer. She closes her eyes and I see her lips moving soundlessly, and I shake my head as I leave the room, giving her the space that I think she needs.

I'm taken aback by her candidness, by the way in

which she has adjusted so well to this world. She is young, so young in so many ways—the way she sucks her thumb and clasps Mr. Bear—and yet she's so grown up in so many other ways.

I make my way back down the stairs, taking a moment to tip my face up to soak in the warmth of the sun that burns through the many windows in this house. It gives me a temporary feeling of safety. Sunlight: our biggest weapon against the monsters, and the only thing that we can't control as a weapon. It's the middle of summer, and the days burn bright and long. Every day is hotter than the last, but I'm glad for the heat and the discomfort that it brings; it makes me feel more human. I only hope that the monsters feel the discomfort of the heat as much as we do.

I continue down the stairs, going from room to room as I do every day. Lilly has learned to relax a little, but I never can. My body and mind are constantly on edge, strung too tightly as if they may snap at any time. And perhaps they will. One day, but not today. My mind wanders to our safe spot on the hill above the ocean, and not for the first time, I wonder if I am doing the right thing by staying here. It had been safe there, beneath the light of the streetlamp, but the fear of that one tiny light going out was ever present. The fear of the monsters or other humans finding their way up the lone road to our retreat is constant. Here in this house, with its high glass ceiling and several exit points, life feels somehow more secure. Or perhaps that is also just my humanity tricking me, longing for some form of normalcy.

I head to the front door to check on our car. Each day I go out to turn the engine over, because one day we will need to leave here and we will need a vehicle that works. If the monsters do find us, we will need to leave quickly. The trunk of our car is now filled with canned food and water, grain, blankets, kitchen knives, and more. The food will only last us a week or two on the road, and that's if we ration it well, but it's better than nothing. It's better than what we had previously—which was nothing at all. We had searched the grounds this morning but found no other car around, but I struggle to comprehend these people, in their big house with all their food and trinkets, not having a car of some sort. But then, so much has happened between those days and these. Who am I to question anything now?

The car is there, as it always is, and I turn the key in the front door before pulling it wide open and letting the fresh air drift into this stuffy, humid house. I relish the air on my face, and give the smallest hint of a smile. Lilly must hear me open the door, because moments later she runs down the stairs, taking them two at a time, excited to go outside for a little while.

She meets me by the front door and takes my hand, and we go outside and down the steps together. I pause on the bottom step, looking toward the shadows of the trees and bushes surrounding the property.

They could be in there, the monsters, their bodies hidden within the folds of darkness, protected by the thick gray shadows. I look for any sign of them—disturbed soil in the long dead flowerbeds, scratches down the bark of the trees, piles of bones—but I see nothing. Lilly tugs on my arm and I look down at her.

"Can I?" she asks almost urgently.

Her speech is coming on so much more since being here, as if this place—this hidden, safe house—has opened her up, like it was the key and her voice a lock. I look into her face—her beautifully innocent face, filled with so much excitement, a beauty amongst the blackness—and I nod. She releases my hand immediately and bounds over to the small island next to our car, her soft curls bouncing around her shoulders as she runs. She lies down on the grass with Mr. Bear and rolls around on it, spreading her arms wide and giggling. The sound melts my heart.

I smile and make my way to our car, unlocking it with the silver car key that has the small key ring in the shape of Mickey Mouse attached to it. Lilly's eyes always light up when she sees this key ring, as if she somehow knows that a giant mouse with red pants would be friendly. I sit in the driver's seat and insert the key in the ignition, and after taking one last glance around to make sure no one is near, I turn it. The engine sputters but rumbles to life and I nod and breathe a sigh of relief. I close the door carefully and begin to drive around the circular island in front of the house. I pause by the entrance road, getting out of the car to check for any disturbance, but I leave the engine running. After a few minutes I see nothing unusual, so I climb back in and then continue in my circle around the island of grass. Lilly runs around the grass, following after the car, her little legs pumping hard as she tries to keep up with me, even though I am only going slowly. She finally collapses, exhausted, and lets out a laugh of total glee while trying to catch her breath.

I pull the car to a stop, and shut the engine off before I climb out and lock the door again. I look over to Lilly and see that she is doing what she calls 'sausage rolls' over and over, and I smile again before walking around the car and checking each of the tires carefully.

We used to have a blue Honda. We had thought it was gray until one night there was a heavy storm and the rain beat down so hard on it that it washed all of the dirt clean off. We had huddled together inside it, trapped, and hating the sound of the noise on the metal roof for the fear that the sound would bring the monsters. The next morning, when we had climbed out of the car, the storm finally over, we had seen the beautiful blue that the car had once been. Lilly had loved it. She had run her small fingers along the sides of it with the first smile I had ever seen from her, and I had almost cried at its beautiful sight. Blue is now Lilly's favorite color.

That day had been good: we had plenty of water

(thanks to the rain), we ate canned tuna, and Lilly had smiled often, her gaze frequently falling to the blue of the car as if she had never seen the color before. Night had fallen sooner than we'd expected, though, and as we tried to drive away I found that one of the tires of our beautiful blue Honda had gone flat. So taken aback by Lilly's smiles and the brightness of the blue of the car, I had missed the flat tire. We really were trapped this time.

We had climbed onto the roof of a 7-Eleven that night, neither of us being able to sleep for fear of being found by the monsters. They had come, because they always came, and they had torn our car apart to get inside, shredding the metal with their sharp claws and teeth and smashing the windows. But of course we were not inside this time, and they had screeched and screamed for us all night. When morning came and the sun rose, they disappeared into the shadows again and we climbed down from the roof, retrieved what little of our belongings hadn't been destroyed, and left on foot. Lilly didn't smile for a very long time after that day, and I swore that I would never let that happen to us again.

I press my palm against a tire, but it's fine. They're all fine. Satisfied, I unlock and open the trunk and check our supplies. I hadn't expected them to change, but I always feel better after checking. By the time I have counted each meal, calculating each ration, Lilly has come back to my side, exhausted and happy. She slips her hand in mine as we make our way back inside the house, and I shut the front door and lock it again.

I look down at her, pulling stray grass blades and leaves from her hair. "Are you hungry?" I ask softly.

She nods and holds her small arms up to me. I reach down and pick her up, and she wraps her legs tightly around my waist. I carry her inside to the kitchen without speaking and set her at the table where she continues coloring the picture that she had begun this morning: the black-and-white image of a cow chewing hay and a farmer with dungarees standing next to it. She colors the dungarees in blue, and I wonder if she's thinking of the blue Honda like I had been.

I open the kitchen cupboard and sift through the various cans until I find something that we can make into a meal with minimal effort. Lilly likes pasta—spaghetti, preferably. She likes to suck the long pieces into her mouth, the red tomato sauce splattering over her cheeks. It only reminds me that we have no cheese, though, because there's no milk, because there are no cows alive now, because monsters are alive and they have killed everyone and everything, and they will more than likely—one day—kill us too. That is, if the infection doesn't change us before then. So I don't make spaghetti and tomato sauce very often.

"How about vegetable broth, Honeybee?" I ask as I turn to her, my hand clutching the can.

Lilly isn't sitting at the table anymore. Instead, a

monster with glowing red eyes and long black talons that gouge the wood of the table sits in her place. The dress with the hearts and flowers on it still lay across what are now wide-set shoulders with twisted bones that protrude from the thin material. The light shines in from the window, reflecting against the soft curls that are still on its head.

I scream abruptly and drop the can of broth. I stumble backwards as my hand reaches for the counter and the knives that I know are there. Though I will never use them on her, only me. Because life without her is pointless.

"Mama?"

Her soft voice rings true in my ears and I blink, seeing Lilly once more and not the abomination. My body sags against the counter as tears burn my eyes and my hand covers my mouth to stifle my terrified cries. Lilly's chin trembles, and she presses down so hard with the blue crayon that it snaps in half.

"I…I'm sorry, Lilly." I clear my throat and stand back up, willing my heart to calm down as I make my way toward her. I reach for her. "I'm sorry."

She climbs down from the chair and throws herself into my arms, and I kiss her soft curls and breathe in her sweet smell as I apologize again and again and again.

Chapter Seven.

#7. Nightmares are now the reality of life.

Lilly sleeps peacefully in the large bed of the master bedroom. Her soft snores make me smile. The small murmurs that escape through her mouth used to make me curious, but not anymore. They are always the same word whispered through her dry lips.

Mama.

I know she doesn't dream of me. She dreams of her real mother—the one she has never spoken of—and that's okay. It makes me happy to know that she remembers her in some way. I'm happy that she still thinks of her. I would hate to think that she forgot her past, her family. Because that would be like losing who she was. And she is such a beautiful, beautiful soul. We have all lost too much already, but really, to lose ourselves is the greatest loss of all.

I don't remember my family; my mother and father are both wiped from my mind. Their faces have long been destroyed by the image of their bodies being torn apart by sharp teeth and long claws. Perhaps because I am older, I cannot wash away the pain and suffering that the people I had once loved had eventually brought me—through no fault of their own, of course, but it was still too much pain for one mind to consume. So I don't think of them anymore. It hurts too much. Instead I have a make-believe past. A family that made it to the helicopters in time and were lifted to safety. Friends that fought back and won. A husband that didn't turn into the monster he feared, a man that didn't kill his only child and try to murder his wife. Instead he's off somewhere safe…waiting for me. And one day we will all be reunited—mother, daughter, and husband.

I look out of the bedroom window, pulling the curtains back ever so slightly to peer outside and into the darkness beyond. Nothing moves out there, but my mind plays tricks on me even so, telling me that there are large shapes moving from tree to tree, and red eyes glowing from within the shadows. But there aren't. We are still alone, and safe. For now. Only for now, of course, because everything is limited now—limited life, limited food, limited safety, limited… Everything is limited—everything apart from love. Because I will love Lilly ceaselessly, limitlessly, until my dying breath.

I leave the bedroom and move to the next room along the hallway. As I do every night, I check each room and each window repeatedly, standing guard, allowing Lilly some peace to sleep. Each dirty window offers a new angle from which to look, a new view of how the monsters could get to us. This is the longest we have stayed in one place, barring the hilltop with the light on it. It has been so long since we saw them—the monsters—and yet, it is not long enough. I am reluctant to leave here, but know that the time will come, and it will be too soon.

I often wonder, in the thick of night, how many people are left in the world. I imagine stories of whole communities somewhere safe, people living lives like we once had, safe and secure and hidden away from the dangers this world has. And there are so many dangers. We had once followed a trail of breadcrumbs to what was supposed to be a safe compound. Upon arrival we discovered that it was nothing more than a dream—false whispers that had spread far and wide, filling people with hope. That hope nearly got us killed. So now I let Lilly hope, because children should always have hope, but I do not. She needs that hope to grow and continue to be strong, but that hope to me is nothing more than a cruel trick.

A long, monstrous scream breaks the silence of the night, and I press my face against the cool glass, my nose squashing against it as my eyes scan the area efficiently and take in every inch of the land surrounding us. I'm just hoping, praying, and begging to make it through another night. The scream of the monster is met with another shrill scream, and then another joins that until there are a chorus of them, singing their terrifying screams into the night sky. I imagine them, their awkward, jutting bones and their red eyes, their claws digging into soft carcasses as they feed. As they kill. As they hunt. Us.

The night falls back into silence again, but I don't breathe a sigh of relief. I never do that. Not anymore. Because there is no relief, there is only another day, and another night to make it through, and the wish that there is another day after that one. I move to the next room. Still hoping, praying, and begging to make it through this night.

*

"Mama."

Her voice comes to me, pushing through the fog, intruding on my dreams. I see her face, so small, so perfect, her smile stretched wide. And then it is gone, and all I see is the blood. It fills the world with its redness, washing away the monsters. But we can never be free of them, they are always here.

"Mama."

Her soft voice alights my heart and I feel myself cry, hot, salty tears pouring down my cheeks. Tears that I have no control over, that I cannot stop.

"Mama."

Yes, I was a mother once. To a child no older than Lilly. A little girl named Jasmine, with light hazel eyes and long brown hair. She used to like dancing to old fifties music that her grandparents played, she ate peanut butter and jelly sandwiches that her father made, and she liked her hair running free and long down her back, trailing behind her as she ran. I was a mother once. But now she's gone, and so am I.

I wake with a start, my breath catching in my throat and my voice choking on my lips. I reach for my knife—the sharpest one I found in the kitchen—and I grip it tightly. My hand only has the slightest of shakes. I look down into my lap and see Lilly lying on me, her small arms wrapped limply around my waist, her head nuzzled against my chest. Sunlight streams in through the windows, hot and bright, and I plead with my heart to slow down—to calm down.

I relax back into the soft chair, placing a protective arm around Lilly's sleeping body. She is hot and sweaty. There's a small, damp patch between my breasts where her sweat has pooled. I stroke her hair, smiling at the softness of it, and I force myself to unwind. I yawn, feeling the long-dried tears on my cheeks, and then I purse my lips as I hug Lilly to me. I love her so much. She is not my Jasmine, but I love her as if she were, because every child deserves love.

I sit in the peace and quiet, relishing in her warm body and her soft breaths, letting the rays of the sun lay claim to my skin. I feel myself drifting, floating on a bed of clouds, lost in the peace of each heartbeat, each breath, each calm moment that we are sharing together.

"Mama?"

I open my eyes and look down, seeing Lilly's smiling face looking up at me, and I smile back.

"Morning," I whisper, my throat feeling dry and tight, my body still sleepy.

She blinks up at me, her small hand reaching to touch my cheeks where my tears had been. She sees me. No matter how hard I try to hide from her, she sees all of me. Lilly hugs me close without saying anything else and I squeeze her back. We sit there in silence for a long time, neither of us wanting to lose this moment—this peace that we share so equally. No birds sing outside the window, and no monsters scream for our blood. We are safe, for now. We made it through another night, together.

My stomach growls loudly, disrupting the silence, and Lilly giggles and looks up at me once more. Her small rosebud mouth stretched wide into a large smile, her eyes are dancing, like a child's should be. Not devoid of life and innocence, lost.

"I need a drink," she whispers.

"I need to eat," I say.

Lilly nods. "Me too," she agrees. "So does Mr. Bear."

"We better get him some breakfast, then, before he gets grumpy, don't you think?" I say, and she grins at me and nods.

She smiles and climbs down from my lap. She takes my hand as we leave the room, and we make our way down the stairs, both of us still weary from a restless sleep, but glad to be here. Together. In the kitchen I settle Lilly at the table, where she continues to color in the coloring book. The picture she has painstakingly been working on is almost complete. She ignores the blue crayon today, favoring the green one instead. I go through the cabinets and take out some of the flat pop, pouring us both large glasses of it, and then I go over to Lilly and hand her a glass.

Our fingers touch when she reaches for the bubble-less drink, and we both stare in morbid fascination at the faint black lines that run down my fingers. I blink sadly, not wanting to feel sad today, but not being able to stop myself. I don't want to die, but further than that, I do not want either of us to become the monsters that we fear so much.

I swallow and turn away, leaving Lilly with her drink as I go back to examine the cupboards while she colors, deciding on oatmeal made with water. I find a small jar of jam at the back of the many cans and packages, and I decide to use it to sweeten the blandness of the watery oats. I pull out the items, smiling as I do, knowing how much Lilly will love the jam.

My hand pauses on the jar as I think about the sweet red jelly within the confines of the glass. It exudes happiness, I decide. Lilly will like this breakfast, she'll smile and eat happily, and things will feel normal and nice. I set to making the oatmeal, my smile fixed as I do. Because this feels good. I am a mother fixing breakfast for her daughter—a child coloring innocently. These things are simple and honest, but they are the things that you miss the most. Not expensive cars or sparkly jewelry. Not televisions and music. But the simplicity of how pleased a little girl will be to taste strawberry jam again.

I heat the oats and water on the small camping stove and when it's ready I set the oatmeal down in front of Lilly. She stops coloring right away, setting her green crayon down and pushing the book to one side. She looks at the oatmeal and picks up her spoon, and then I place the jam in front of her and I grin. She looks at it for a long moment without speaking, and then her face looks up at me with a smile so bright it almost extinguishes the sun.

I grin wider as I open the jar, the loud popping sound as it opens makes her giggle. I spoon a large amount into her oatmeal and she stirs it for a long time, making it turn pink, but she seems hesitant to try them, to taste the pink goodness.

"Eat it now, Honeybee, or it will go cold," I say on a happy whisper.

She looks at me with those big wide eyes that pierce my soul, and then she pushes her chair back and throws herself into my arms. I hug her tightly, another smile playing on my lips, and I kiss the top of her head, tears choking my throat. Tears of happiness.

"Come on, into your chair now," I say. Because I don't want to cry again today—not even happy tears.

I help her back into her seat and she picks up her spoon, eating the oatmeal with an excitable groan of delight. I watch for several minutes, leaning my cheek into my hand while my elbow rests on the table. I enjoy seeing her happiness, enjoy her being the child that she should be, that she could be. When she is almost done, I stand to go eat some of my own oatmeal. I spoon a small amount of jelly into mine—just enough to give it flavor and sweeten it a little, but not so much to make it turn pink. I want to save it all for Lilly. I want to see this smile on her face every day for as long as I can. Because all we are left with at the end is a handful of memories to brighten the darkness.

I look out the kitchen window while I eat, looking for any sign that *they* have been here in the night, but as is becoming the usual, there is none—no scratches, no blood, no disturbance outside. I smile and realize that they—the smiles—are coming easier each day. This both frightens and excites me. The tentative tendrils of hope are beginning to grow inside me, and I'm struggling each day with dampening them back down. I don't want to hope, but it's hard to stop the buds from blooming.

After breakfast, Lilly goes off to the bedroom to play and I pace the house, checking each room for broken windows or a disturbance of any kind. When I find none, I open the back door and take the bucket of pee from last night out to the drain and pour it away, happy to see that both of us are not dehydrated anymore. Lilly has even put on a little weight; the hollowness to her cheeks is filling out, and the big gray bags under her eyes are almost extinguished.

Perhaps I can lock us away here forever, trapped in this house's magical safety. I would like that, I think, and so would Lilly. There is a bike leaned up against the side of the house. It's rusty and old and has a brown wicker basket on the front. I imagine that the woman who had lived here would ride her bike into town. She would probably go to the butcher's and the baker's, perhaps even the post office. She would fill her days with small trips on this bike, a smile on her face and the sun on her back. On her way back home she would stop and pick some flowers from the roadside, filling that brown wicker basket up with them. And when she got home she would put them in a vase with some water and place them in the kitchen.

I lean down and pluck a small yellow flower from the edge of the path. It's a weed, really—not a real flower—but it's pretty all the same. It reminds me of the sunflower field where I found Lilly hiding. The monsters had been scared to go into that field. The brightness of the flowers had confused them. Perhaps I can plant thousands of these yellow flowers, all around this house, to keep them out.

I bring the flower back inside, putting it next to her coloring book, and then I take the bucket back to the bathroom. I walk back along the hallway, examining the books on the shelves. I pluck one off the shelf that has maps of the United States on it, and I take it back to the kitchen. I sit down at the table with it, using one of Lilly's crayons to mark where we are and where we have been. I use the blue, and the color looks strange against the white of the paper for some reason. Too vivid, almost as if my eyes are still growing accustomed to colors, like they have been blinded to only muted grays and blacks for too long. Like the world has been washed free of its color but it is slowly being colored back in by a little girl with golden curls.

Our journey has been long, but I'm grateful for that. This place has given us roots—roots that we didn't have for a long time. We have been wandering the country for months and months, driving or walking from one place to another. Because no place stays safe for long. My thoughts drift back to our last location, with the light that still worked at the top of the hill, and I mark it on the map. I worry about staying here too long, especially since I could hear the monsters last night, yet the desire to stay here pulls strongly at me. What life is it if you are constantly running? So I think maybe another day here will be okay. I leave the map book on the table and go upstairs to look in on Lilly and see that she is playing a happier game than yesterday, her smile truer and broader, her voice more content.

"I'm going to check on the car," I say from the doorway.

She looks up with happy eyes.

"Are you coming?" I ask.

She jumps up from her spot on the floor immediately and skips over to me, and we make our way down the stairs, taking them two at a time and giggling. When we get to the front door and I unlock it, and we stand in the doorway as I open it wide, the warm air rushing in to greet us. We wait, listening for sounds of the monsters, looking for signs of them everywhere, but there is nothing. Just the stillness of the day, and the sun hanging full and heavy in the sky.

She looks up at me expectantly, a huge grin on her face, and I forget where we are, the world in which we now live. I imagine that this is our life, our home, and that there is nothing to fear but the pettiness of each day. These are our things—our clothes, our toys, our furniture, our food. Food that I went into town on my bike with a wicker basket to get. I visited the butcher's and the baker's, and I sent a letter to my husband at the post office. He's away at war, fighting and winning, but he'll be home soon. And he and I and Lilly will live here happily, forever.

"Go on then," I say, and gesture for Lilly to go and play.

She releases my hand and skips past me, heading straight to the circle of grass once more. Like yesterday, she rolls around on the grass happily, giggling in that way that is both addictive and alluring. A laugh that only children have. I stand and watch her, admiring her resilience to this world—this life—floating above myself to watch her innocence as she rolls around and around and around. Like yesterday, the dried grass clings to her hair, and I smile as her curls tangle and she looks up at me, begging me to come and play with her. But unlike yesterday we are not alone.

A loud crash sounds from the road—the one that is obscured by the trees—and the screech of metal can be heard. A minute passes and smoke begins to rise from over the tops of the trees. Lilly jumps up and scampers over to me, her eyes open so wide that I see the whites around her irises. I pull her up into my arms as we watch the smoke rise higher and higher and we listen to the soft cries of a woman's voice for help.

Chapter Eight.

#8. There is truth in the unknown.

"What is it, Mama?" Lilly asks, her fingers curling against my skin and digging into me painfully.

I don't stop her, though; I enjoy the pain she gives me. It keeps me alert, it stops me from folding in on myself and giving way to my fear…to her fear. What is it? I wonder that myself. I don't want to go down there and see, but the cries are becoming more insistent, more urgent and pleading. We go into the house and lock the doors, and then we go upstairs and hide in one of the bedrooms. I stay by the window, looking out to see if the people find the road, to see if they come up it, to see if they find the house and us and…

Lilly cries in the closet. She doesn't like it in there—it's dark and stuffy—but she is safer hidden than not. People are bad. Monsters are bad. This world is bad. And I don't know how to protect her and keep her safe. The cries from outside are quiet now. They must be trapped, I decide. Whoever is down there is growing tired, possibly dying, and I'm here, hiding away to protect Lilly and myself.

Lilly has stopped crying and a stillness has settled over the world. The air barely moves. I can hardly feel the pulsing of my heart within my chest, the ache of indecision gnawing at my gut. But I know that my heart still beats, that the breath still leaves my lungs, and that my indecision could kill someone. The smoke has dwindled, thankfully. At least there won't be a fire that will burn away the trees, our cover and protection. I chew on my bottom lip, tasting copper and flesh, my eyes aching as I watch the trees for any movement.

I hear the creak of the closet door and I turn to see Lilly peeking out. Her cheeks are blotchy and red because she knows—she *knows*—how dangerous other people can be. But she's also good, her soul undamaged and still trusting. She knows that someone down there needs our help—my help.

"It's dangerous, Honeybee," I say softly, my patience with her as constant as ever.

She nods and blinks slowly, but the guilt eats away at me. She doesn't need to voice the words for me to hear them. They are borne within me. I turn back to the window, looking for the smoke once more, but it's gone now, and so are the cries for help. The silence is thick and oppressive. I look back to her, to Lilly, still feeling unsure. Her innocent face watches me with morbid curiosity.

"Are they dead?" She whispers so quietly I can barely hear her.

I avert my eyes. "I don't know. Possibly." I shrug and turn away from her sweet pools of brown. Her eyes make me feel like I'm drowning.

She joins me by the window, her hand finding mine and clutching it tightly. Her skin is warm and soft, and my hands are cold. "I feel bad," she says.

"Why?" I ask.

"Because it will be my fault if they die, won't it?"

I frown and look down into her face, before pulling her up into my arms. "No, Lilly, no it will not be your fault. Nothing is ever your fault. This world is what's wrong, other people are what is wrong. Not you, never you."

"You would go and help them, if it weren't for me," she says, speaking the truth that she knows so well.

My heart is racing, my words bubbling to escape from my lips. I don't want her to feel the heavy responsibility of someone's death. That would be worse than letting someone physically harm her. Because those scars—the ones that burrow deep down into your veins—they never go away. Those scars will grow vicious, crude bumps across them to try to disguise themselves. But they won't be hidden. They'll be ugly, and I'll see them every time I look at her, every time she cries, every time she wakes screaming from a nightmare about the person that I let die. I'll know that she blames herself for someone dying, and it is those feelings that will destroy my sweet, innocent Lilly. She continues to stare into my face, blinking every once in a while, her eyes telling me a story.

"If I go see, you'll have to stay here, on your own." I wait for her reaction but she tucks in her bottom lip and nods at me. "Okay, I'll go see," I say with an almost inaudible sigh. I put her down and urgently gesture her back to the closet.

She turns to look at me. "Will you tell them about me? Will you bring them here?" she asks.

"I don't know, Lilly. I'll see if I think they are good or not."

She climbs inside the closet, pulling the thick coats up around herself and wrapping her arms around Mr. Bear tightly. "Will you be able to see? Can you tell if they are good or bad?" she asks me innocently.

"I hope so" is all I can say.

"Mama?"

"Yes, Lilly?"

"Am I good?" Her question hurts, and I answer her without missing a beat, because the answer is the most truthful thing I will ever say.

"Yes. You are good."

She nods and I close the door on her, trapping her into the darkness that I know she hates so much. I leave the bedroom, shutting that door also. I wish it had a lock on it. I'd lock and shut every door in this house if I had to, to keep her safe, to protect her from whatever and whoever is out there. I make my way down the stairs, and I unlock the front door and leave, locking it behind me and placing the key in my pocket. I grip my kitchen knife tightly in my hand, holding it in front of me as I walk straight across the middle of the circular island, across the green grass that offered Lilly so much happiness, and straight onto the gravelly path that we drove up over a week ago—a path I had hoped to avoid going back down.

The road is long, longer than I remember, and my heart beats heavily with each step I make. As I draw close to the hidden exit, I can hear quiet sobbing, murmurs of someone down here, and the ticking of an engine. I slow my pace, eager to see who is there but not eager to welcome them into our lives. I want to go through the dense trees, using the undergrowth as my camouflage, but I don't dare. It's dark in there, and the monsters may be hiding in them—though it's unlikely, given that they haven't come for us.

I take careful, cautious steps to the end of the road and look out to my right, not seeing anything, but to my left is a mangled car. It has crashed into a tree, the metal twisted and crushed. The hood has been flung open from the impact, and the windshield is no longer intact. I can see someone moving inside. I can hear them crying. I squeeze my eyes closed, listening to their soft murmurs, and recognize that they are praying, wishing for death before nightfall.

I open my eyes back up and move toward the car silently, cautiously, carefully. Watching, always watching. I can tell from the back of the person that it is a woman in the car. Her hair is long and light, a soft brown that reminds me of honey and caramel. It hangs in a low ponytail, dangling between her bony shoulder blades.

"Please, please…" Her soft murmurs make me swallow, thick emotions making my mouth dry. "…let me go, let me die…please, please…" She begs and begs, because everyone knows that death is better than the monsters getting to you. Much better than the violent death that they will thrust upon you.

My shadow falls across her window and she stills, her whispers abruptly stopping. Slowly she turns her head, her face pinched with worry and possible acceptance of her forthcoming death. Her eyes meet mine. Gray eyes, dead eyes, remorseful, sorrowful eyes, which flood with relief when they see me.

She looks me over, her dead gray eyes examining my skin, my fingers, my face for any sign that I am one of *them.* I try to speak, but my throat feels tight and dry and my words come out choked.

"Are you infected?" I finally ask through her closed window, my words direct and to the point. There's no point in being anything but.

She slowly shakes her head no, her ponytail swaying behind her, and I step closer to the car. She is trapped inside. The airbag has deployed, the dashboard crumpled and pinning her legs in place. There's blood coming from her nose, thick and red, an invitation for the monsters.

"Are you?" she asks, and a dry laugh leaves my throat.

"Aren't we all," I say. Not a question.

She stares blankly at me, accepting my answer for what it is: fact. I'm alive right now, and I'm me, that's what matters. If I was one of them, I wouldn't be able to talk to her, because they don't talk.

"I can't get out," she sobs, her voice breaking on

the last word. Her chin trembles. "I'm stuck." She says this as if I can't see her predicament.

"Where did you come from?" I ask, startling myself with the cold edge to my voice. "Who are you?"

She pauses, looking confused, and this should have put me at ease. The fact that she seems so confused by my questions. Who are you? Where did you come from? Such simple questions in such difficult times.

"I came from Oklahoma. I was a human rights lawyer," she states, wiping at the blood under her nose with trembling hands. "Most of my family died after the first attack, and I—,"

I shake my head. "No, who are you…now? Where have you been?"

It's important that I know this truth of hers, because I'll leave her here to die if she doesn't tell me. Her past is not relevant to me or this situation, but who she is now is key to her survival. And ours. Is she a murderer? A cannibal? A helper? Has she been with a group—will they come for her? Was she a loner? These are the things that are important to me now. Because I don't trust people. No one but Lilly.

"I'm Sarah. My husband died a month ago." She says her words short and staccato, and then looks down into her lap. "I'm alone now."

I believe her. I don't know if I can trust her, but I believe her. Lilly would want me to help her, because she would think that this woman—this Sarah—is good. I don't know if she's good, but I believe that she's telling me the truth. I walk to her door and try to pull it open, and she looks up at me sharply, her eyes meeting mine in a silent *thank you*. The door is stuck, the metal jammed into itself. I move to the passenger side and that door opens with a loud groan. I climb in and use my knife to cut her seatbelt off her. The steering wheel is pressed up against her chest painfully, and I wonder if it has done any internal damage to her. I look down, seeing the black plastic from the dashboard and steering wheel column cutting into her legs. Blood is pooling around her feet, but she is unaware of it, of the jagged black plastic slicing into her flesh.

I push on some of it to try and give her room to free herself, but she screams loudly so I stop. I sit back in my chair, unsure of what to do next, of how to free her, and she begins to cry again.

"Don't leave me here, please don't leave me here for them."

I watch her carefully, her deep gray eyes looking at me and my knife in pleading desperation. I know what she is saying—what she wants from me—with that one look. Death. She wants me to kill her so that *they* can't take her. I blink sadly. I'm not a killer, this isn't me, but I don't want her to become one of them either. I don't want her to suffer at the mercy of their teeth and claws and their red, red eyes. And because she will be just one more monster to add to their growing horde. I breathe out softly, the whooshing of my blood loud in my ears.

"Please," she whispers. "Please." Tears bleed from her eyes, and I know that I should feel something for her, but I don't. I can't. And yet…

I bite my lip and reach down between her legs again, pushing on the plastic more carefully this time. It scrapes against her skin, peeling some of it back like sandwich meat to reveal the redness of tender flesh underneath. She hisses through her teeth in pain, but she doesn't ask me to stop, and she doesn't scream this time. I reach further between her legs, underneath the seat, my fingers grasping on the metal lever that moves the chair backwards and forwards. They slip from it and I lean down further, my shoulder pressing against the wheel and making her gasp in pain, but I finally press it down and push with everything I have. Her chair screeches as it moves fractionally. The metal wheels have come off their runners, but at least it moves.

Slowly by slowly, inch by inch, the chair moves, the grind of metal upon metal making me nervous, but there is eventually enough of a space for her to get out. I climb back out of the car and she moves her bloody and damaged body out of the wreck, almost falling to her knees as she escapes the confines of that metal coffin. I catch her before she falls, and hoist her upwards, and she leans heavily on me.

"Thank you, thank you," she sobs out repeatedly. "Thank you so much."

Blood is escaping from her wounds—not pumping

or spurting violently, but a slow trickle coming from somewhere on her. I consider leaving her to escape on foot, to get herself as far away from here—from Lilly and me—as possible, but with her wound I know she won't make it very far. And come nightfall, the monsters will find her body. With a heavy heart I decide to bring her back to the house. To our safety, our sanctuary. To Lilly.

We begin to walk, her leaning heavily on me and grunting with every step, and me keeping look all around us. The day is still bright, the sun burning high in the sky, yet still I worry, still I panic. She doesn't question where we are going; she only seems glad to be free of the car wreck, glad to be moving out of the shadows and into the bright, burning sunlight.

We escape up the path, the house coming into view, and my nerves build in the pit of my stomach. My frown deepens the closer we get. However, Sarah doesn't look up. Her head hangs low to her chest, each step making her face contort in pain. The cut on her leg is bad; blood is still trickling from where the skin now hangs loose on her calf like sliced lunchmeat. I should feel sick at the sight, but I don't. I have seen too much in this life to get queasy over blood or a little flayed skin.

We cross the small island of grass at the front of the house, pass our car, and climb the three steps to the door. I lean Sarah against the wall while I retrieve the key from my pocket and unlock the door, and then I help her into the house. I kick the door shut behind me, making a mental note to come back and lock it as soon as I can, and we stumble down the hallway toward the kitchen, leaving a trail of coppery red blood behind us.

At the kitchen I help Sarah sit on one of the wooden chairs around the breakfast table, and she sighs with relief at getting the pressure off her leg. I watch her for a moment, unsure of what to do now that we are here. Her gray eyes meet mine for a brief moment before she slouches forward, rests her head on the table, and takes a deep shuddering breath. I chew on my lower lip, deciding upon my next move.

A small line of blood is trickling down her leg while another is soaking through the middle of her thin sweater. The blood is trailing down her body and amalgamating around her feet. I don't want Lilly seeing all this blood—it might frighten her—so I decide the best course of action is to stop her bleeding, bandage her up, and clean the blood away. I jog down the hallway, locking the front door as I pass, and head into the downstairs bathroom. In the lower cabinet there is a small first aid kit, and I take it out and head back to the kitchen. I pause when I get back to the kitchen, because Lilly is standing in the doorway looking at Sarah.

"You should still be hiding, Honeybee," I say quietly.

She doesn't look away from Sarah, however, Sarah looks up sharply at the sound of my voice. Her eyes widen at the sight of Lilly, her mouth open in wonder.

"A child," she gasps.

Because, you see, there has not been a child seen alive in such a long time. The children were the first to go: the weakest, the least immune, the slowest…the easiest to catch. How quickly we gave up our children to save ourselves.

Chapter Nine.

#9. The mystery of life.

"She's…there's a…how old is she?" Sarah tries to get to her feet, but her leg is still painful and she is too weak to stand without help. She gasps and falls back into her chair, a shaking hand going up to cover her mouth.

Lilly looks at me, turning her back on Sarah, and then she steps forward and wraps her small arms around my leg. She looks up at me with eyes full of sadness and worry. Because she knows the look Sarah is giving her; she understands the awe that her survival brings out in people.

"It's okay," I say to her. But still she clings. "Go sit over there." I point to the tall stools at the breakfast bar, and she goes automatically without question. I turn back to Sarah. "I need to look at your leg," I state simply, coldly, "I need to stop the bleeding."

She nods, but her eyes never leave Lilly, following her across the kitchen.

I kneel by Sarah's feet and open the first aid box, pulling out gauze and bandages, antiseptic wash and tape. I look up at her face and see her still looking at Lilly, and I don't like it. It makes me feel nervous and worried. I shouldn't have brought her here. It was a mistake, I decide. I have to put my knife down to clean and bandage her wound, another thing that I don't like. But I can't have her bleeding everywhere, or she'll die in here and we'll be trapped with a rotting corpse.

I place the knife down next to me, right next to the bandages so it is easy to grab if I need to, and I grasp the antiseptic solution. I grip Sarah's leg and tear the dirty material of her jeans away from it. The jeans were already badly torn and hanging open, but now I can see the full extent of the injuries. I pour the solution over the wound without warning, and Sarah yelps and pulls her leg free from me. She looks down at me, her gray eyes full of tears again, her chin quivering.

"Stop staring at her," I say quietly through gritted teeth. I hadn't meant to scare her. My action wasn't supposed to be a threat, but she deems it as one and I'm glad.

Her chin trembles and she blinks, the tears trailing down her cheeks leaving clean tracks on an otherwise dirty face. She nods and looks away from me, but also away from Lilly, and though I continue to scowl, I feel better knowing that she isn't staring any longer. The wound is bad: the plastic from inside the car has sliced through and up, separating skin from flesh so that it now hangs in one loose flap. I wrap gauze and bandages tightly around the wound after cleaning it and then tape it all in place. The bleeding has stopped, or at least hasn't seeped through the thick layer of bandages yet. I ask her to lift up her sweater and she does, but the cut there is only minimal, a thin red line across her stomach, and the bleeding has already stopped. I clean it and place a Band-Aid over the top, and then I pack everything back into the first aid box and stand up, grabbing my knife as I do. There is nothing else I can do for this woman. I can't stitch her skin back together; I can only hope that it doesn't get infected and possibly her skin might knit itself back together.

I retrieve two of the precious painkillers and hand them to Sarah, and she takes them with a mumbled "thanks." I don't like giving out our rations, especially not painkillers, but Lilly is still watching and I don't want her to think that I am cruel. Lilly brings over water to help Sarah swallow the dry, powdery tablets, though I frown at her until she goes back to her stool.

This world has made me selfish and greedy. When you have nothing, you don't want to share it.

"You should sleep," I say abruptly, pulling Sarah up from her chair without waiting for her reply. "You can stay for tonight, but you'll need to leave tomorrow." I leave no room for disagreement.

She nods and leans on me again, though I can feel that she isn't placing all of her weight on me like previously. We move slowly down the hallway, and I see that her blood has trailed all along the wooden floors, and I feel guilty that Lilly had to see any of this.

The stairs are hard to climb, but between pulling herself up using the banister and clinging onto me, Sarah makes it onto the landing. I guide her along to one of the bedrooms and help her into the bed. She's shaken up by both her accident and the sight of Lilly, but her adrenalin is wearing off and the blood loss was quite substantial, so she's tiring. I help her under the covers and she stares at me with wide eyes, reminding me in many ways of Lilly, her look of confusion and wariness, uncertainty washing over her features. She lies stiffly in the bed, almost afraid to get comfy or to move in any way.

"How did you crash?" I ask, now that Lilly is out of earshot.

Sarah swallows before replying. "I fell asleep while driving," she says.

I nod, because I can understand that. I've almost done that many a time. I turn to leave but she grabs my arm, and I snatch it back and stare at her in anger.

"I'm sorry, I didn't mean to startle you. I just wondered…is it safe here?"

Her voice is soft and shaky, but her meaning is clear: Is it free of monsters? Will she be okay to sleep with us guarding her? Will we, in fact, guard her at all? I think about all these unspoken questions, deciding for myself what I will do before I speak, before I voice my answer to this stranger.

"It's been safe so far," I reply calmly. "You can sleep. I'll wake you for supper."

A small smile plays on her lips, not quite giving itself over to a full-mouthed expression of happiness, but close enough. She nods and closes her eyes, and I turn to leave.

"Thank you," she whispers to my retreating back.

I don't bother to reply. Her thanks isn't needed. Her leaving here tomorrow is what I want. Downstairs, Lilly is exactly where I left her: on the stool by the breakfast bar. She's waiting patiently, scared of strangers but also excited for new company, new interactions. She looks up when I come in, her eyes dancing with eagerness. She waits patiently as I make my way to her, reaching over to hug me when I get within distance. I take her hug, hungry for its warmth, the reassurance that it provides, and I kiss the top of her head.

"She's sleeping," I murmur against her hair.

"Is she bad?" she whispers back.

"I don't know," I answer honestly.

Silence falls around us, but I know that Lilly is still thinking about what I said. She may be a child, but her brain is more accustomed to this world, to the decisions that a person must make in order to survive. Yet she is much more understanding and forgiving than me.

"She has to leave tomorrow. We'll give her some food and send her on her way."

Silence…

"You understand, don't you?"

"Yes, Mama," she replies. "You want to keep me safe."

I pull out of our hug and look down into her pretty face, her large eyes looking up at me unblinking. Like twin pools of darkness, her brown eyes suck me in, absorbing me until I feel lost. I cup her cheeks in my cold hands, finding strength in her as I always do.

"I have to keep you safe," I croon, hoping that she will understand.

"Okay," she replies.

I let go of her face and look across at the blood on the floor. "I need to clean this up. I'm sorry that you had to see it." I gesture to the mess, but I know that she has seen much worse than this. Yet somehow this seems almost as bad. Because she was beginning to soften here, her walls coming down. She was settling, and was almost at peace, but I can feel it now, the iciness in the air. This woman, her blood, they have invaded Lilly's space, and she is lost again. And that makes me feel bitter resentment toward this woman. Intruding on our lives. Of course it wasn't by her choice, but I don't care.

I gather some large towels and wipe the blood away as best as I can. It takes a long time—some of it has already started to dry—and when I stand back up and look along the hallway, I see that the floor still looks stained by the blood. But it's the best I can do. My back aches as I gather the bloody towels and place them in a clothes hamper in one of the bedrooms, and before I come back down the stairs, I check on Sarah.

She's sleeping soundly, soft snores only punctuated by the occasional murmur. I click the door closed quietly and contemplate putting a chair under the handle just in case she is dangerous, but at the last minute I decide against it. I can protect Lilly and myself from this woman—of that I am sure.

I clean my hands with some of the hand soap in the downstairs bathroom and stale water from the toilet cistern, watching mesmerized as the bloody water swirls away. There isn't very much left in there, just enough to cup in my hands. I realize that neither of us have eaten since breakfast, and since our bodies have quickly gotten used to three meals a day since arriving here, I feel desperately hungry and presume that Lilly will feel the same way.

The day is nearly over, and night will be falling soon. I hurry to make both Lilly and myself something to eat—spaghetti and canned Spam —because she likes spaghetti. I don't use any tomato sauce today, though. I've seen enough red. We devour large bowlfuls with greedy smiles, both of us wishing for cheese to sprinkle on the top and make it even more perfect, but at least when we are finished, we are full. Our rumbly tummies are blissfully silent, and I'm once more left feeling like I've accomplished something by being able to fill Lilly's stomach.

Lilly moves back to the table and continues coloring her picture, and I set about cleaning our bowls—which involves wiping them out with a slightly damp cloth. I don't want to waste what little water we have on properly washing things, but if I don't clean things, at least a little, we could get sick from infection.

When I'm done with cleaning them, I get the small map book and look at it again, wondering where we will go next. I hope that we can stay here for a little longer, but the time will come when we will have to leave. Of that I am certain.

Sarah comes slowly into the kitchen with a shy smile on her face. She looks pale, but she's moving easier now. She smiles wider when she sees Lilly, as if she had forgotten about her, or thought that maybe she was a dream. Her smile falls when she sees me watching her closely.

"I smelled food?" She poses it as a question, and from across the room I can hear her stomach growling loudly.

"Mama can make you something," Lilly says, her words so soft, so innocent.

They're both looking at me expectantly now, and I incline my head to Sarah to sit at the stool at the end of the breakfast bar, far away from Lilly. She hobbles over and perches on the stool, and I boil her some of the spaghetti. The water bubbles in the pan, the spaghetti softening and dancing in the scorching water. I drain it into an empty pan, intending to use the water tomorrow for some more pasta. Pasta is great: it's a good source of carbohydrates, it releases the energy slowly, and it's filling even when you only have a little. But the best part is that we have lots of it. The worst part is that you need water to cook it. I open another can of Spam, chopping half of it and putting it in with the spaghetti, and then I push the bowl toward Sarah.

She takes it with a "thanks," diving in with her

fingers. She's noisy as she eats, sucking up the pasta with a slurp and licking her fingers hungrily as if she hasn't eaten for weeks. I watch both transfixed and fascinated as she eats. Her cheekbones are jutting, her eyes hollow, and I don't understand how I missed that she was quite obviously starving. Had this been us—Lilly and me—only last week? I suddenly feel guilty for withholding food from her and insisting that she sleep. Last week I couldn't have waited another hour for food. I was weak and tired, aching all over, my head pounding…

"How are you feeling?" I ask, giving her some of our flat orange pop.

She eyes the glass warily, picking it up with greasy fingers and sniffing the contents.

"It's juice," Lilly says matter-of-factly, startling both Sarah and me as she comes to stand with us.

Lilly has been watching Sarah too, and she hands her a fork with a shy smile.

Sarah takes it with a soft blush. "I'm sorry, I was just so hungry," she says by way of explanation. "It's been days since I ate." She drinks the flat pop down in one go, but I don't give her any more. It's Lilly's favorite.

Sarah starts to eat again, this time using her fork, though I can see how much it frustrates her to do so. Her stomach grumbles noisily, the food being digested easily as she eats. When the bowl is empty, she looks into it longingly, wanting more but not daring to ask me. I refuse to cook any more of the pasta, though. Things have to be rationed if we are to survive. Instead I grab a handful of the dry crackers from the pantry and let Sarah eat those. They are stale, but I have been eating them and they are better than nothing.

"Thank you," she mumbles, picking one up and biting down on it.

I fill her glass up with water and watch her take sips in between mouthfuls of dry, stale crackers. She finishes them and looks up with a little more color to her cheeks than before. She gives me a tentative smile, which I don't return. I want to, though, but I can't. This woman makes me nervous, though she seems harmless enough and Lilly likes her.

Lilly runs around the breakfast bar and pulls on my top. "I need to pee," she whispers, glancing with embarrassment at Sarah.

I smile down at her. "Okay." I take her hand and we leave the kitchen. I give Sarah a wary glance as we go because I don't like leaving her alone in this house—not with our food so close. I take Lilly to the downstairs bathroom and she quickly squats over the bucket. I do the same after her and pick up the bucket, bringing it back with us to the kitchen. Sarah hasn't moved from her place at the breakfast bar, and she watches us as we enter. Lilly goes straight back to her coloring book and I go to the back door before glancing over at Lilly.

"I'm going outside for a moment, Lilly."

She looks up at me and then nods once before

returning to her coloring.

I unlock the door, ready to take the bucket outside. I look over at Sarah as I leave, waiting for her to scoot off the stool and follow me.

I pour the pee away and then pull my cigarettes from my pocket and light one up. I haven't smoked once since we arrived here—I haven't felt the need—but I feel stressed today. Worry is eating away at me like cancer. The sun will be setting any time now, and the long stretch of night will begin. The night is our death sentence, when the monsters come out, hunting, screaming, searching. There is no escape from them in the night.

Sarah stands by my side and I turn to look at her, examining her features more carefully, trying to decide if I can trust her or not. I want to, but so many times I have been tricked, led to believe something that isn't true. And now that I have Lilly, I don't dare take any risks. I have only done that once since we have been together, and it turned out badly—very badly—and I vowed never to trust again.

"I used to have a child," Sarah says quietly. "A little boy called David." Her eyes are far away. Though she's looking directly at me, she sees through me as she speaks. She looks down suddenly, breaking our contact with a soft shake of her head. "It doesn't matter now."

But I see her tears splat on the ground below, one landing on her white sneaker and loosening some of the dirt. I don't want to hear about her little boy. I don't want to learn anything about her. It doesn't matter that she had a son, because he is dead, and I know that she probably let him die. That's what most people did: they sacrificed their children for their own lives.

"You have to leave tomorrow," I say, still watching her. Still smoking. Still unsure.

She nods, another tear falling. "I know."

"What will you do?" I ask, suddenly curious.

She has no car—none that works, anyway. No vehicle to get from one place to another. We only have our car, mine and Lilly's, already loaded up with our things in case of emergency, but she can't take that. It's ours.

"Can I borrow your bike?" she says sarcastically with a bitter laugh.

She kicks the wheel of the bike that's leaning against the house. It's rusty and old, but its tires are still inflated. Lilly had a brief go on it yesterday, though she was too small to reach the pedals. I pushed her around the garden until my back hurt. There's a small basket on the front, it's a light brown wicker and makes me think of my grandma and smile. Sarah looks up at me with a grimace.

"No," I say, feeling childish.

Sarah looks up into the sky. "The sun is setting," she says.

"Where will you go?" I ask, curious. Because I know the sun is setting, but I don't know where this woman will go when I send her away, and I'm curious.

"I was headed to Colorado. I met some people a month or so back. That's where they were heading." She looks up, and this time it's her examining me, seeing if I'm trustworthy. She must decide I am, because she continues talking. "There's talk of a safe place, without the monsters. My husband was too sick, though. I couldn't leave him and they wouldn't let him come with us." She frowns as she says it, as if she herself doesn't believe her own words. "But he's gone now, and if there's safety, well, I'd be stupid not to go."

I shake my head. "I've heard all this before." I stamp out my cigarette, already wanting another. I'm not angry, not even a little, but it's the truth: I *have* heard all of this before. I risked everything to find a safe place, and it got everyone I knew killed.

"Me too." She shrugs in agreement. "But at least it's a destination." She looks away from me, across the yard, squinting directly into the sun hanging low in the sky. "It's hope at least." Her last words are a murmur, but I hear them all the same.

"Hope is what gets you killed," I reply, softly yet defensively.

Sarah turns back to me. "No, hope is what keeps us alive."

I laugh, a dark, low chuckle. "If you say so." I light another cigarette, needing the nicotine to get me through this conversation.

"I can write down where it is for you, if you like.

Just in case."

I shake my head. "No, we'll be fine here. We have our car out front packed with supplies, enough food in the house to last us a couple of weeks, and we have each other." I shrug on a smile.

This is all I need to survive—not false hope and promises of safety.

Just Lilly. Just my car, and our supplies.

"But aren't you at least curious?" she asks, looking genuinely confused.

I shake my head. "No. Not even a little bit."

Chapter Ten.

#10. I don't want to say I told you so…

The sun has begun to set, its orange glow dipping over the tops of the green trees, and worry has begun pooling in my tummy. We are all nervous, but we are all prepared—as we are every nightfall. We keep our weapons close and our shoes on, because you just never know.

Lilly has fallen asleep on the big bed, her soft curls splayed around her head like a halo. She sleeps fitfully tonight, and I hate that—hate that her only escape has been stolen from her. A child should be able to dream of faraway lands and fairies. Instead, her dreams are invaded by monsters with red eyes and nails as sharp as knives. I hate that.

I stand by the window. The curtains are closed, but I stare out of a small crack on one side. I haven't heard their calls yet, their angry screams of hunger and hate. But I will, anytime now. Sarah is at the other end of the window, looking out of another small crack. She, too, seems nervous, and for the first time I'm grateful to have her here. Grateful that I don't have to do this alone. The nighttime hours are long and frightening. They can drive you insane if you listen too intently, if you let the screams and growls of the monsters get inside of you. At least tonight I will have someone to share that burden with.

"Do you ever think where they came from?" she

asks, still staring out the window. "Or how the virus started?"

I shake my head no, but then realize that she can't see me. "No. Not anymore," I answer. "Because it doesn't matter."

Silence, and then: "I do. It's in my nature to be curious, though, to try to find the pieces of a puzzle. I often wonder if we knew, if we could end it—end them."

Her last words sound angry and bitter, and I understand that. I can make sense of the misplaced anger and bitterness that eats a person up. I have been there, and I have come out of the other side until I am now indifferent. I hate them, but without emotion, because I understand that it isn't their fault. They don't like this any more than we do.

But things are the way they are. And there is no changing that.

"I'm going to check the other windows," she says, and turns to leave.

We have been taking it in shifts to check the windows, and it's another thing that I'm glad to have help with. I wonder about asking her to stay with us longer, but then I change my mind.

"Keep quiet," I say, without turning away from the window.

"Not like I'm going to be blasting music or revving the engine on your car," she says back, and I hear the humor in her voice.

I like her humor. I like that she makes Lilly laugh

and smile.

"I have the keys to the car with me, so no, you wouldn't." I turn to her and I jangle the keys in the air between us. There's humor in my words—not much, but a little. And I'm shocked at myself.

Sarah smiles back, happy, I think, to see some other form of emotion from me than just indifference or distrust. She leaves the room without another word and I turn back to the window and continue to stare into the darkness.

It's not long before the growls start—the long, drawn-out, piercing screams that punctuate nightmares. I imagine them running around in the night, their bodies glorifying themselves in the darkness, rolling around and embracing the touch of the black night upon their leathery skin. I look back toward Lilly and see her sitting up and staring at me.

"Are they here?" she whispers, her words carrying across the room to me.

"They are awake outside somewhere, yes," I reply solemnly, hating that I have to say this to her. Just once I would like to say no. Just once.

I hear her swallow. The sound is loud in our darkness until another scream and growl cuts through it. I look back toward the darkness, hating the noise, hating that they fill each nighttime hour with dread. The darkness is everlasting, enveloping the house in its blanket of blackness, and even here doesn't feel safe.

But we are.

Here is safe.

They can't find us here.

I stare at the shadows outside, seeing them moving, and knowing that it's just me—my imagination. Just the wind in the trees, blowing the branches and making the shadows move. The eyes glowing red are not real; the monsters creeping up the long path from the road are just my mind's resurrection of my nightmares.

I stare into the darkness…

Staring, staring, staring.

Lilly's hand touches upon mine, her warm fingers slipping between my cold ones.

"Mama?" she asks, looking out, and I pray that she never gets to see the demons that live inside my head. "Mama?" She shakes my arm, squeezing on my hand, her voice more urgent.

Teeth as sharp as knives, biting, tearing, stretching. The night brings everything to life. My visions burn my eyes and I want to join in the chorus of screaming outside.

"Mama?!"

I look down into Lilly's face, reaching to pull her up into my arms. I kiss the top of her head, feeling guilty for my morbid thoughts.

"I'm sorry, Honeybee." I kiss her again. "I'm sorry."

She wriggles to free herself. "They're here," she whispers, and I stare into her face, my own features contorting in confusion. "They're here." She grips my face and forcibly turns my head to look out of the window.

I stare into the darkness, seeing the shapes moving, the red eyes glowing, and my heart freezes. They *are* here. They have found us. But how? I think of earlier, of helping to free Sarah from her car. I remember the pool of blood at her feet, and the way it had trailed down the hallway downstairs. The way it had dripped on the steps outside, across the lawn and down the path.

"Mama, they are here," Lilly sobs.

"They are here," I say back numbly.

I hear Sarah coming up the stairs. She rushes into the room, and I know that she has seen them too. She stares at me and Lilly, her eyes panicked, her breathing shallow.

"They're everywhere," she says on a whisper.

"My car—we need to get to my car," I reply matter-of-factly.

"But how? They're at the front." She rushes to the window, as if to confirm the fact.

"We need to distract them, to draw them to the back of the house so we can get to the car."

Sarah nods, her fingers gripping her knife carefully.

I look down at Lilly, her chubby face staring at me full of innocence and hope, and then I look at Sarah. I walk forward, Lilly feeling like the lightest thing in the world, but my heavy burden.

"Take her. I'll distract them." I try to hand Lilly

over but she clings to me fiercely, her whimpers growing louder. "Lilly, you have to. I'll distract them and run to the road, and you and Sarah will be there, waiting for me in the car. I'll get in and we'll drive away." I look at Sarah to confirm and she nods.

I have to do this. Because I know that Sarah will not. And I will not risk Lilly. Sarah had a son, and she cares for Lilly. She'll protect her as best she can. But if it came down to a choice between herself and Lilly, she would save herself. So I need to guide the danger away from us all. This is what I tell myself. The screeching outside gets louder as more monsters join the first ones. All drawn by the same thing: blood. Sarah's blood.

Sarah reaches over and pries Lilly from me. I want to cry, because Lilly is scared—and I don't like Lilly to be scared. I don't want her to be sad. But she has to stay safe. I hand Sarah the car keys, our eyes locking as I try to get her to understand that she must look after Lilly for me, that she can't let anything happen to her. That she must get rid of all selfish thoughts now, and protect this little girl.

"I love you, Honeybee," I say, and head to the bedroom door. I can hear the monsters down below, scratch-scratch-scratching… They're unsure if we're still here, but they know we *were*, and that will be enough to make them stay.

"Wait!" Sarah says, coming forward. She hands me something: a piece of paper folded up.

I frown at it and shove it in my pocket,

disinterested. There is no time to question it or wonder what it is.

I run across the landing to the back of the house, passing closed doors, until I reach the room farthest away. I'm not sure what I'm going to do until I get there, until I turn and see Sarah with Lilly on her back standing at the top of the stairs, waiting for me to cause a distraction loud enough and big enough to make the monsters move away from the front door.

I look around, seeing all the normal things that belong in a normal life: a dresser, a bed, a cabinet, and a lamp. I pick up the lamp and grip it in my hand, pulling the plug out of the socket, and then I go to the window. There are one or two down here, all sniff-sniff-sniffing for something. For us…for our blood. I take a deep breath, reach back with the lamp in my hand, and throw the lamp as hard as I can at the window.

It smashes through the glass, both lamp and window breaking simultaneously upon impact. The monsters all at once scream loudly for their brethren. With the window broken I can't hear anything but their screams and growls, their nails scratching to get to me. I can't know if Sarah and Lilly have made it to the front door, if they make it to the car, to freedom. I can only buy them some time.

I grab anything within reaching distance and begin to launch things out the windows: photo frames and artwork from the walls, ornaments that smash as they crash down below. I throw and throw until there are so many down below that the glow from their eyes is like the setting sun.

I back away from the window, wanting to run far and wide but needing to know that Lilly is safe first. I dart across the landing, making it back to our bedroom, and I run to the window and look out. I see the taillights of the car heading down the path and I pray that there are none left down there.

I clutch my knife tightly and run out of the room and to the stairs, and then I run down them, taking them two at a time until I reach the bottom. The noise down here is insane, the scratching sound of their nails on the walls and doors sounding like a million mice trying to gnaw their way inside my head. I get to the front door and open it, warily looking out, but see nothing but darkness—no glow of eyes to still my rapidly beating heart and freeze the blood in my veins. I step outside, the smell of the monsters hanging thickly in the air, and I'm about to run down across the lawn when one of the monsters slinks its way around the corner of the house.

It sees me and hisses, but it doesn't scream for attention. It looks injured, and I remember how I once saw one monster eating another. It had been injured and dying, and its brother had clearly been starving. I realize that this one doesn't call out for its brothers and sisters because it fears them as much as I do. However, it does not fear me.

It charges at me, diving when it is within reaching distance, and I lift my arms to shield myself from its attack. I collapse under its weight, its muscle mass pressing my back against the cold concrete steps as the air leaves my lungs in a loud *whoosh*. My head cracks against the steps and I cry out in pain as stars dance before my eyes. Its body is a limp, dead weight on top of me. Its mouth is agape, its sharp teeth centimeters away from my face. Its blood drenches me, and I'm frantic as I try to shift myself out from under its corpse.

I slide out from beneath its heavy body and realize my knife has pierced its belly and slid all the way up to its chest, and as I move, its insides tumble out on top of me. I think of the monster I killed when we first got here and for a second I think on what a peculiar coincidence that is. I stagger backwards, hearing the telltale scratching and clicking of nails on the path. The monsters can smell the blood, and they are coming.

I press my back against the wall of the house, willing myself to calm down, to be invisible and to not release the scream of terror I feel trying to tear its way up my throat as the monsters come around the opposite corner of the house. I blend myself into the shadows, the first time they have ever been my friend, and I pray. I pray for it to be quick, for my death to be immediate.

But they don't see me. They are too busy with the dead monster at their feet—sniffing, scratching, biting, and tearing. They hold no mercy for anyone or anything; they are soulless beasts that only mean to destroy. I slide along the wall, my eyes fixed on them the entire time, my legs shaking with the urge to run away. But I hold steady and continue to slide my way slowly along, feeling the bricks digging into my back, until I reach the corner. I look away from the group of monsters for a split second and I peer around the corner, seeing nothing but shadows, and I slip around and out of their sight.

I run along the side of the house, not knowing where I am going to go but aware that I can't get to the road by way of the front of the house anymore—not until the monsters go inside. Around the back, several of them have smashed a lower floor window and I see the tail end of one enter the house. They are inside now, inside what was once our home, and that thought makes me so angry. They have ruined everything. Again.

My eyes fall to the bike now lying on the ground. One of the monsters must have knocked it over, I decide. Its back wheel is spinning mindlessly, and I almost laugh at the irony that it is I that will be using the bike for my getaway, and not Sarah.

I hurry over to it, keeping low and out of sight in case any of the monsters look out the window. I pick it up quickly. It's lightweight and I wheel it quietly away from the house and toward the bushes, where it is dark. They're murky, and not somewhere that I want to enter, but as more windows smash, and I hear the screaming and growling of the monsters inside the house, I know my best bet is in the dark grey shadows—somewhere I have avoided for a long time now. I climb on the bike, sitting on the saddle, and I take a deep breath before pedaling away quickly. I stick to the shadows as much as I can until I am at the front of the house once more, and I pedal as fast as I can around the island of grass and down the long, gravelly road, following the trail of blood left by Sarah earlier today, staying in the shadows.

I look back at the house when I reach the bottom of the road. The noises coming from inside the house are loud and obnoxious as the monsters break and destroy everything we had come to cherish so much. I say goodbye to our peace, our sanctuary, and our supplies. It was good while it lasted. But nothing ever lasts forever. Not anymore.

At the bottom of the gravel road, I turn onto the main strip of blacktop that was once a perfectly good road. As time has passed and the elements have taken their toll, the roads have begun to crumble and crack. They are dangerous to drive on at night, the giant holes left in some of them almost begging for you to drive into them and crash. I start to pedal quickly, the sound of screeching and smashing still echoing down to me from the house. I feel sad that we have lost that home, sadder still that Lilly didn't get a few more days of peace there. But our supplies are my greatest loss. The food that we have had to leave behind. I had known it would happen—I had prepared, packing the car with water and food rations to last over a week—but the loss of the food left behind is still acute.

I look around, my heart sinking when I don't see my car. I have been left behind, and that should hurt more than it does, but I am just glad that Lilly is safe. I will mourn my loss when I am safe. I see Sarah's beat-up car up ahead, the hood still crumpled around the base of a tree where she crashed. The car is in worse shape now than earlier. The monsters have torn the metal apart trying to taste the blood. I pedal to the side of it and stop, taking a second to witness the destruction. Blood is still pooled around and inside of it—Sarah's blood from earlier today. It is dried and hard now, yet to the monsters it will still smell fresh. I feel stupid for not realizing that it would attract the monsters to us. Stupider still for not being prepared for them or packing our things and leaving before they came.

And as I hear the soft whimpering of Lilly coming from underneath the wreck, I feel stupid for ever trusting that woman and allowing her into our lives.

Chapter Eleven.

#11. Hold tight to that which you love.

I let go of the bike and drop to my knees, seeing the tiny form of Lilly underneath the car. I can't make out her face, nor her arms or legs, but I know that it is her. I know her cry. It is like a brand on my heart and soul.

"Lilly!" I whisper and reach under. My fingers graze her hair and she shrieks and backs away. "Lilly!" I whisper again, more urgently.

Her eyes open, almost glowing in the darkness under the car. And she reminds me of a cat.

"Mama?" she asks, her voice so soft, so scared. Almost as if she is afraid to believe that it is me.

"Yes. Come quickly."

I don't have time to ask Lilly where Sarah is or why she is hiding underneath the car, but anger, raw and hot, burns in my stomach at the thought of Sarah leaving behind my Lilly—my Honeybee.

Lilly scrambles out, blinking away her tears as she looks into my face before burying herself in my arms. I scoop her up and squeeze her tightly, kissing her hair and breathing in her life. Sobs work up my throat but I push them back down. There will be time for that, but not now.

"We need to go," I say, and Lilly nods against my neck.

I pick up my bike and straddle it, all without

putting Lilly down. Because I will never let her out of my sight again. Her little legs and arms tighten around me as I begin to pedal, but after five minutes I decide that it is almost impossible to ride like this. We are getting nowhere, and the monsters will be out in force tonight, especially here, brought by the scent of blood.

I stop the bike and think what to do. "Lilly, I need you to sit in the basket if you can," I say, deciding on my plan.

She shakes her head, not wanting to let me go, and I don't blame her. I can't blame her. The urge to ask what happened after she left with Sarah is strong, but the knowledge will do me no good right now. I would get angry and emotional, and I need to be strong. I need to have a clear head. I need to be quick.

I pry Lilly's arms away from me, which spurs a fresh bout of tears from her. I push her tangled curls back away from her face and I look into her eyes, my heart breaking at her sadness, wanting and needing to take it all away, but all I can do now is try and get us to safety.

"I need to be quick. We need to get away from here. You have to sit in the basket, please." I beg her to understand. My voice is forceful and calm, but she seems to find some comfort in it.

Her chin quivers, tears pouring down her cheeks, but she nods. She loosens her grip on me, and I lift her and place her bottom into the basket. She's facing toward the road, her legs dangling in front, and though she's not comfy in any way, it is the safest way for her to ride for now.

"Hold on tightly," I whisper, to which she nods solemnly and grips the handlebars. She looks awkward and uncomfortable, but it's the best I can do.

I give a quick glance behind me, almost certain that I can see the dark shadows moving around at the site of Sarah's earlier car crash. I turn back to the way we are facing and begin to pedal as fast and as hard as I can. It's much easier like this, though it's still too slow for my liking. Especially compared to a car. But we are moving away from *them*, away from the death that they would surely bring.

My muscles are tight with worry and anxiety, and anger still burns in my stomach—a quiet fury that I want to release, but can't. Yet when I look at Lilly, the pale profile of her face looking up to the trees that hide the moon from our sight, I breathe a sigh of relief. Because she is here. She is safe. I have her with me again, and I will never let anything happen to her. And that is all that matters. Not my anger and my rage, or the dread I feel growing inside of me. I will keep Lilly safe, no matter what. And I will kill Sarah if I ever run into her again.

The night is a blur of blackness and monster screams, though thankfully, we do not see any of the monsters. But their screams are enough to chill me to my core. I say a silent prayer of thankfulness as the trees open up and give way to a wide open highway. I can see on either side of us now. The ground is flat on both sides, allowing me to take a shaky breath as the realization that we are truly alone settles in. We are not being followed, or stalked through the night. There are no monsters waiting for us. It is just Lilly and me right now. The moon is glowing full and round in the blackened sky, another thing that calms my fractured nerves.

I slow my pedaling, feeling hot sweat beading down my spine and across my forehead. My muscles are aching, tiring after riding so hard for so long without a break, but I can't stop now. Not yet. Lilly's body slowly slouches sideways as she finally falls into a deep yet troubled sleep. I hold the handlebars tightly with one hand and keep a grip on her body with my other. It makes pedaling twice as hard and makes the bike wobble, but it's the only way for her to sleep. And damn it, she's a little girl, she should be safely tucked up in bed somewhere, with a fluffy pink blanket in her little bedroom filled with cuddly toys and Barbie dolls. She should be dreaming sweet dreams of cotton candy or riding on flying unicorns. She should be looking forward to going to school, to playing in the park, to seeing her friends, to eating Pop Tarts for breakfast. But she's not. She's running for her life through the night, being chased by monsters and slowly turning into one of them herself.

We're doomed. No matter which way that I look at it, no matter which way I try to decipher the problem. We. Are. Doomed. Yet I still try, my heart refuses to give up—to give her up—even though there really is nothing to give up on anyway. The end is inevitable. It is death, and one way or another, it will come for us.

The night is humid and quiet, leaving me to the darkness of my bleak thoughts. My worries swim around in it, never-ending, restless, warring for something that I cannot give to them or myself: peace.

We have nothing now.

Nothing at all.

We are worse off than we were previously. Tears sting my eyes, the world blurring as I fight to hold them back. What will we do now?

We have nothing.

My body shivers, trembling up and down as it begins to give in—give up. We have nothing, there is no escape from this. Only time…such little time left with each other. It will never be enough. Lilly's soft snores interrupt my downward spiral into the blackness of my internal misery. I stop pedaling, my mind more exhausted than my weak body. I place one foot on the ground to balance us and the bike, and then I watch her. Her little pink mouth is slightly agape as her soft breath leaves her lips. Her eyes move behind her closed lids, and I wonder what she is dreaming of. She seems so peaceful, and yet so thoroughly exhausted. The tears from earlier are still evident on her cheeks, and I grip my chest—the place where my heart lies just beneath my ribs—as pain burns deep within it.

Is this what it feels like when your heart breaks? I

wonder.

A screech in the night echoes out loudly and I jump, the tiny hairs on my arms tingling with recognition of the danger. I look behind us, seeing nothing but darkened blacktop and empty fields. Up ahead there is a large square shape in the distance—a barn, I think it is. I look at the bike and contemplate climbing back on it, pedaling to get us there quicker, but my legs and butt are sore and aching. So I stay standing, choosing to push the bike forward while still awkwardly holding onto Lilly and stopping her from falling out of the small wicker basket.

Despite the adrenalin and the fear, I yawn as I push us onward through the night. My eyelids feel heavy, my body weary. I walk and push and I ignore the dark thoughts that wander my mind until we finally, mercifully, reach the barn. The shadows surrounding it scare me, the shadows that I know will be inside it are even scarier, but I simply can't go on any further. We have to stop…*I* have to stop. We've been going for hours, and no matter what hunts us, my body needs sleep. I lean the bike against the wooden wall—the side that is currently bright with the glow of full moonlight shining down on it. Lilly mumbles as I pull her from the basket, and she automatically wraps her little arms and legs around me, her face burying into the space between my shoulder and my head, and she falls back to sleep.

I move slowly, cautiously toward the door, dread filling my gut, heavy and foreboding. But I'm at the point of no return. There is nowhere else to go. There is no more I can give right now. One hand is planted beneath Lilly's butt as I hold her to me, her little body going slack in my arms as sleep takes her deeper. With my other hand I grip the handle of the barn door and pull it open fractionally. I breathe in the warm, rank air that slips out through the small crack, smelling straw and mildew. I pull the door open some more and peer inside, my eyes taking in what they can.

Nothing moves.

Nothing screams.

Nothing comes forth from the blackness within.

I carry Lilly inside and shut the door after me, standing still as my eyes adjust to the deep blackness. I am glad that she is asleep now. She wouldn't like this place. This is everything we should run from. But I can't run anymore tonight; I need to rest.

The moon glows bright through a gap in the broken roof, a window or hatch I think that was once there. I see steps leading up to a hayloft and I step on the bottom one, testing my weight against the aged wood and finding that it is still sturdy after all this time. I climb, holding onto the wooden ladders with one hand, my other still holding onto Lilly. My body shakes with the strain, but still I go on. I reach the top, and know that I need to put her down to climb up onto the ledge.

"Honeybee," I whisper against her hair, kissing her softly until she stirs against me.

She slowly looks up at me, her eyes half closed as

they drowsily find my face in the darkness. She looks past me, taking in our surroundings, but I don't know if she knows what is happening right now; she is still too sleepy.

"I need you to get down a moment," I say, and she nods and clambers from me until she's standing on shaky legs in the middle of the wooden ledge, swaying with sleep.

I climb all the way up and then move to her, taking her hand in mine as I guide her over to some haystacks. I move some out of the way, until I can make a small fort of sorts within them, and then I pick Lilly up and we lie down together. The moon shines down on us like a beacon of hope, protecting us—or so it feels like. But the moon, like most things, is an illusion. The monsters are frightened of the moon, but only because they see its light. The moon's light, however, cannot harm them. But still I find comfort from the soft glow.

I lick my lips with thirst, my eyelids already growing heavy. Lilly snuggles up against my body, already drifting back into unconsciousness, and I afford my heartbroken mind and somnolent body the same relief. My eyes close and I feel myself being sucked down into a sleep like no other.

I dream of nothing. I am floating along on a cloud of blackness. But then a tongue whips through the air, large and thick, and slick with black blood. It curls around us, around Lilly and me, and then I am running, pulling on Lilly's hand as I drag us through the dark. Running, running, we are forever running. Hiding from the blackness that grows within us, that calls to the night, that is slowly stealing our souls. Stealing everything we are and will not be. I am panting and breathless, my legs tired and aching, the dull throb of sadness filling me to the brim as I scream blindly into the dark and pray for the end to come quickly.

I look down at Lilly, and she looks back at me with a devil's smile and eyes as red as hate. Her tongue darts out, thick and long and black, and I'm screaming and screaming and begging for anything and everything. Because it can't take her... not my Lilly. Not my Honeybee.

Chapter Twelve.

#12. Our gift is the sun.

I wake with a start, my heart already hammering heavily in my chest, ready to burst out and escape through the broken space above us. Lilly's arms tighten around me as I stare unblinkingly up at the bright yellow disc in the sky: the sun, our savior. The warmth of its rays are draped across our entwined bodies, and I take a small, self-indulgent moment to enjoy it, the warmth and the security that the sunlight provides. This is our gift. Our gift for surviving another night: the sun.

Lilly's soft snores are all I hear, and my shattered nerves begin to soothe on their own accord. I relax myself against her, all thoughts of my nightmare subsiding. I remember singing to Honeybee when she had nightmares, the mellow and soulful tones I would produce to try and vanquish her sadness—her fear. She has a more beautiful voice than me, though I have only heard her sing once. One day when we were eating wild berries by the roadside, the warm sun on our backs and the delicious, bitter tang of berries on my tongue, she started abruptly. No warning, no slow buildup. She just opened her little heart shaped mouth and began to sing, the stain of berries still vivid on her chin. I had smiled, watching her as I continued to eat, listening to her sweet voice sing a lullaby that I had never heard before.

I smile now as I clutch hold of the memory as tightly as I can.

The smell of the sweat on our bodies and the hungry gurgle of our empty bellies brings me back to wakefulness. Back to the life that I don't want to be in. I open my eyes and look down at Lilly, pushing back the tangles of her hair. The black lines of poison beneath her skin come into view, and I swallow. They trail down her throat, black and ugly and slowly changing her—killing her. I squeeze my eyes closed as I pull her tightly to me, kissing the top of her head. I work hard to suppress the sob that hangs in my throat, refusing to give up on her yet. I have the same poison running through my veins, but I don't care about that. I only care about her.

"Mama?"

I open my eyes and see her pools of brown staring up at me. She's still sleepy, and I realize that I must have been squeezing her too hard. I force a smile.

"Morning, Honeybee."

She watches me carefully, blinking every now and then as she gazes upon my heartbroken face. Because she knows. She always knows. She's so clever for someone so young.

"I love you," she finally whispers.

I smile affectionately and stroke her cheek. "And I love you."

She grins back, and like that—like a snap of the fingers—the mood between us is better. Our morbid thoughts are pushed away for the moment, because what good is morbidity to you? It doesn't help. Though of course nothing really helps, but morbidity even less so. It is like an infection—a disease if, you will. It destroys you from the inside out, making you sick with sadness and rage.

I sit up and Lilly pulls away from me, giving a small stretch of her thin body. She lifts her arms above her head and her top lifts fractionally—enough for me to see that despite all the food she has eaten for the past week she is still all skin and bones, and enough for me to see that the black veins are slowly working their way across her stomach. I look away as she finishes her stretch and casts her glance back to me.

"I like it here," she says, tipping her face toward the sun that is still burning down on us through the broken hatch. "It's warm."

"Me too," I say. I give a small shrug. "But we can't stay here, it's not safe."

She looks away from me, her eyes sad. Sad because she understands. She knows that today will be hard, that we have lost everything, and that we need to start again. Yet when she turns her sweet face back to mine, a small smile plays on her lips.

"What is it?" I ask, curious.

"I think I stink," she says, the smile growing wider.

I can't help but smile now. Our chances of survival, even for another week, are now minimal. Our chances of survival at all are nonexistent. Yet here she is, my sweet Honeybee, smiling—smiling because we smell bad.

I grab her and she giggles, the sound erupting from her mouth and making me laugh right back with her. We lie in the loft, rolling around in the hay and tickling each other, giggling insanely for several minutes until my sides ache from laughing so much. I look into her perfect little face, her beautiful, wide brown eyes and her rosebud mouth, and I smile. I feel the smile right down to my toes when she smiles back at me.

"I love you, Mama."

"I love you too, Lilly. So so much."

A low hiss breaks through our declarations, and my smile falters. The hiss comes again and I frown, hard, and scamper over to where the wooden ladders are and look down. I blink, once, twice, and then I give myself a small shake to make sure that I am awake and this is not another nightmare.

"Mama?" Her voice is a soft whisper, but it's enough to get their attention.

The monsters lie beneath us, hidden in the shadows of the barn. Curled together like vipers ready to strike. Their nest a warm bed beneath the sun, hidden in the refuge of this barn. They pace back and forth, avoiding the square of light from the broken hatch in the center of their darkness. They stare up at me, their eyes glowing red and hateful, and a tremor runs through my body from head to toe. I push back from the ledge, stumbling to my feet as their growls grow louder. Lilly's hand latches onto mine, and I look down into her face.

"They are here," I say, quietly. Matter-of-factly.

She blinks in understanding. We are trapped.

I put a single finger to my lips and she nods. Her chin begins to tremble, but she doesn't cry or whimper. We've been here before—she knows what to do: keep quiet and stay in the sun. I look around us, searching for an escape, a way out of here, but all I see are wooden walls and hay. The hisses are becoming louder down below as they alert one another to our presence, and my searching becomes more frantic. I grip Lilly's wrists and pull her into the center of our small space so that the sun is shining directly down on her. This is where she will be safest.

I feel along the walls, testing the durability of each plank of wood, my fingers attempting to pry the boards loose, but they do not budge. The barn is old and rickety and yet I cannot pull out even one small plank of wood. There is a small window at one end of the loft, cracked, dusty, and small. I push on the lock, trying to free it, but it is jammed in place. I bite my lip, glance toward Lilly, and then I abruptly ram my elbow against the glass. It shatters noisily and the monsters below begin to screech and scream. I look out the window, seeing more hay on the ground below. It's dangerous. The fall is short, but Lilly is fragile—humanity is fragile. I run back to Lilly and kneel down in front of her, but no words will come out.

She places a hand on my cheek, her chin still quivering as she seeks out the problem, stealing the truth from my eyes. Scratching of nails down below makes us both jump. Because this isn't scratching, it's clawing. Urgent and deadly as it—they—try to get up to us.

"Stay here," I whisper, and I creep to the ledge and look down once more.

They are all awake now, bumping and jostling each other, all eager to get to us. Thirty pairs of red eyes stare up at me from the shadows, and it is all that I can do to not scream out in fear and anger. One of them attempts to climb the rickety ladder, but their limbs are not made for climbing ladders, and it stumbles and falls backwards, hissing in frustration as another monster takes its place.

I grip the wood and shake the monster free from it, and then I begin to drag the ladder up, pulling it away from their reach, cursing myself the entire time for not dragging it up after us last night. The ladder is heavy, but I eventually lay it flat amongst the hay. I'm hot and sweaty, and trying not to panic. I look at Lilly, who is still standing in the center of the square of light. She's watching me carefully, picking up on my every emotion. Though she's trying to stay calm, I can see her own anxiety peeking through the cracks.

I fall to my knees, gripping my head as panic begins to consume me. Every breath feels like it is poison, the stench of the monsters hanging thick in the air, so much so that I can taste them in my mouth, on my tongue, bitter and vile and evil. I fix my gaze on the hay and the wooden floor, attempting to get a grip on my emotions before I lose control completely. The noise from below is almost deafening now and I can hardly think, but I hear Lilly. I hear her call my name and I look up through the tears that blur my vision. Her eyes meet mine and she points her small finger toward the ladder.

I blink, looking at it and then back at her. And then I get it. I stand back up and grab the ladder, dragging it across the landing and toward the window. I have to angle it to get it out of the small gap, and I grip it with everything that I have so it doesn't fall over. We only have one chance at this. The ladder is too small to reach all the way from the window to the ground. There is a gap of almost three feet that I somehow have to navigate. I lean out the window as far as I dare and hang onto the ladder as hard as I can, not letting go of it until I am absolutely certain that it is the best position for it, and it won't just fall over. My fingers gently slide from the last wooden step, and I hold my breath as it clanks noisily against the side of the barn. I think it might fall, but then it balances and a small sound of thankfulness escapes my lips. I turn back to Lilly, gesturing for her to leave that small space of safety in the sun.

She does, reluctantly, once again putting her entire trust in me. When she is by my side, I hug her, using her to compose myself. Her body is trembling in my arms but I refuse to cry. Not now. She needs me strong, and I need her calm.

"Lilly, I am going to lower you as much as I can."

She blinks at me, confused, so I get her to look out the window so that she understands.

"The ladder is too short. But it will only be a small drop. You can do this, Honeybee." I kiss her forehead, holding back the words that I so desperately want to say: *You have to do this.*

She nods, but her eyes show vibrant fear, so I pull her into another embrace and kiss her head. Her small arms cling to me almost painfully, but I don't care. I would take any amount of pain for her. We finally pull apart and I take her hands in mine and kiss her knuckles.

"Are you ready?" I whisper, ignoring the screams that echo below us. The monsters that are calling for our blood.

She nods but still looks uncertain.

"Just be calm, concentrate, and hold onto me until the very last second."

I help her up to the window and grip her fiercely as she turns around, letting her legs dangle over the edge. I can feel her small body trembling beneath my fingers, her ribs sharp and jutting. I grit my teeth and begin to lower her, stretching myself out as far as I can go. I lock my hips in place, my feet pressing against the floor to stop myself from slipping. She stares at me the entire time, her wide eyes never straying from mine. Her grip is firm, stronger than I could have hoped for her, and it gives me the belief that she will be okay. That she can do this.

A noise from behind has me breaking our stare,

and I turn to see one of the monsters' clawed hands gripping the ledge. The skin is bubbling, burning up in the glare from the sun. It screams loudly in pain but it presses on, almost as if it knows that we are escaping and it will be worth the pain if it catches us in time. It drags itself up, and I realize that the other monsters have sacrificed this one in favor of themselves. It drags its rapidly burning body toward us, the flames igniting and catching hold of the hay around it. Its eyes burn pure red and hateful as it holds my stare, its teeth snapping at me as it drag, drags, drags its body forward.

I turn back to Lilly, but the resolve has gone from her eyes, and now she just looks like a petrified little girl.

"You have to let go."

She shakes her head at me.

"You have to, Lilly, you have to." I try to free my hands from hers, but she starts to cry and clings to me, all the while shaking her head fearfully. "Let go, Lilly, drop! It's there, it's right there. An inch, two at best," I lie. "You can do it." I look away, checking behind me, and seeing the barn alight, the angry flames licking against the ceiling, and the monster, aglow with fire yet still coming for me—for us. I look back at Lilly, her knuckles white with the fierceness that she holds me with.

"I'm sorry," I say, watching as her pupils dilate, and I finally pry my hands free from hers. "I'm sorry," I say, breaking all the trust that she has in me as I let her go.

And then she's falling.

The sun, our savior, is bouncing off her soft golden curls in the morning daylight. She's an angel as she falls, her arms going wide, her mouth open in a silent scream. My arms are reaching for her, wishing I could take it back. And then her feet find the wooden step of the ladder and her hands are clawing against the side of the barn to hold herself steady as she screams painfully, fear filling her body. She stares up at me, frightened and happy all at the same time.

"Go, Lilly!" I yell to her.

She climbs down, taking the steps quickly but carefully, and I'm so proud of her. I turn at the sound of a growl, a growl far too close to me. And it all happens so quickly.

It lunges.

I move.

It falls through the open window.

I turn and watch as the monster explodes into flames when the sunlight hits it, its mutilated body shattering midair. Too much sun for this monster—flames alone were not sufficient this time. It lands on the ground in several pieces, each one of them twitching, but very dead, and fire engulfs it.

Lilly is finally on the ground, ignoring the monster and staring up at me expectantly. Her tears have ceased as she waits for me to join her. She knows she is safe outside, away from dark corners and shade. I climb up onto the window ledge and turn around, squeezing my body through the small opening and dangling my legs over before finally lowering myself down. The tips of my toes find the first rung of the ladder and I let go of the ledge and grip the wooden panels of the barn for support.

The sun is hot on my back, but the wood is hotter under my fingertips as heat, both inside and out, protects me. I breathe steadily as I climb down, my feet finally finding purchase on the dusty ground. I step away from the ladder just as the roof begins to collapse, and the screams from inside intensify. They chorus their pain together almost beautifully, a high-pitched chant of death.

Lilly's hand slips into mine and we walk backwards, afraid to look away from the burning barn. Away from the monsters trapped within. Away from the place where we just nearly died.

Again.

Because it feels that if we look away, perhaps this won't have been real, that perhaps we did die in that place, that barn full of hay and monsters. So we walk slowly backwards, our hands entwined, our breathing rapid, as we watch the wooden building burn, the screams and cries from within filling the sky.

Chapter Thirteen.

#13. It's always the little things.

The barn burns to almost nothing. Small pops and explosions can be heard as it collapses in upon itself and the monsters fry in the sun. Their deathly smell hangs in the air like toxic fumes, and I encourage us to begin our walk. The daylight won't last forever, and the stench of their bodies will no doubt attract others if they are hungry enough when night comes.

We walk, placing one foot in front of the other. Our steps are timid, almost, quiet in the now equable daylight. I watch our shoes, dirty and worn, moving over and over, disturbing the dusty road that we walk upon. We don't speak. There are no words for or from either of us. Our fingers are wrapped around each other's, and those are the only silent words that we need. We are here, together, once more. So we walk. The minutes tick by, the hours drift past, and we don't stop.

The sun is warm, sweat clings to our skin, trickles down my face and into my eyes. I rub it away, feeling the smear of dirt and grease. Was it really only yesterday that we had been in a house? Fed, watered, clean? It feels like a lifetime ago, a dream upon where we once existed and now we don't. That reality stolen. That home gone. That peace we had shared lost once more.

My eyes follow Lilly's feet. She is becoming tired. Her shoes drag a little with each step, a scuff growing larger on the front of each small shoe. I stare, watching fascinated, almost too numb to do anything about it as we walk, walk, walk. A slow trickle splashes off the end of her left shoe as she lifts it, and as she lifts the right one to take her next step, a splash of urine drips off the end of that one too. I watch for a few more steps, as she pees herself but doesn't stop walking. I finally look across at her face, my neck and shoulders glad that I have moved my neck and head.

Her eyes are almost glazed over as she stares straight ahead. Her face is paler than snow, and her eyes lost. I stop walking, but she doesn't realize that I've stopped and her arm jerks backwards when she takes her next step forward. She slowly turns to face me, blinking twice as she stares calmly into my face, coming back to the here and now. Large black rings circle under her eyes, heavy shadows of exhaustion and weariness, and without a thought I scoop her up into my arms.

She clings to me weakly and falls asleep almost instantly. I glance up at the sun, seeing that it is at its highest, meaning that the day is halfway done. I look back the way we have been walking. The barn is completely out of sight now—not even the smoke can be seen—but it still seems too close. We still need more distance. And so I continue to walk, with Lilly's small sweat-and urine-soaked body wrapped around mine.

My arms ache after several miles, burning with a pain and intensity that is unlike anything I've ever felt. My leg muscles twitch for relief, begging me to stop and rest. The day has been almost silent, apart from the sound of my footsteps, and I wonder how many nests of monsters we have passed. How many have heard us walking, how many will wake up when night falls and follow our scent, hunting and tracking us through another night. I shudder and almost drop Lilly, collapsing down to one knee, the gravel tearing through my pants and digging painfully into my skin. I don't gasp, though. I don't make a sound. I just wait, poised on one knee, feeling the slow trickle of blood trail down my leg.

Lilly's face breaks free from my shoulder and she looks up at me groggily, the remnants of sleep still evident in her eyes. The corner of her mouth quirks up in a small smile, but I can't smile back, no matter how much I try. She senses my weariness and climbs down from me, and then she holds out her hand. I push myself to standing and take her small, warm hand in mine. I stare unashamedly at the intricate black veins that peek out from under her cardigan, wishing that there was something I could do to save her, to save me. But I can't. It's just a matter of time. Our hands are clasped, and my own blackened veins seem stark and obvious against her pale skin. It frightens me.

My stomach rumbles loudly and Lilly smiles

again. I finally find the energy to smile back as her stomach joins in with mine, and we both stand there, our stomachs wailing in hunger. Looking up the road, I see nothing. Just more empty fields, more highway, more broken cars, more overgrown plants, more sunlight. To the left is a field, overgrown with tall weeds and grass, and to our right is an empty, dusty field, as if the very life has been sucked right out of it. Stark contrasts to one another. One full of life, the other not. Neither providing us with what we need: food.

I look back at Lilly, seeing that the wet stain from where she had peed earlier has almost dried. Her face is dirty, dry tracks of tears trailing down her cheeks, and her hair is a tangle of knots. But she's alive. She's still smiling. She's still my Lilly—my Honeybee. For now, at least.

"We need to find food," I finally say as she watches me expectantly. My throat feels sore and painful when I speak; like there's sand on my tongue.

She nods in agreement.

"And something to drink," I add on, to which she nods again. I take a deep breath and look up the road once more. "I think we should go this way," I say decisively.

I light a cigarette and we start to walk once more, just one step in front of the other. Because this road has to end somewhere, eventually. Every road leads to something, or someone. And this road is no different. Dusty, lonely, and unused.

I inhale the nicotine, feeling my hunger pangs subside but my thirst grow. I finish my cigarette, throwing it to one side as we come up on one of the many rusted cars at the side of the road. The door is hanging open like an invitation. I approach it carefully, but there is nothing and no one inside. No food. No water. No clothing. Nothing of use. And so we continue to walk.

Heat rises from the road like a mirage, and I fix my eyes on the distance, staring, hoping, waiting. What for, I don't know. Anything. Anything at all. In the distance, at the very end of the road, I see something. A shape of something. I blink several times, trying to clear the fog from my eyes, but the shape is still there. Hope leaps in my heart. I stop and point.

"Look!" I say excitedly.

Lilly looks up, following my pointing finger, and then she looks at me confused. I scoop her up and point again. She narrows her eyes, and just as I am beginning to think that my mind is in fact playing tricks on me, she sees it.

"What is it?" she asks quietly.

"A gas station."

"Will it be safe?" she asks.

"I don't know, but it could be. And there could be food."

We pick up speed, both of us excited and nervous to reach the gas station. The sun is hot, but neither of us complain about it, even though I am so thirsty that it makes my throat sore, and I know Lilly must be feeling the same way. As we get closer to the gas station we see two abandoned cars in the forecourt, and we approach them warily. I check each car carefully, because people leave the silliest things behind, forgetting things in side pockets or under seats. These cars are not like that, though. There is nothing of use in either of them.

We slowly approach the gas station. The doors have been wedged open, allowing light to shine into the darkness. The windows are all dirty, inches of thick dust and grime covering each one. The glass in the door has been broken, and as we step closer it crunches under our feet. The sound echoes around us, and I look down to Lilly with a grimace. I hear her swallow, and then it is as if every sound has an echo loud enough to wake a beast. Her swallow is loud but her breathing is louder, the crunch of glass reverberating around us, the wind whistling through the open door.

Lilly tugs on my hand and I nod as we go inside. It feels like dusk inside—not quite day and not quite night, that strange color that the world goes when it is almost time for bed, the stillness that settles over the earth as it readies itself for sleep. But it is neither of these times right now, and so it is even more unnerving as everything grows still.

I let my eyes adjust to the dimness and I take in our surroundings. Lilly stays by my side, unmoving. She knows to stay still and silent. I look across the room, the remnants of civilization a stark reminder of what we have lost. There is no food on the shelves—at least none that I can see from here—so we must venture further inside.

I take a timid step forward, and then another, becoming more emboldened with each one. Lilly follows, her hand in mine and her eyes looking everywhere as mine do the same. But each dark corner is empty, free of monsters. Our shoulders relax as we find the place empty. Even the storeroom and the breakroom at the back of the gas station are empty of monsters, and they only had one dirty window in apiece, making their spaces darker still. Happy that we are alone, I turn to Lilly.

"Let's look for food," I say.

"Okay," she says.

Lilly stays with me as we traipse each aisle, looking at everything, searching for food and drink, but the store has been pilfered and there is nothing left for us to eat. My heart aches with disappointment, but I don't let her see it. We go behind the counter and I sit Lilly on the stool there. She pretends that she works in the store and is serving a customer while I search the small cabinets. I find another pack of cigarettes. They were damp once and the pack is still misshapen, but I don't mind. I search right to the back of the shelves, moving old, damp papers to one side, a pen, a stapler, and then my hand lands on something else. I grip it and pull it out. I smile and turn to Lilly. She is still playing her game of shopkeeper, but she stops and looks at me.

"What is it?" she asks.

"Gum," I say proudly.

There are only four pieces inside. There were once seven, and the ones that are left feel a little stale, but I don't mind. My mouth waters at just the thought of gum, of its flavor. I unwrap a piece a hand it to Lilly. She takes it and stares at me blankly, so I unwrap a piece for me.

"You put it in your mouth and chew it. You don't swallow it, though," I say.

"Why not?"

"Because it can give you a tummy ache. It isn't meant to feed you."

She examines the hard, thin strip of gum with curious eyes and then looks back at me, another small frown puckered between her eyebrows. "What is the point of it then?" she asks.

I smile at her. "Just chew it, and you'll see." I put my piece in my eager mouth and begin to chew.

At first it doesn't taste of anything, and the strip of gum snaps and sort of crumbles, but then as my saliva softens it, it begins to form a small ball of flavor in my mouth and I groan in satisfaction. Lilly watches me and then does the same, grimacing as the gum crumbles in her mouth, and I know that she wants to spit it out.

"I don't like it," she says.

"Keep chewing, Lilly," I say, and she does.

A moment passes and slowly her grimace softens until she starts to smile. She chews and chews and then returns to her game of shopkeepers but this time she is smiling. I continue to search the store for anything else while I chew my gum, the saliva in my mouth soothing the scratch in my dry throat.

There are some old magazines, mostly ruined from damp, but one of them is a comic and so I take it, deciding that I can try and read it to Lilly later on. There are some moth-eaten T-shirts in the storeroom. The box has some mice living in it, and I manage to catch one and crush it by knocking another box over on top of it. I think I will cook it and then we can eat it, but when I look at the tiny lifeless body, I decide that I won't. I hide its body so Lilly doesn't see it, because I know that she would be sad if she saw its lifeless body, and I know that she would be sadder still knowing that I was the one who had killed it.

I take two of the T-shirts, and a cap for Lilly. I find an old carrier bag and pile our meager supplies inside it: the magazine, the T-shirts, and the cap. There's still nothing to eat or drink though, no matter how hard I search. I go back to the front of the store and look out at the day, seeing that the sun is lower, nighttime is coming. Lilly comes to stand next to me and we go outside and look up and down the road, the way we had come and the way we were going, but there seems to be nothing in either direction for miles.

"I think we should stay here tonight," I say, the gum still in my mouth. I chew it thoughtfully. The taste is almost gone but still I chew, as if the very idea that I can chew and my stomach feel full is a real possibility. Of course it's not. But I still chew it relentlessly.

I don't want to stay here. I don't want to stay anywhere, really. Everywhere frightens me, and Lilly. But we have to stop for today. I'm tired and hungry and I know Lilly is feeling even worse than me, though she hasn't complained—not once. But we have to stop. Better to stay here than end up trapped out in the open with nowhere to hide. That would be worse. Lilly nods an okay at my plan to stay, and we go back inside.

I force the doors closed and barricade them with some of the portable metal shelving. Then I go to the breakroom and check that the back door to the gas station is locked. It is. I look around, trying to find access to the roof, because that is actually the safest place to sleep. Up on the roof, away from the dark of the gas station, away from the reach of the monsters. This won't be the first time that we've slept on the flat roof of a gas station. I finally find it and then I use the tall stool from the front counter to climb up and I push open the little hatch. It's stiff, but it eventually opens. I look out to check that it is safe, and when I decide it is, I reach down and hoist Lilly up onto the roof.

"Mama?" she says.

I climb up, and then I lower the hatch door back in place and I turn and smile at her. She's getting anxious and so am I, but we need to stay calm so I do all that I can to relax her—which isn't much.

"Are we safe?" she asks, her eyes looking tired,

with deep black rings below them.

I look around us, seeing the sun getting ready to dip below the trees. The air is cool up here, and I know that we will be cold tonight. Cold and hungry. Lilly holds up her arms to me and I pick her up. She nestles into me, and I kiss the top of her head.

"Right now we are," I say to her.

"What about when it goes dark?"

"I hope so," Is all I can say. "Do you want some more gum?"

"Not yet. We should save it so that it lasts."

I nod. "Yes we should. Do you like it?"

She nods, her face still scrunched against my neck. "Yes I do," she mumbles, and then I feel her breath hot against my neck as she yawns.

I find a spot to make a makeshift bed, and then I gather some of the leaves that are scattered across the roof. I pile them up and lay Lilly down on them, hoping that they will soften the hard ground for her. I use the carrier bag with the T-shirts inside as a pillow for her, and she lays her sweet little head upon it. The bag gives a small rustle, and then she falls asleep right away. I stroke her hair as I watch the sun set, my thoughts empty of anything useful. I don't even have the energy to feel worried or sad anymore.

I just am.

Chapter Fourteen.

#14. A new dawn.

I wake fitfully throughout the night, the sound of screeching and claws scratching hanging in the air like a stench that you can't wash away. Minutes later it goes quiet again, and I slip into unconsciousness. An hour passes and I wake to the sounds again. On and on it goes: I wake, I tremble, I squeeze Lilly close, and then I slip back to sleep when it all goes quiet.

They are searching for us—for anyone, really—but they don't know we are up here, and I am too tired to worry too much about anything. There are places that your mind will take you when fear takes hold, horrible places where you will scream into the darkness and beg for it to end. And then there are times when you are just a black void of nothing. You suck the air into your lungs and you breathe it back out. You blink, you stare, you feel your heart beating, but there is nothing else. It's a place beyond exhaustion but not without compare.

I am there right now. Drifting in and out of consciousness. Hoping that Lilly gets to sleep the full night through. Hoping that we find food tomorrow. Hoping, hoping, hoping. Even though it pains me to do it. Hope seems to be the only thing left.

The final time I wake to the screeches, I cannot get back to sleep. So I lie there, staring up at the stars, blinking every once in a while. I cuddle Lilly's warm body to me, feeling her breath on my neck. She is silent, barring the soft noise of her breathing. I stroke her hair and let my thoughts wander aimlessly until the sun begins to rise.

The soft orange glow builds slowly in the distance at first, the night being banished for another day. The monsters go back into hiding, and everything is as it should be again. I slide Lilly's arms from around me and sit up. I creep to the edge of the roof and look down. There are signs of the monsters' presence but nothing that is impactful—no shattered glass, no blood or dead bodies. They came, and they moved onward to another destination before morning.

I pull my cigarettes from my pocket and light one. I take a deep drag, pulling the nicotine into my lungs, and then I release it slowly. My stomach hurts with hunger, and there is a low throb in the base of my skull. I turn to look at Lilly, seeing that she is still sleeping, and I'm glad. She will be very hungry when she wakes, and I have nothing to offer her but stale gum. I feel bad—wretched, even. I feel like a failure to her. What kind of mother lets her child starve to death?

I finish the first cigarette and light another one immediately afterwards, needing the buzz they give me. I hear the rustle of leaves as I finish the second cigarette. Lilly comes to join me at the edge of the gas station roof. We dangle our legs over the edge as we look into the distance, imagining all the things that could be just over the horizon.

"I'm hungry," she whispers.

I know that she feels bad for telling me that, because she knows that I can't do anything about it. But I'm glad that she tells me nonetheless.

I hug her and kiss the top of her head. "I know, Honeybee. So am I."

She goes silent after that. No point in wasting energy talking about the things we do not have. We eventually climb back down from the roof. I take some more of the dirty T-shirts and put them in our carrier bag. There is an empty bottle, which I take as well. *If we find water then we can fill this bottle and keep it with us*, I think.

We push our barricade out of the way of the doors and step out into the warm sun with heavy hearts. Lilly slips her hand into mine and wordlessly we begin to walk again.

We need to find water. And soon. That is even more important right now than food, even though my stomach angrily disagrees. But we are very quickly dehydrating. Lilly is hot, so I help her out of her tatty cardigan and tie it around her waist. I note the thick black lines that run down Lilly's arms and I squeeze my eyes shut, not wanting to have seen them. She smiles up at me, unaware, and I see that her gums are bleeding. I don't say anything, though. What would be the point? Instead I smile back and we start to walk again.

I think that we might be getting close to a town.

There are more cars around now. I check each one but don't find anything useful in them. None of them work anymore, either, which is disappointing. There's a small bridge up ahead and I am both anxious and happy when we get closer.

A bridge means water, and water means we can drink and wash. But there may be shadows where the monsters can hide. I give Lilly the carrier bag to hold, and I make her stay in the center of the road while I go to check.

The bridge is small—only big enough to get over on foot. It's rickety also, and I don't think walking over it would be a good idea at all. I climb down a small embankment carefully, seeing that there are no shadows, and there is a small stream of water running underneath it. I climb back up and gesture for Lilly to come over. She does, and I help her down the embankment.

She looks unsure of what to do, but she stares at the water thirstily. It isn't clean water, but it is coming directly from a stream somewhere, so it's fresh. We decide to drink it because we are really thirsty now, and we are dehydrating, and I don't have anything to make the water sterile for us anyway. I take the carrier bag from Lilly and pull out the bottle, and then I fill it with water and take a sip to show her that it is okay. She smiles when I hand her the bottle and then drinks it greedily, letting it spill down her chin and T-shirt.

I scoop handfuls of water up, and drink and drink and drink until my stomach feels weird and sloshy. I smile as Lilly fills the bottle back up and drinks some more. When she's had enough she hands the bottle back and stares at me wide-eyed.

"We should wash now," I say, and she nods.

We undress until we are in just our underwear, and I rinse our dirty clothes in the water. I lay our clothes down on the embankment to dry a little and then I begin to wash myself. Lilly is splashing in the water, kicking it and giggling as the cold droplets land on her head. I smile. It comes easily. I try not to look at the thick black veins that now cover almost a third of her body. I look at my own body and see the same thing, though my lines are much darker. But I don't care about me. Only her.

"Mama!" Lilly whispers urgently.

My eyes look up to meet hers. "What is it?" I ask.

"Something touched my toe," she whispers, sounding worried. She looks back down into the water, watching in fascination.

I stand up quickly. The water is only a couple of inches deep, so it can't be the monsters. I splash over to her, looking into the water the entire time, but don't see anything. I stop next to her, waiting for the water to settle, and when I do, I see a little fish. It's only a small one. Barely the size of a sardine. We stand there in the water, watching as more of the little fish come out from wherever they were hiding. They swim around our toes and Lilly smiles happily at the sight of them.

"Fish," I say.

"Fish," she repeats, still smiling.

We both watch in silence for several moments. Their little silvery bodies reflect the light off them every time they turn with a small flip of their tail. Lilly's smile grows every time one swims over her toes.

"We should catch them and eat them," I say.

Her smile falls. "Okay."

I look across to her. "We need to eat, Lilly."

"I know," she says sadly.

"I'm sorry," I reply, but she doesn't say anything back.

I use the carrier bag to catch some of the small fish by scooping it through the water. They flip and splash in the bag, and I lift it out of the water and let it drain away. I take them to the embankment and I tip them out onto the mud there. We watch them flip some more as they try to get back to the water, but I don't let them. Their movements become slow, their gills opening rapidly as they struggle for breath. I can't stop staring, fascinated at their fragility as they suffocate.

Lilly puts her hands over her eyes and begins to cry, and I look up at her, at her skinny body, her ribs protruding almost painfully. Thick black veins trace up and down her body, some faint, some vivid. Her hair is a mess and her skin is pale. I look back to the small fish. They no longer move. They are dead.

I gather some sticks to make a fire, but then I remember watching a program once and that it said that you could just eat fish raw. I pick up one of the little slimy fish, placing it in my palm. It doesn't look very appetizing, but it has nutrients in it that will give us energy. It might stop the painful tug in my stomach. It might help to stop the ache in my head and let me think properly. I pick up the little fish using my thumb and forefinger and I drop it into my mouth, and then I crunch down on it.

It wiggles and I realize that it wasn't totally dead, and I feel bad as my teeth crunch down on its insubstantial little body. It tastes bad. Like really bad, and I gag and grimace, my body giving a little shudder as its broken body slides down my throat. I look up at Lilly who is watching me carefully with her wide brown eyes.

"It's not too bad," I say—a big lie, because it tastes really bad. I pat the ground next to me and she sits down. "Pick one," I say.

She looks at the little dead fish—that might not be totally dead—and she counts them. Her lips move slowly, the whisper of numbers falling from her lips. Seven little fish. Eight including the one I just ate. That makes four each. I pick up another one and she does the same, and then we drop them into our mouths quickly. Our eyes are locked as we crunch our way through the fish. At one point I think she might be sick, but she holds it in.

Afterwards we drink lots more water, and then we each have a stick of gum to try and get rid of the taste of dead fish from our mouths. I rinse her hair in the water, tugging my fingers carefully through the knots, until once again her hair is full of ringlets and not just one giant knot. I hand her one of the musty T-shirts to wear and she slips it over her head, smiling at the picture of a cow's head on the front. Apparently this used to be a big milk district called Collier County. That's what the T-shirt says, anyway.

"We sure do love our milk!" Lilly says with a giggle, as she guesses what the smiley-faced man on her T-shirt might have once said.

I laugh with her and I slip mine on. It's the same picture of a cow, but the words are different.

"Ain't milk great!" I say with a smirk.

We laugh some more and then I fill up the bottle of water and we put our pants back on. I give Lilly one of the caps that I got from the gas station and she puts it on. Our pants are still a little wet, but that's okay—neither of us mind, because at least they don't smell like pee and sweat anymore. We climb back up the embankment, feeling better than an hour ago. I carry the carrier bag full of our sort-of-clean old clothes, the bottle of water, and the comic I found yesterday.

My stomach gurgles loudly, and feels a little swishy with all the water we have drunk. The fish tasted bad, but they have made my head feel a little clearer so I'm glad that I ate them. I blow a bubble with the gum and look down at Lilly. She stares in amazement at the pink bubble coming from my mouth and smiles widely. She tries to copy me but can't manage it, so we stop and sit down right there in the middle of the road and I show her how to do it.

Half an hour later, we are both walking again and blowing bubbles happily.

The small milk town comes into view, and we stop as we look at the shadows of houses and stores in the distance. I glance down at Lilly but she doesn't look up. She's still blowing bubbles, almost like right now she is trapped in her own little bubble.

I tug her hand a little and we begin to walk some more, and I try to ignore the anxiety that builds in my gut. Because while this is good—houses, stores, cars, all ripe for us to look through and hopefully find supplies—it's also bad. Because it could house the monsters.

We pass the first car. The skeleton of a man or woman are still inside, hunched over the steering wheel as if they were still driving. The monsters have picked this one clean. I think it is very old, right from the start of the outbreak. The monsters were less frantic back then. Less starving. So they were more careful. Not like now. Now they tear their prey apart. The next car must have been on fire, because it is a mere shell, the metal burnt and fragile-looking.

The first storefront comes into view. It's a small souvenir store that was once filled with milk products and tacky gifts. The sign says it was once called Milk Products by Flo. There's a picture of a cow hat with clapping hands. I strangely hope that I can find one of these hats for Lilly to wear, because I know that she will like it more than the one she is wearing.

The town finally comes properly into view, and I find myself smiling despite the fear that trembles in my gut and makes me feel nauseous—though that could also be the raw fish digesting. This town looks picturesque. Like every town, there are buildings that are destroyed—either by fire or by the elements, there is old garbage everywhere, and the remnants of bones. It is dirty, dusty and not as bright as I'm sure it once was. Yet there is something that is quite sweet about it.

The storefronts each have red and white awnings, and there is a strip of grass running through the center of the main road, with small trees. Some are dead and some are alive. Cars are crashed, burnt out and destroyed, luggage is strewn across the sidewalks, suitcases flung open, their contents now missing. Same old, same old. Yet I have a good feeling.

I look down at Lilly and see that she is unaware of my happiness right now, but that's okay. I don't mind that either. I reach over and poke a finger into the bubble that she has just blown and she looks up at me. The gum is stuck to her lips, and I smile and she smiles back.

Chapter Fifteen.

#15. In this house of straw I cried.

We rummage through burnt-out homes and found things. Things we didn't want to see. Things we would never be able to un-see. But in amongst those ruins, we also find things we can use: another lighter, some canned food that has no labels on it, a book I once read in high school, before all of this began. We find a blanket, and I fold it neatly and put it inside my carrier bag.

We rummage through old stores: a grocer's, a shoemaker's, a dairy shop that only sold milk. *How did they run that business?* I wonder. A shop that only sells milk and cheese, yogurts and such. The store must have at one time smelled foul when the produce began to decay and rot away, yet now it only holds the familiar scent of emptiness and loneliness that everything has.

The sun is beginning to set, and we find shelter in an old dress shop. It's sufficiently lit with a skylight in the roof. A skylight makes it sound so fancy, but the skylight is, in fact, merely a hole in the roof. Through it you can see the sky—the sun, the moon, the stars, whatever else might be up there looking down on us. There is no shelter for us on the roof, of course. It would be too unsafe, I decide. Instead we find a trapdoor which still bears the heavy metal lock on it that it has held since it was put there, however long ago that was.

I smash the lock off with a block of wood after a fruitlessly long search for the key. It is dark down here, and neither Lilly nor I want to go down, but night is settling in and so I flick my old Zippo lighter and we make our way down the concrete steps. The place is dank and ugly, a storeroom of sorts. I flip a couple of switches, but the lights don't work. I hadn't really expected them to, but I always check, just in case. Habit, I suppose.

There are small rectangular windows, only an inch or so deep—enough to cast a little light in the space, but not big enough for anything or anyone to either get in or out of. And they are dirty. Really dirty. Years of dirt and grime, both inside and out, has built up on them—from even before the infection hit, I would think—so I don't worry too much about the monsters seeing us down here. It does mean that we will be in the dark for the night, though.

As our eyes grow accustomed to the dark, we search for whatever else might be down here. There are piles of materials, all neatly stacked and ready to use, apart from the heavy layer of dust upon them. There are also racks of dresses and suits, and I flick through them. One dress catches my eye, and my hands stays, fingering the delicate material. A cream lace dress, knee-length, with little round pearls sewn into parts of it. It's beautiful and I think of when I would have worn something like this. A wedding perhaps, or a christening, maybe. It isn't the sort of dress that you would wear just any day. No, this is the sort of dress that you would put on to feel special.

"Pretty," Lilly says from next to me.

"Yes, it is," I say.

My hand falls from it and takes hers, and we continue around the room. There is a sewing machine and a desk and a high-backed chair, which looks incredibly uncomfortable. The room stretches out, almost never-ending and opening up into another room. A single mattress is on the floor, with blankets and pillows and an old rocking chair in the corner.

"It's like they knew we were coming and made up the room for us," I say jokingly.

"Who?"

"The people."

Lilly cocks her head to one side. "Which people? Everyone is dead."

Her words chill me, and I nod solemnly. I put down the carrier bag next to the bed and then turn in a circle. I grip the edge of the duvet on the mattress and pull it off, shaking it in the air to get rid of some of the dust, and then I do the same to the pillow.

"It should be okay for you to sleep in now," I say absently.

I go back into the other room and get the high-backed chair. I carry it over to one of the thin windows and I climb on top so I can look out. The window is filthy, and I do not want to wipe any of the dirt away so I put my face really close to the glass so I can properly see out. The moon and the sun are currently fighting for leadership, but the moon will win. It always does. The town is silent, nothing moves. Yet.

I climb down and tell Lilly to stay on the bed. I make my way back up the stairs we came down and I open the hatch that leads into the store. I look around for something heavy, finally seeing a large chest that holds material. I climb out of the basement and begin to pull the chest over to the hatch, and I place it as close to the opening as possible. Then I grab some of the material and I tip some of it out around the opening. I climb back inside the basement, gripping some of the material, and I carefully close the hatch, at the very last second letting go of the material. Then I pray that the hatch cannot be seen from the shop.

There is a small latch on the inside of the hatch. It won't really do much good if the monsters know that we're down here, but I slide it across all the same. Any lock is better than no lock.

When I get to the bottom of the concrete stairs I see Lilly standing and waiting for me.

"I told you to wait by the bed," I say.

She stares at me but doesn't say anything, and I frown. This is the first time she hasn't done as I've asked. Certainly the first time that she hasn't cared about not doing as she was told. I frown some more and then take her hand, leading her back into the other room.

I sit her down on the bed. "Are you okay?" I ask, standing in front of her.

"I don't feel well," she says quietly.

I put a hand on her forehead, but she doesn't feel hot. "I think you're just hungry," I say.

I pull the cans with no labels out from the carrier bag. And then I look around for something to help me open the cans, because I don't have a can opener. Obviously. I find a large pair of dressmakers' scissors on the desk, along with some smaller scissors and a knife. I use the scissors to stab a hole into the can, and when I pull the scissors free I hold the can up to my nose and sniff.

My heart plummets. Sinking into a bottomless pit. I drop the can, my hands shaking angrily. The room spins and I lower my head, putting it between my knees as I try to catch my breath.

"What's wrong?" Lilly asks, "Can we eat it?"

I take deep, slow breaths, and when I feel less panicky I look up at her, forcing myself to dam the flow of tears that I can feel building up.

"It's dog food," I say to Lilly.

"Can we eat it?" she asks again, innocent, always so innocent.

I shake my head no and tell her that this is animal food, and we can't eat it, and then her sad gaze drifts toward the floor. I stab through another can and find it is also dog food, and I want to yell in frustration. By the third can, my palm is sore from using the scissors to split the can open, and when I find it to be another can of dog food, I give up. I don't want to dull my scissors on dog food.

I help Lilly into the bed and I climb in next to her,

lying in front so I can get out quickly if I need to. We face each other in the dark, the musty covers draped over us as we stare into each other's eyes. Our stomachs are empty and gurgling noisily, screaming for food. Minutes pass by, and then an hour or two, or maybe it is just mere minutes. The noises begin as they do every night: the scratching, and clawing, the hissing and screaming. But I feel almost numb to it tonight.

Lilly places an arm across my waist and holds me tightly, trying to be brave. I know that she hates these sounds. I do too. But I think these sounds must be so much worse for a child. As a child your fears are more irrational than when you are fully grown. But what she doesn't understand is that the noises are just as scary for me, a full-grown woman, because I cannot rationalize them away. They are real, living, breathing nightmares.

Nevertheless, I kiss the top of her head and then I hum quietly into her ear to try and drown out some of their horrible sounds. It seems to work. Yet just as Lilly seems to be about to drop off to sleep, she speaks. I jump, just a little, as the sound of her voice in this interminably dark basement fills the space.

"Sarah wanted to leave you behind," Lilly whispers.

"It doesn't matter now," I whisper back.

"She said I should go with her. That I could go somewhere safe."

Silence.

"But I didn't want to leave you," she continues. "Even though she said it would be safe where she was going. I wanted to stay with you."

I kiss her head again. "You should have gone with her. It would be safer than this." Tears fill my eyes at the truth of my words.

She shakes her head no and goes silent again, and I realize that my words must sound horrible to her—though I hadn't meant them to be. She's only a child. I forget how young she really is sometimes. Especially now, traveling on foot and without her small teddy bear to cuddle. She seems so much older, so much wiser than her short years.

I ponder on how to make her feel better, on what I can say that might make things not sound so cruel. But then her soft snores fill the silence that her voice left behind and I put it all to the back of my mind and hope that she won't remember what I said when she wakes up.

The night stretches on for eternity, since I cannot sleep. I do not feel safe down here in this basement. Shadows pass by the windows every once in a while, shrill screams filling the air. I jump at every new sound. Eventually I get out of bed and go into the other room. I sit in the large corner chair and I light a cigarette, feeling better with the nicotine in my system. My stomach aches, my head pounds, and my thoughts whirl.

Sarah tried to take Lilly from me, my Honeybee. That makes me hate her all the more, yet I know that is wrong and selfish. So incredibly selfish. The most selfish thing ever.

If she had left Lilly because she wanted the car, that would be one thing. She didn't want the burden of a child—I hated that I could understand that, but I could. But she had tried to take Lilly *from* me. That was very different. Because I was Lilly's and Lilly was mine. It had been that way since we had found each other in the sunflower field, both lost, both frightened, both ready to give up.

My hands clench angrily. Sarah had tried to take Lilly away. To take her somewhere safe. But there is nowhere safe. Sarah is delusional. I would have nothing if I didn't have Lilly. I would *be* nothing. I would be alone in this nightmare without purpose, and I don't think I could continue on without her. What would be the point? It is all so incredibly inevitable anyway. I only keep going for her. So in a way, I see Sarah as trying to take Lilly from me as a death threat of sorts… or perhaps I'm just really really tired and hungry.

I smoke another cigarette. They taste strange since they are the ones that I had found in the gas station and had gotten damp, but nicotine is nicotine. I smoke it in four long pulls, and then I stub it out on the floor. I stare into the blackness of the basement, barely able to make out my own hands in front of my face. The darkness doesn't play tricks on my mind, because I feel like perhaps this is all one large trick—this life, this existence, if you can even call it that. I rock back and forth, and I don't realize that I am even crying until the sun begins to shine through the small, dirty windows, the light reflecting off the silent tears that have pooled in my open palms. The screams have stopped and a dull gray light now shines in the room.

I wipe my hands down my pants and stand, and then I go back to where Lilly is still sleeping soundly. I wipe my damp cheeks dry with the sleeve of my sweatshirt and then I climb onto the bed and lie next to her. She automatically nestles up against me as if I had never gone, and I kiss the top of her head and close my eyes. Blackness takes me, dragging me under to blissful unconsciousness.

The mattress smells musty and old, and the air in the basement is stale, but all I can smell is Lilly. The sweet smell of this little girl who loves me, and whom I love in return. She didn't leave me. She chose me over Sarah. That makes me both happy and sad. Because one day soon we will have to leave each other. The infection is spreading. I can feel it in my veins, I can taste it in the very air that we breathe. One day soon this will all be over, and we will be the ones screaming through the night and hiding from the day. I hate that truth, but it is fact.

We will both become that which we fear.

Chapter sixteen.

#16. Find help in what is provided.

I awake far too soon. The arm that Lilly is lying on is tingling. I slowly slide it out from under her and I flex my fingers to get the blood flowing again. I can't see her face. Her curly hair is long and ratty and is covering most of her cheek and forehead, an arm slung above her head. The black veins are clear and prominent, running down her neck like track marks to hell. I stare at them, willing them to disappear, to leave us alone. But they don't go.

They are here to stay.

I brush the hair back from her face, jolting when I see her staring back at me, and for a second I think she is dead already. But then she blinks. And then she attempts a smile. It turns into a grimace as her stomach growls hungrily. Her sweet lips part and she speaks.

"I'm hungry, Mama."

I look away, not able to look at her any longer. I feel guilty. I have failed her. I should have been more careful. I should never have allowed that woman into our lives, but I did. I trusted again, and look where it has got us: starving.

We're starving to death, and there's nothing I can do about it.

"I'm sorry," I say. I don't wait for her reply, instead

I sit up. "Let's go see if we can find something to eat. I think we'll have better luck today," I say, though it's a lie. Our luck feels just as hopeless as yesterday and the day before that one.

"Okay," she says, and sits up. She's always so resilient.

Her hair is a nest of knots and I laugh, a small squeak of happiness escaping my misery. I reach over and ruffle her hair, and she blinks back at me questioningly.

"Let me do something with this first. You don't want to get bugs living in it, do you?"

She shakes her head and then scoots over to me. "I do not want bugs in my hair mama." She blinks those big brown pools at me and a rush of love runs through me.

Slowly and methodically, I begin to run my fingers through her hair. My fingers catch and tug on some of the bigger knots. "I think I need to cut some of it off, okay, Honeybee?"

"Okay," she replies without care.

I stand and find the dressmakers' scissors from the desk. They are big and cumbersome, my fingers unused to wielding them. I sit back down and slowly begin trimming away some of the larger knots, and then I cut some of the length away. I stop when her hair reaches just above her shoulders, and I put down the scissors. I continue running my hands through the curls until my fingers glide through easily. I kiss the top of her head.

"There you go. All better."

She stands up and runs her own hands tentatively through it, her pupils dilating when she sees all the hair that I have cut away covering the bed and floor.

"It is just hair. Hair grows back," I say.

"Okay," she says with a small pout.

She stands and stares, waiting for me to do something else, to tell her what we are doing now, and I realize that she is going back inside herself again. As if all of our time at the secret house had never existed. I am losing that Lilly again, and it pains me.

I stand up, gathering our meager belongings and taking the few extra items that we have found, and then I take Lilly's hand and we go to the concrete stairs and climb up them. I push open the hatch a fraction and look around, checking for monsters. If there are any inside the store, I cannot see them, so I push the hatch all the way open and we climb out. I close the hatch after us and put the material and chest on top. We may end up using it again tonight, or perhaps someone else will find it one day and it can provide them with somewhere safe to sleep. That thought makes me feel both good and bad. Good because I am helping an unknown person, and bad because deep down, I don't want anyone else to be living this way and going through what we are going through.

Deep down, I'm not sure I think it's worth it.

We step out into the daylight, and both take deep breaths of the fresh morning air. It's dull today, the sun not glaring down with its usual beautiful bright heat, and I wonder if there is a storm coming. That would be bad. If a storm were to come, it would be best at night, not during the day. I think it might have rained a little in the night because I can smell damp in the air. The ground is dry now, but I still hold out some hope that water might have collected somewhere that we can drink it.

I look left and right, deciding on which way to go, when I feel Lilly tug on my arm. I look down at her, and she points to a garbage bin. I nod and we walk over together and begin to rummage through it, but there is nothing. Just empty cartons and long-rotted food.

"Come on," I say, and take her hand again.

We walk through the small town, weaving in and out of buildings and around rusted out cars, piles of ash, and bones. Plants and trees have continued to sprout up amidst the destruction, like the earth is showing us the sick irony that is our life. Mother Nature will take with one hand and give back with another. The human race is slowly being wiped from existence, one brutal monster at a time.

What will come after us? I wonder.

A patch of yellow catches my eye as we step around a pile of rubble that was once a shop that boasted that it sold the town's "best milk souvenirs," and again I wonder at what a strange town this is. I walk further around the rubble and toward the patch of yellow, tugging Lilly along with me. I smile when

I see the small patch of dandelions.

"What is it?" Lilly asks.

"Dandelions."

A pause and then: "Can we eat it?"

"Yes," I say.

I sit down and she sits next to me. I dig around the flower, the dirt sticking in my nails. All the while Lilly watches me carefully. I finally free the weed—root, leaves, and sunny yellow head—and I smile proudly at it. I pluck out a leaf and hand it to her. She takes it, examining it before putting it in her mouth and beginning to chew. I do the same and we both watch each other as we sit and chew the very bitter-tasting leaves of the dandelion. Lilly swallows hers first and I offer her another. She's hesitant, and I can't blame her. We're hungry, close to starving again, but we still have taste buds, and these don't taste very nice.

"I'll cook them for us. We'll have dandelion soup," I say.

I gather some twigs and rocks, making a small circle of rocks and putting the twigs in the center. I get out our bottle of water and then look around us for something to cook the flowers and water in. I stand up and a dizzy spell hits me, making me sway, and the world tilts sideways. I try to focus on a spot in the distance to steady myself, but it doesn't work so I close my eyes instead.

"Mama?" Lilly's hand touches my leg and I blink away the dizziness.

I look down at her. "I'm okay. I need something to cook them in." I look toward the collapsed souvenir shop. "I will find something in there." I hold out my hand and she takes it, and together we walk over to what was once the doorway.

I look in, seeing dark and dirt and dust, wood and rubble, glass and trinkets that are no good to me. But there is a counter, and underneath the counter I can see what I think is a can of something. The building is too dangerous to try and get inside by walking in, so I lie down on my front and pull myself along the ground. The debris scratches my stomach, and I think I hear my clothing tear before the sharp pinch of my skin scraping on rocks. I wince but keep going until my hand can reach under the counter and touch the can.

I look back to Lilly, her feet visible to me. "I have it," I say to her, and she bends down and looks in at me. I smile and then look back to the can. I stretch and reach, my fingers flexing for a little more space to grip it. However, the area is tight and restrictive, and no matter how much I try, I cannot reach it. I stretch until my shoulder feels like it might dislocate, until my fingers feel painful, but still all I can do is scrape my fingertips against the can, but not grasp it fully.

I curse out my whispered frustrations and then slide myself backwards, my stomach and chest scraping along the ground again. When I am back out into the daylight, I look down and see that my sweatshirt has torn and a small circle of blood is on me. I lift up my top and look, but the cut is only very small. I look back to Lilly and shrug in frustration.

"I can't reach it," I say with a frown.

Lilly kneels down and looks inside. Seconds pass as we sit in silence and then she looks back to me, her wide brown eyes meeting my cool gray ones.

"I can try."

"No," I say immediately. "We'll think of another way."

Another dizzy spell hits me, and I decide that we will just have to eat the bitter weed raw, whether we like it or not. I tell Lilly this and she grimaces.

"I want to try," she says stubbornly.

I turn around on hands and knees and look back into the gloom of the shop. I can see the dull metal of the can, but I cannot read the label. It could be dog food again, I think. But then, it could be food—real food. If we get it, we could eat. I could stop the hollow, painful feeling inside Lilly's stomach. We would have the empty can to make our soup in. That can represents two meals, not one. It represents two more days of life. It represents everything about our current existence—how our life, a true life, is just out of our grasp. That's pitiful, but true. I look at Lilly again. She doesn't seem afraid, only hungry and determined.

"Okay," I relent. "Get the can, quickly. I will be right here," I say, pointing to the edge of the entrance. Because there isn't enough room for both of us in the space. "Don't go too far into the dark. Get the can and come straight back out."

She seems almost pleased, and nods before getting down on her belly. She takes a deep breath and begins crawling her way into the small space, her small body moving easier in the confines than mine had. She reaches the can, grips it, and pulls it free with a small tug. The counter and some rocks move around her and I gasp as I wait to see if it will collapse, but it doesn't. She glances back at me with a smile, proudly holding the can for me to see.

"I got it, Mama," she whispers to me, the whites of her teeth glowing against her dirty face.

I smile back, and then my attention is drawn to the glow of two bright red eyes that shine out of the darkness close to her face. "Lilly," I whisper.

She looks back ahead of her, and I hear the short intake of breath she takes as she sees the eyes too. I crawl in after her, and grab her ankles just as the monster begins to move toward her with a hiss and a snap of teeth. I pull her legs, not caring if I scrape her face or hands, not caring if she drops the can, only caring that I need to get her out, now.

She doesn't cry as I pull and pull, and it feels like she will never make it back out into the sunlight—until finally she does. We stagger backwards on our hinds, clinging to one another as the monster comes forward, forgetting itself for a brief second and daring to come out into the daylight. It screams in pain and darts back inside, and we can smell the stench of burnt flesh as smoke rises out of the dark hole of the shop. It watches us as it licks its wounds, hissing every once in a while.

I grip Lilly and pull her to me, and she climbs on my knee and wraps her small body around me. I stand up and back away from the hole of the store, still watching the monster within. I take us back to our dandelion patch and I sit back down. I can't see the monster anymore, and it can't see us, but it knows that we are here now, and we know that it is there. We will need to leave now, quickly and quietly, putting as much distance between us and this place before nightfall.

"Are you okay?" I whisper against Lilly's hair.

Her arms give me a small squeeze to let me know that she is okay.

"I need you to help me dig the plants up. We need to leave, but we can take these with us."

She nods but doesn't move, and I hate that I have to pull her away from me and get her to do this. She wants comfort, but I need her to dig. She looks up at me, her eyes full of hurt that I can't allow her a few more seconds in the safety and solace of my arms.

"We need to hurry," I say urgently and apologetically. Her face is grazed, a little blood trailing down her left cheek, and I wipe it away gently with my sleeve. "Help me," I say.

Lilly nods and then holds up the can in her hand, and I want to laugh and cry at the same time. It's pinto beans. Of course it is. She hands it to me and I put it in our bag, and then we begin to dig. She is slow at first and then she becomes almost frantic, her breaths coming short and sharp, and I can see her eyes building with unshed tears. We dig and dig, and she copies me when I pull out the plants and put them in our carrier bag, being sure to get all of the roots.

When all of the weeds have been dug up, I take her hand and we stand. I peer around the rubble cautiously and see the red eyes of the monster still glowing near the doorway. It hisses as if it knows that I am watching it, and I dart back away. I take Lilly's hand and we begin to walk quickly away from here, from this town and its little broken stores filled with monsters and souvenirs.

As we reach the outskirts of the town, I see a cap on the ground. It was white once but is now more of a gray. It has little cow hands on the peak and they clap in the breeze. I pick it up and slap it against my thigh to free some of the dust from it, and then I take Lilly's cap off her head and place on this new one.

She looks up at me with a smile. The red grazes on her cheek are stark against her pale skin. She takes my hand once more and we begin to walk again, the cow hands clapping with each step she takes.

Chapter Seventeen.

#17. Fill those hungry holes.

We walk for several miles in total silence, nothing but the breeze in the trees to occupy the hush, until abruptly Lilly stubbornly refuses to walk anymore. She stares at the ground at her feet, unwilling to look up at me. I give her arm a small tug, but she still doesn't move. I get down on my knees and try to look into her face, but still she stares at her shoes, her eyes unwilling to meet mine. I remove the flapping cow cap from her head and she finally looks up at me, her expression defiant as she snatches the cap back and puts it firmly back on her head with a small pout.

"What's wrong?" I ask her softly.

She waits a beat before replying. "I'm hungry, Mama," she whispers back. And then she begins to cry.

"I know you are," I whisper, as I pick her up and she wraps her arms around my neck.

I carry her, singing to her softly as I walk, the sound of my voice floating in the slight breeze. I make the song up as I go—the tune, the words, are all spur-of-the-moment fiction from my own mind. I can't remember music and how it once sounded. Not the sound of guitars or drums, or any of the lyrics from songs. It is all gone, blanked out from my memory as if it were too painful for me to remember.

Yet I somehow string some words together that have some semblance of a tune, and I sing a song that she likes. My voice carries an unknown tune that eventually calms her, and she stops crying.

In time we come to a children's park, and I point to it and whisper to her to look. After much persuasion, she lifts her head from my shoulder to see what I am talking about. She doesn't smile, but she's interested, and that's good enough for me.

I push open the little green gate and we go inside. There are two swings, which are both broken, and the merry-go-round squeaks loudly when I push it around, so I tell her she can't go on that as it could draw attention to us. But the slide still seems good and strong—safe—so I tell her that she can go and play on it. I begin to gather stones and twigs to build a fire, and she climbs the steps, her footsteps sounding loud yet hollow on the metal stairs. She slides down without even smiling, and I wonder if she likes it at all, but then she goes back around to the stairs and climbs them again before going back down the slide once more. She's here, and yet not. Her body is on a continuous loop, going up and down that slide, yet her mind is unaware, blissfully or perhaps ignorantly somewhere else. I don't blame her; I want to be somewhere else too.

The park is only small, enclosed by what was once a green metal fence, and I search all around for twigs and stones. I find a child's backpack near the picnic benches. It has a small brown stain near the zipper that I think could be blood. Inside the backpack is a well-loved brown teddy bear with only one eye, a piece of paper and a pen, some loose change and a small knife that doesn't look very sharp. I take the backpack, feeling annoyed that there wasn't any food in it but knowing that Lilly will love the teddy bear, and then I keep on searching the park. I rummage through the green trash can by the entrance and find an old polystyrene container that probably once held a Starbucks coffee in it. I dig a little deeper and find a shattered coffee thermos. The silver reflective material that was once on the inside of it, is broken and it tumbles out, the sunlight reflecting off the shards when I tip it up. The sound is actually quite sweet—like tiny sparkling stars falling to earth. I bang the side of it to make sure all the glass is out, but still worry just that some remains inside, so I drop it back in the trash can. I find an old Pepsi can and I take that instead.

I watch Lilly as I walk across the park. She's stopped sliding now and is staring off into the distance as if transfixed by something. I look to where she stares, but see nothing. There are houses across the field, but they are very far away, too far for her to be able to see anything in them—but still she stares like she knows something that I don't, some secret that she is being whispered to by the wind, that I am not privy to.

I cut the Pepsi can in half using the dressmakers' scissors, and then I sit down on the grass and begin to build my fire with stones and twigs. I use my lighter and watch the twigs and leaves begin to burn, and then I open the can of pinto beans and pour half of them into the Pepsi can. I tear apart the dandelions—the heads, roots and leaves are all edible, even though they are bitter—and I put them in the tin can and then add some of our precious water. I set the can on top of another circle of rocks in the center of the fire, so as not to smother the flames of the fire, and then I wait while the food slowly cooks.

Lilly is still staring into the distance when I hear a gunshot somewhere. The sound makes me flinch even though it is far away, and Lilly breaks her trance and scampers over to me. She sits down, looking at me with those soulful eyes of hers that see everything.

"It's okay," I say. "It was far away. Sound travels in the open like this, especially when the world is so quiet."

She doesn't say anything. Instead, she looks at the food bubbling away and licks her lips. I give her knee a squeeze as a sign of reassurance.

When the broth and beans are good and boiling I distribute them between the Starbucks cup and the can, handing Lilly the largest portion.

"It's hot," I say, and she nods as she takes it.

Lilly blows on it before she tries to drink some of it. She winces as it burns her tongue, and I offer her the bottle of water.

"I told you it was hot," I say.

She takes a small swig of the water and then gives

it back to me. When she picks up her cup of broth again, she blows it a lot more before trying to drink any this time. We eat in silence, each of us staring off into the distance as we slowly sip the bitter broth. It doesn't taste very good at all, but it should make us feel better, because any food is good food right now, and there are plenty of nutrients in the dandelions. I think we're both feeling numb and empty—hungry to the point of exhaustion. I hope that after we've eaten we'll both be feeling a little better. I'd like to keep on walking today, put some more distance between us and that strange small town that sold only dairy products and the monsters hiding in its depths like dark family secrets.

I slurp the last of the broth down and then stare into the empty can longingly. It's not enough, but then, it will never be enough because nothing ever is anymore.

I watch Lilly drinking the last of hers. She doesn't eat without restraint, but with care, as if every last drop of the broth is some amazing, life-giving force that needs every flavor to be experienced and enjoyed. And maybe it does. But other times it's just bitter dandelions and out of date pinto beans in boiled water, and it is nothing more than there to fill the hollow hole where our tummies are.

Lilly finishes the food and sighs, looking satisfied, and that makes me happy—to know that she is full, that I have done a good job today of feeding her, especially since I could have gotten her killed back at the collapsed store. Her eyes meet mine, a small spark of something within those beautiful brown orbs, and she tentatively smiles at me. Not a full-mouthed, toothy grin, but a shy, contemplative smile. I reach behind me and get the child's backpack, and I hand it to her. She looks at it like it's possibly the greatest gift she's ever received. Her small fingers clasp the smaller zipper, and she slowly opens the bag up before looking inside. Her face tilts up to look at me, and there it is: the smile that fills me with such joy.

"Can I keep it, Mama?" she whispers, one of her little hands reaching in and grasping the teddy bear. She pulls it out of the bag, showing it to me, even though she must be aware that I have already seen it. "Won't someone miss it?"

"You can keep it," I nod, "I don't think there is anyone to miss it anymore." She looks into the face of the bear with only one eye before promptly bursting into tears.

I scoot over to her and place an arm around her shoulders. I know that she's thinking of Mr. Bear and how much she misses him. He had been with her since the start of everything. He was her longest memory, and like a fallen family member, she has lost him to the monsters. In the rush to escape the house, he was left behind in the bedroom. And I hate Sarah even more for making us lose that teddy. I kiss the top of Lilly's head and hum to her until she calms down.

"Hush, Lilly, hush. It's all okay," I murmur, though this life is anything but okay.

"He smells different from Mr. Bear," she says, pulling out of the hug. She holds him up for me to sniff, and I do, taking a deep lungful of him in.

"He does, doesn't he."

She nods.

"Different isn't always bad though, Lilly. Sometimes different can be good."

She blinks twice and then looks down at the teddy. Her mouth quirks in a very tiny smile and then falls away, but then she hugs him to her chest. I wonder if she feels like she's betraying Mr. Bear by keeping this one. The way she clings to him is both angry and happy.

"It's okay to love him, Mr. Bear would want you to be happy." I say and she wipes at her damp eyes and nods. "We need to keep walking," I say with a heavy heart. "We need to put some more distance between us and that place."

"From the monsters?" she asks.

I nod and she bites her lip to stop herself from crying again.

I pack away our things, noticing how my headache has eased now that I have eaten. Lilly places the backpack clumsily over her shoulders, and I adjust the straps so that it fits her more snugly. The previous child must have been older than Lilly, I realize with sad indifference.

We begin to walk again, Lilly's hand once more slipping into mine. The silence is heavy and oppressive around us, like thick smoke, until Lilly's voice cuts through it.

"Will you sing to me?" she asks.

I look down at her with a small frown. "Sing?" I say, and she nods.

"The song you sang before," she explains.

I huff out a breath because I really don't want to, but I nod as I try to recall the words to my made-up song from earlier today. Parts of it come to me, but I'm still struggling to remember exactly what I had sung. It was just a jumble of words that made no sense, and then I realize that it isn't the words, but the sound of my voice that she likes. It's the sound that soothes her when she has nightmares, or when she is feeling sad and missing her real family. So I nod again, just to confirm that yes, I will sing for her. And then I open my dry lips and I sing in the same tune, but with different words from earlier:

> *I never knew—how could I know?*
> *That you and I would see the world.*
> *We walk the roads, so very long,*
> *We walk the roads, and they pass us by,*
> *Because they do not know—how could they know?*
> *They don't see us as we sneak on by.*
> *My love for you is what sets me free.*
> *It gives me breath, and it gives me wings,*
> *To lift me high, above the roads.*
> *I never knew—how could I know?*
> *That the world would end tonight.*

I stare up at the clouds, watching the twirling white tails of their innocence drift lazily across the sky, oblivious to our pitiful existence, and I picture a world that I once loved so much. I blink past the faces of the people I have met, both old and new, and I feel my soul scorching, set on fire with the memories that beat down on me. The world is hollow and empty, but not as empty as me right now. My emptiness echoes for all the world to hear. I think it would have been so much easier if I would have died when all of this began. If I would have ended at the start.

Lilly tugs on my arm and I blink sluggishly, still staring up into the distance. My lips are moving, but barely a wisp of voice leaves them. She tugs on my arm again and I look down at her, realizing that I have stopped walking altogether. I realize that it was a selfish thought, because if I would have died, Lilly would be all alone now. Or perhaps not even here at all.

"I'm sorry," I say, cupping one of her small cheeks in my dirty palm. "I'm sorry," I say again.

She still looks uncertain, and I force a smile—which is possibly more frightening.

"Did I scare you?" I ask.

Lilly nods, and I drop to my knees in front of her, cupping both of her cheeks now as I stare into her face and get lost in her eyes.

"I'm sorry, Honeybee. I was thinking of the past," I say sadly. And I was, sort of. I was thinking about death and how sometimes I wished that I had never lived. That I hadn't hidden so well. Because if I hadn't hidden so well, then I wouldn't be here now, starving, dying of this disease, being chased by monsters every night.

"You shouldn't do that," she whispers back.

I nod, and tear my gaze away from hers. "I know. It doesn't help. It's just hard sometimes."

We stay there in silence for several minutes, me on my knees in front of her, and her staring down at my pitiful form.

I finally take a breath and stand back up. I take her hand in mine. "I won't do that again," I say, and we begin to walk. And I know that I won't do that again, because I was supposed to live. If I hadn't lived, then Lilly wouldn't have, either. My life gives her life.

She doesn't ask me to sing anymore, and I'm glad, because I can't stand the sound of my own voice right now.

Chapter Eighteen.

#18. ...

It will be night soon. Again. I sigh, feeling more frustrated than I would normally. I should be feeling anxious as the day draws to a close, as our savior—the sunlight—goes to bed to rest its weary rays of light. Yet I don't. I just feel frustrated because the days are never long enough.

We stand outside a squat, red-bricked house, both unsure of what to do. It could be safe inside. But it might not be. Monsters may be inside, waking from their daytime rest, hungry and eager for the night's gentle caress on their skin. There could be other humans inside. Bad humans. Vicious humans. Humans with bad intentions.

But the house could also be empty. We could rest here for the night. We could hide—sleep, rest from our long day, hopefully… but there could be humans or monsters…It's so hard to tell the difference between the two sometimes.

So many frightening possibilities.

I see Lilly and I as separate entities from other humans now, since none have proved anything to us but how corrupt their souls really are, showing that they are no better than the monsters we all run from. As if we are the only true living humans left on earth. As if the black poison that grows in other humans, threading and weaving its way through their veins, destroying their bodies, has ruined everything that they are. And perhaps even though they are still physically human, they aren't really—not where it truly matters: inside. Of course it doesn't help that we haven't seen another human in almost a week now. Not since Sarah. Not since she stole all of our things and abandoned Lilly at the roadside. I growl, my nostrils flaring at the memory of what that horrible woman did to us.

Yes, Lilly and I are our own race now. Still human. Still pure and fundamentally good, for the most part. For now, at least.

I stare at the darkened windows of the house, willing my eyes to penetrate through the glass to see inside, to see if there are dangers that lurk within these walls. But of course I can't see inside. Of course I'll have to go and look. Of course I'll have to risk our lives searching for somewhere safe to spend the night. Of course, of course, of course!

I sigh again. The beginnings of a new headache making itself known. Or an old headache. I'm not sure that the previous one ever really went away. They all just sort of roll and tumble into one now, like the days, and weeks. Everything is a blur of facts and things that happen, decisions that are made and not. A big blur of *what ifs* and *whatevers*.

"Mama?" Lilly whispers questioningly, urging me to make a decision soon.

"Come on, Honeybee," I say, pulling on her arm gently as I guide her to the back of the house.

The front yard is full of long, dying brown grass, and I suck in a breath thinking about what could be lurking in those long grasses. The never-ending sunshine has turned the grass to brown straw, crisp and fragile as we walk through it, brittle and snapping as we brush against it. The bright sunshine that scorches my skin and steals my hydration. But I am not allowed to despise it, not even once, because it saves our lives. Every. Single. Day.

I clutch my blunt knife in my left hand and follow the rocky path to the backyard, all the while holding onto Lilly's small hand tightly. I almost laugh when we reach the backyard, my eyes widening as I take in the image that awaits us. There is no back of the house. At all. The entire back of the house is not there—where it should be. The back walls have collapsed in a heap, and I can't fathom how the front of the house is even still standing, but standing it still is. It's unfathomable logic. I finally let loose the laugh as I see a skeletal body sticking out of some of the debris that was once the bathroom. They never made it out alive, but it doesn't seem like the monsters got to them, either. This place was possibly safe. Until it wasn't.

I sigh again, unsure of what to do now, my bitter, sardonic laughter dying on my cracked lips. It's getting late, we don't have much time, and yet still the urgency hasn't hit me. I look down at Lilly, seeing her small curls sticking out from either side of her cow hat, one arm wrapped around the teddy bear with only one eye and her other hand still wrapped in mine. She's staring straight ahead, looking anxious. And that's how she should look. That's how *I* should look. I bite my lip.

"I don't know what to do," I say, my words almost stolen by the wind. At first I think they are, but then slowly she looks up at me. I shrug, because I don't know what else to do and honesty is the best answer for her. I gesture around us with the hand that holds the knife. "I don't know what to do," I say again. I feel bad, guilt eats away at me, because this is not the sort of thing that you drop on a young child. But I can't help it. I'm lost, and confused, and so very very exhausted. And I really don't know what to do.

"We need to hide," she says matter-of-factly, looking at me like I am possibly the stupidest person alive.

"I know that. But where?" I say, feeling frustrated.

Lilly looks around us and then back up to me, understanding our predicament. "Somewhere safe," she says with a small frown, and I have the urge to laugh again.

Somewhere safe. Is there even such a place?

"There is nowhere safe now," I say morbidly, feeling bad as soon as the words leave my lips. Because again, this is too much for a child to have to take in. Yet Lilly just blinks up at me, her expression anxious but her eyes calm.

"I'm tired, Mama," she whispers.

For some reason, those words snap me back to

reality. I give one more sigh, just for good measure, and then I give myself a good mental shakedown. I see the setting of the sun. I see the ruins of the collapsed house. I see the long, overgrown grass that hides a multitude of secrets. I feel Lilly's warmth, the sensation seeping through her small hand and into mine. I hear her shallow breaths. And then I see a pile of something at the back of the garden. I squint, looking closer, and think it might be a car, mostly hidden by wooden fence panels and garbage.

"Quickly," I say, and start to move toward it.

Lilly follows close behind, her small hand never leaving mine. We finally get to the car—or what I hope is a car. I pull one of the fence panels back and look more carefully, expecting to see the face of one of the monsters looking back at me through the glass, but as I peer into the gloom of the car, I only see another skeletal body. It's sitting on the other side of the car, in the driver's seat. It's staring out the window, its eyes expressionless and its hands still clutched around the steering wheel, ready to drive off at a moment's notice.

I pull the wooden board back even more, the dying of the light urging me on quicker. I step around to the driver's side of the car, my feet crunching on something, and when I look down I see both monster and human remains, my foot crushing through the bones of a misshapen monster skull. I flinch and jump back, almost falling on my ass. Lilly yelps and does fall, and then she yelps again as she lets go of my hand

and begins to scoot her way backwards away from the bones of monsters and men.

"It's okay, it's okay," I say, reaching for her.

She whimpers but takes my hand and stands back up, and I dust off the bone fragments on her backside. I look back to the car, to the wooden panels concealing it, to the bones surrounding it, and an idea forms. I clutch the handle of the car door, a satisfied smile daring to cross my face when the door clicks open. I pull the door open wide, looking inside and seeing the keys hanging from the ignition. There were actually two people hiding in the car, not one, and now there are two sets of bones hiding inside it. I reach in, worrying about how to get them out carefully, but in the end I decide that there isn't the time to be careful or considerate. I grip the clothing of the first body and drag it free of the car, forcing myself to look at the dried-out face of this person that was once alive.

The second body is in the back of the car, still huddled on the back seat in a fetal position, its face buried into its own arms. But it doesn't move, not a fraction. There's no way to get it out without removing more of the wooden boards, and I don't have the time to do that, nor do I want to disturb what was obviously a good hiding spot for so long.

"Come on," I say to Lilly.

I throw the carrier bag of our meager possessions in the footwell and help her clamber inside. Lilly climbs over to the passenger seat, oblivious of the body in the back. I run back around the car, putting all the panels that I've disturbed back in place and making it as hidden as it was before—maybe even more so. Then I move to the driver's side, and before I get in I pull the last panel back around the car, concealing it again, and then I shut the door and lock it from the inside.

I look over to Lilly, her brown eyes staring back at me from the passenger seat.

"I think we'll be safe in here for tonight."

"Are you sure?" she asks innocently.

I keep my gaze on hers, letting her see my truth. "No. But we can never be sure of things like this, can we?"

She shakes her head but doesn't reply. She knows that I'm right. We can never be sure of our safety. Not anymore. I reach in the bag and pull out the half bottle of water and offer it to her. She takes a small drink, aware that we need to ration everything right now, and I am in awe once more of her ability to understand things like this.

"Do you want some gum?" I say, and she nods, so I get one of the stale pieces out and give it to her.

"Do you not want any?"

"No," I say, forcing a smile because I don't want her to worry. I want her to chew the gum, enjoy the flavor, and forget the danger we are in for a little while.

She chews and chews, humming mindlessly to herself and to me, and then she starts to blow a large bubble. My eyes go wide when I see it.

"Oh no, Honeybee, you can't do that," I whisper.

She blinks back at me, confused, the large bubble still on her small, pink lips.

"It will pop," I continue to explain. "It will be loud."

Her eyes finally widen in understanding, and she tries to suck the air back out of the bubble.

I grin despite the danger we are in, because the image of her trying to suck the air out of the bubble is actually quite funny. Slowly the bubble deflates, and I nod an okay as she continues to chew more slowly. The car slowly descends into darkness just as the screaming begins outside—the high-pitched screech of the monsters as they awaken and set about finding their next meal. An involuntary shudder runs down my arms, goosebumps breaking out all over my skin despite the humidity of the summer evening.

And so it begins: the long night of waiting. Tonight, I feel, will be longer than any night that has come before this one. Something feels different, but I don't know what. I look in the rearview mirror, my eyes finding the body still curled up on the backseat. Ice runs through my veins, my heart stopping in my chest as slowly, the head of the body turns, and eyes full of death stare back at me.

I blink at it. Once. Twice. Three times. And those eyes blink right back. Once. Twice. Three times. Neither of us move, the air stills, and all that can be heard is the chewing of gum coming from Lilly's sweet mouth as the deathly face of the passenger on the backseat stares back at me. My hand clutches onto my knife, and though I know it's blunt as hell, I'm also more than certain that this dull piece of metal will kill the thing in the back seat.

"Hel…p m…e." The voice echoes forward, and I feel Lilly still next to me. "He…lp me," the person says again.

I turn slowly in my seat, one hand gripping my knife and the other blocking Lilly.

I look upon the face of death, and the bitter realization floors me. This person is not a monster. They are human. They are not dead. But they are barely alive. Like us, but more so.

"Mama?" Lilly murmurs, her nails digging into the soft flesh on my arm, and I'm almost certain that she is going to break the skin at any moment. "Mama," she says again.

I can't look away from the face of this person. This person that is hollow and empty, much emptier than I am, and hollower than I thought someone could ever be. They blink, the movement sluggish, their eyeballs rolling into the back of their head before meeting mine again with a crackling breath.

"H...elp m…e," they say again. Their voice is barely audible, and yet I hear the words clear inside my head. *Help me*. They want me to help them. But how can I possibly help them, when I'm barely alive myself?

The screams are right outside the window. Right

outside the wooden panels that conceal us. All of us. All *three* of us. I swallow, my throat burning with the resistance. I want to take a sip of water, yet it feels wrong to do this in front of this person. This person that is dying. Starving. Dehydrating. Yet I don't want to share our things with whoever they are. They are dying, almost dead. I cannot help them, a little water will not help them. Yet it would be cruel of me to deny it to them, even though the loss of the water could play a heavy part in both mine and Lilly's downfall.

So I ignore the parched scratching in my throat, the panting thirst in my mouth, and the tickle of a cough. I ignore it all, and I turn back around in my seat. I face forward, away from the eyes of death on the back seat of the car. Away from the person that I cannot help. I glance sideways at Lilly. She is watching me carefully, trying to decide…something. Perhaps trying to decide if I am one of the good people or the bad people now for my cowardly act. For my cruelty. I place a finger to my lips as she opens her sweet mouth to speak, to question me.

Monsters are outside the car, merely a sliver of wood and metal away from us. Now is not the time to judge me. Now is the time to hush and sink into the darkness. To forget the person on the backseat. To forget to judge me, and forget to choose between good and bad. Now is the time for silence. I need the silence. I need to believe that what I am doing is for the best.

Let Lilly's thoughts be loud in her beautiful head

but silent on her lips. Because there truly can be no greater punishment than hearing her disappointment in me.

Chapter Nineteen.

#19. The longest nights are the ones I hate.

The person, whoever they are, stopped asking for help once we turned back around, as if they knew that it was futile to waste their energy on pleas for help from us. I wonder if Lilly and I are perhaps not the first people to do this to them—to ignore them and view this person's death as inconsequential to their own existence. That unfathomably makes me feel worse, and yet better almost simultaneously. I check the mirror every once in a while, seeing their cold, lifeless eyes staring back at me.

As the night grows heavy, it becomes harder to see them, hiding away there on the back seat of this tragically decrepit car. Lilly fell asleep a little while ago, her cheek pressed against the glass of her window. I woke her the first time she fell asleep, because she looked so deathly still, almost like the person on the back seat, and I freaked out that she might have actually died.

The screams have turned distant as the monsters roam further away for food. They came, our scent pulling them toward us, but the bodies outside of the car—both of their own kind and those that are human—masked us. And so now they are moving on, confused as to where we have gone. Yet I still don't make a sound. Still I don't leave the car.

The person seems almost frozen in their position. And perhaps they are. Maybe they are too weak to move, to escape from this car, which was once their refuge, their sanctuary, and has now turned into their tomb. Their horrible metal tomb. With that thought I shiver again. I pray that this won't end up our tomb also. I pray that morning comes soon. I pray for the person to close their eyes and sleep, or to die and let them find peace there. But they don't. They continue to stare at me, and the night draws on, and my prayers go on unanswered.

The person blinks. I have counted their blinks thus far. Twenty in the last hour, give or take the minutes. You would have thought that this person would have blinked more, but they don't, and it seems wrong because I know that humans blink more than this. But they don't. They just stare, their lips occasionally moving, whispering something I can't make out. I know they're not asking for help anymore, I can tell by the shapes that their mouth makes, but still I puzzle over what they are saying. I try to outstare them, to only blink when they do. But I am more full of life than they are and so I blink several times in the time between their blinks, and eventually I look away, ashamed of myself for playing this wicked game with them.

Because the truth is, though I feel like I am at death's door, I am not. I am alive, Lilly is alive, but this person is dead.

Lilly jumps, a short, sharp squeal escaping her lips.

She sits upright, looking around us in panic. It's dark, and she hates the dark. I reach over, my hand finding her arm.

"It's okay, Honeybee, I'm right here. We're safe," I whisper reassuringly.

"For now," she replies.

"Yes," I nod solemnly, "for now, and that is what matters most." My words feel like a shadow from some other time, a time when I said the same thing to her.

My heart plummets as I think of our safe haven below the streetlight at the top of the hill. We had been safe there, the monsters trapped down below us, out of reach. I wish we had never left there, I wish we could go back, but I know that we can't. So much has happened—too much, in fact. Other than the light, there was nothing left there for us. The light protected us from the monsters, but it did not feed us or quench our thirst. I'm once again brought to the conclusion that yes, we are going to die. It's just a matter of when.

"Do you want to sit on my knee?" I ask Lilly.

She doesn't answer, but I see her turning in her chair to look onto the back seat, at the person behind us. I hear the sharp intake of her breath as she watches the person that equally watches us. As if she had forgotten that they were there.

"Lilly?" I say again. "Do you want to sit on my knee?" I whisper, my hand reaching out to touch her cheek. I think she must nod because in the next moment she is climbing over to me, and I hug her close as she tries to go back to sleep, wrapped safely in the warmth of my arms, with the gentle *thud thud thud* of my heartbeat to reassure her that I am still alive, and I will protect her.

I look up in the mirror and see the person staring back at me, and I look away shamefully once more as Lilly and I take solace in one another's arms. I haven't offered this person comfort of any kind, because I know that there is no point. They will die no matter what now. So I don't waste my time. But this person was once a person—a woman, it would seem, by the string of pearls around her neck—someone's daughter, someone's friend, someone's sister or a wife perhaps. Who really knows anymore? I bet she doesn't remember. A tear breaks free from my left eye and trails silently down my cheek. I will feel shame forever.

The woman blinks, I blink and then I look away, and I'm almost certain that she continues to stare at me. I kiss Lilly's sweet curls, tightening my grip around her. I will never let this end be Lilly's.

The hours drip by, like water from a leaking faucet. One drip, two drip, three drip, slowly, slowly, the night stretches on, seeming to never end. Lilly sleeps fitfully, waking every once in a while, looking over my shoulder at the woman on the back seat and then cuddling herself closer to me.

The woman doesn't sleep. Or maybe she does, but her eyes remain open, awake, staring, seeing into my blackened and wicked soul. The virus that grows in my body must have destroyed some of my humanity, for I know that it is wrong to ignore her—to pretend that she is not even there. But I can't stop myself. I'm an ostrich, sticking my head into a big pile of sand and pretending that there are no monsters outside my window, and there isn't a dying woman on the backseat of this car. Watching me. Always watching me.

There is a flurry of activity from somewhere outside, some screeching and scraping, and then a minute later the first crack of light begins to descend on us, slipping in the through a fissure in the wood panels that surround our car. The small slit of light pierces our darkness, and I blink lazily, feeling exhausted but grateful. I am always grateful to have made it through the night, to be alive for another day, no matter how pointless I know it is. Morning is here, the night has gone, and we can finally leave this wretched car. How can I not be grateful for that?

As the heat of the sun begins to penetrate the car, Lilly squirms on my lap, slowly rousing from her sleep. Her cheek is still pressed against my chest, but she looks up at me, her face devoid of emotions. She blinks slowly, sleep still thick in her eyes and comprehension of where we are working its way across her pretty features.

"Good morning, Honeybee," I say. But I cannot form a smile for her today. My mind, my body, my soul feel chilled to the bone, despite the heat of the new day trying to warm me. This coldness is bone deep and will not go away so easily. Lilly doesn't reply. She just stares at me with empty brown eyes, so I speak for her. "Are you okay?"

The words leave my mouth, and I feel the clench of guilt in my tummy again. It's a pointless and insensitive question, and I look away as shame and grief bury me under their heavy burden. Lilly rubs at her eyes as though she's still tired, and I push the guilt away and help her back into her own seat for a moment while I check outside. Things can change so much overnight. The monsters can knock things over, drag things to build new nests. You never know what you might find, so I am always cautious, just in case. You can never be too cautious.

The door creaks loudly when I open it, which is strange as I hadn't noticed the creak last night. I push back some of the wooden panels surrounding the car and blink against the bright light of day. Outside there are signs of the monsters everywhere, from the bones of the human at my feet, to the splash of blood across the grass, to the deep gouges in the mud. One monster lies flat on its back, its legs in the air as if it is a dog lying in the sun and warming its belly. Its body is burnt to a crisp, but you can still see its humanness—what it once was. It has legs and arms, a head and a torso. But its fingers are elongated, its nails sharpened claws. Its feet are not covered by shoes anymore. Instead the nails of each foot are long like that of the nails on the hands, and the feet are stretched longer than they should be. There's no hair on its head; that happened before this monster met the sun. That is one of the signs of the infection—the loss of hair, the misshapen skull. Deep black veins are threaded through its skin, but it's the reddened, bloodshot eyes that always frighten me the most. They are the thing of nightmares. This monster's mouth hangs open in a silent screech of pain, its teeth blackened and sharp, still deadly despite its death, but I feel no sorrow at its violent and painful death.

I shudder and look back in the car. "Come on," I say, holding my hand toward Lilly.

Her eyes flit to the woman on the backseat, a silent request to rescue this tortured person. How do I tell her that there is no point? That they are already dead, they just haven't quit breathing yet.

"Come on," I say again, my voice more forceful this time. "It's time to go."

Lilly climbs across the space but she doesn't let me help her out of the car. She pushes past me and flinches against the bright daylight. I turn away from the door, ignoring the whispered pleading from the woman to help her. I can't help her. Doesn't she see that? Doesn't she understand? There is no help—no hope for her! No help for any of us. She should just accept her death and be done with it. Lilly turns to stare at me, and for once her eyes aren't full of love, but full of something else. Something akin to dislike burns in her eyes.

"Lilly," I say, but then no more words come. Her

name falls from my lips like air from my lungs, a sudden gust of sound and breath leaving me in one word. I look away from her, feeling the shame creep back up, heat traveling up my neck, leaving me flustered and depressed. I look down at the ground, seeing the dead body of the human and the monster there, a crowbar still held tight in the human's grip, even in death.

How hard he must have fought, and for what? Nothing. He's still dead, just like the rest of us. What are we even fighting for anymore? A butterfly beats its wings as it flies between Lilly and me, and we both look up from our respective staring spots. It is orange and black—nothing uncommon about its appearance. In fact, it's a very average-looking butterfly. And yet it's not. It is beauty, wrapped up in freedom. It can flap its wings and fly away in the blink of an eye, leaving behind every nightmare and demon that it comes across. Its life is a blip in the existence of mankind, and then it dies and is reborn once more.

How I wish Lilly and I were butterflies.

"Lilly," I say, "I want you to put your hands over your ears and watch the butterfly. Watch the sun. Watch the sky and the clouds. And keep your hands over your ears, and do not turn around no matter what."

Lilly stares at me silently.

"Okay?" I ask, knowing now what I must do.

"Okay," she says, and then her hands come up to cover her ears and she turns around, no doubt her eyes following the butterfly as it flits from flower to flower.

I look back in the car, seeing the woman still staring back at me. Though now she looks different. Now her eyes glisten with dampness, and I understand how hard it must have been for her to produce those tears. I glance back at Lilly, checking that she isn't looking, and then I bend down and retrieve the crowbar. I slide another wooden panel out of the way and I pull open the back door. The woman tries to turn her head to look at me, but she can't move, her body has hardened in place and only a low, throaty sound like dead air escapes her dried lips. I hang the crowbar from my back pocket, feeling the metal, warmed by the rising sun, against my ass. I reach in to the woman, tucking one arm gently below her neck, and the other I hook under her legs. Then I lift her and clamber backwards out of the car. She weighs almost nothing—less than Lilly, it seems—and though I am weak, I don't struggle to carry her.

I look down at her, seeing a woman in my arms, and yet not. Her head is cradled against the crook of my arm and I see the string of pearls around her neck, almost like a sign of her perfect life before this terrible one. But now she is no more alive than the dead man on the ground.

I turn to look at Lilly, seeing that she is still doing as I asked, and then I look down at the woman as I walk to the very back of the yard. Her cheeks are hollowed, her eyes gaunt and her skin gray and sickly. But the black veins are still so clear, slowly working their evil into this poor woman. Even as she starves to death, it is trying to change her. She blinks at me, her eyelids moving slowly, sluggishly, her pupils dilating painfully against the brightness of the day.

At the back of the garden I set her down on a lonely and decrepit bench. Despite the ugliness of the bench, the view of the horizon is quite spectacular, and she stares at it in wonder. I even suspect a small smile gracing her lips as she blinks and stares at the sun hanging low and heavy.

"I am sorry that we didn't find you sooner," I say, my words sounding rough in my mouth, like filthy lies. But sometimes you have to lie to make people feel better. "You can let go now, you can be with your family. In the sun." I point to the sky for some inexplicable reason. Inexplicable because I don't believe in a God, and if we were to try and touch the sun we would burn up before we even reached it. Much like the monsters we fear so much.

She breathes heavily, her eyes still fixed on the distance. It's now that I notice how little hair she has, how many black veins she has, how long her nails have grown on her elongated fingers, and I'm suddenly so very angry with her. She asked us to help her—she asked me to help her, yet she must know how close to turning she is. She could have even turned last night and killed both Lilly and me in that metal death trap. What is wrong with her? Why would she do that? Why is mankind so intent with destroying everything and everyone? I don't understand people anymore.

I reach in my back pocket, feeling the heavy metal of the crowbar beneath my fingertips and then I grip it and slowly I slide it out of my pocket. I'm not a murderer, but we have to do things we don't like to protect the ones we love. And I love Lilly. This person could have harmed her, and for that reason alone she must die. This isn't murder, this is self-preservation. After it is done, it will mean one less monster to try and kill us in the world. One less monster to destroy another person's life. Yes, this is the best thing for everyone, even for them. I am putting them out of their misery.

I hold the crowbar above my head, ready to slam it into her skull, my arms and shoulders feeling so heavy with the burden but the strong decision to do this. But then Lilly suddenly calls my name, and I'm not so certain anymore.

"Mama?"

I turn and see her walking toward me, her eyes on me and not the crowbar above my head, though it's obvious that she's seen it. How could she not? She reaches me and slips her skinny arms around my equally skinny waist, hugging me as hard as she can. I slowly lower the crowbar and then hug Lilly back. The bile that has risen in my throat slips back down the way it came without making a full appearance.

"I'm sorry, Lilly," I murmur.

"I'm hungry," she whispers back, ignoring my apology and what I was about to do.

I kiss the top of her head, her curls soft beneath my dry lips. Then I take one last look at the woman—who has turned to look at me, the sunlight glinting off the string of pearls around her neck—and then we turn and leave. I think I hear her say something, but I ignore her, like I had done all night, and we leave. My hand finds Lilly's as we make our way back to the car. I climb in the driver's seat and turn the key in the ignition. It splutters and whines, smoke coughs out of the exhaust, and then it goes dead.

"Try it again," Lilly says.

So I do. I try it three more times, with the same result: a splutter, a whine, and then some black smoke. I slam my hand on the steering wheel in frustration.

"Try it again," Lilly asks softly.

"It's dead. It's no good to us," I say, trying to not let my frustrations into my voice. I reach down to the footwell of the car to get Lilly's backpack and hat.

"Just try," she pleads, her bottom lip quivering.

I huff out a breath and straighten my back. I look over to Lilly, keeping her gaze so that she knows I am serious. "Just one more time," I say, and then I try the key again. But of course it doesn't work. "Sometimes, Lilly, you have to know when to let go," I say and look away, feeling guilty, though none of this is my fault.

She stares at me, her forehead creased in

disappointment. But she doesn't complain or whine. She accepts the decision as she always does. "Okay" is all she says in response, her sad eyes looking downward to her feet.

I grab our meager supplies and then help Lilly put her backpack on. I take her hand in mine as we leave this wretched place and continue to walk.

Chapter Twenty.

#20. Luck will find you in the end.

We walk for miles, the road long and winding. We never know what will be around the next twisty bend, so we make it into a game, trying to guess what could be around the next one. A windmill, a boat, a man, a cow. We of course find none of these things, but Lilly enjoys the game, and she smiles frequently. Her smile lightens my heavy heart. We come across a ripe blackberry bush heavy with fruit and we put all of our belongings from the ratty carrier bag into Lily's backpack and then fill the carrier bag with as many berries as it will hold. We eat while we scavenge, plucking fat berries from thorny branches and chewing them contentedly. The juices sate our thirst and our hunger, and I can almost feel myself being revitalized with each mouthful.

Lilly's hands are purple from the berries, her lips and chin also, and I smile for the first time in days as she eats and eats and eats. There was a day like this, long ago, where we ate berries and she sang to me. Her voice was sweet and carried in the wind. Yet today I hope that she doesn't sing. I think the silence would be best today.

I suck on my forefinger as I prick it on a thorn, the copper taste of my blood mixing with the berries, and I wonder if a well-fed human tastes better to the monsters than a starving one. If they can taste our ripeness, much like we taste the juiciness of the berries. Or if when we are starving and weak we taste of bland pinto beans. I frown at my morbidity and push away the horrible thoughts.

When our tummies are full and our bag is heavy with the fruit, we begin to walk again, our steps happier now that we've eaten. Lilly's hand is clasped in mine and she swings them back and forth as we walk.

"A robot," she says as we near another bend in the road. She looks up at me, her eyes shining happily.

I feel happy today. Happy because she is happy.

"A can of Spam," I say. And she giggles because she knows that I hate Spam.

We turn the next bend, the trees overhead blowing in the breeze, shading us just enough to stop us from getting too hot in the early afternoon heat, but not enough to offer shelter to the monsters. *Today is a good day,* I think.

The road straightens and I see a car up ahead. It's old, of course, but its door is wide open and it looks like it might not be totally useless.

"Look, Lilly," I say, and she looks to where I point.

"Will it work?" she asks.

I shrug, unsure.

I almost jog to the car, and then I remember that I'm still weak from lack of food and I'm tired since I didn't sleep all night. And, well, of course, the car isn't going anywhere, and it's not like anyone is around to steal it from us. So we walk to it—slowly, sure-footed and cautious as I look around, checking that nobody is going to jump out at us.

The car is a mixture of brown rust and white paint, though I'm sure at one time it was a handsome car—a car someone would have been very proud driving, with its long hood and chrome rims. The driver's door hangs open, and I see why now: there's a shoe trapped in the doorway. And when I look closely, I see the bones of a foot still in the shoe. I sit in the driver's seat, but the keys aren't in the ignition so I check behind the visor and under the seat, but they aren't there either. I'm ready to give up when Lilly squeals, and I jump out of the car sharply, clutching at my crowbar.

"I found them!" she says excitedly, and stands up.

I hadn't noticed her getting down on her hands and knees, but that's where she found the keys: under the car. She hands them to me proudly, her chin raised, and I take them and smile.

"Well done, Honeybee," I say, and then I put the metal key in the ignition, watching for a second as the little key ring of a Hawaiian doll dangles from it, before turning the key.

It starts immediately.

There's no choke or struggle or black fumes. Just a strong healthy, growl from the engine. I grin as I look at Lilly, seeing that she is looking decidedly like the child that she is today. Some days I find that she is growing up right before my eyes. I can look at her—this sweet, curly-haired child—and then blink to find that she is all of a sudden a terrified teenager with no one left in the world. That thought scares me as much as the realization that she will never get to become a teenager.

"Get in," I say, reaching around and putting the carrier bag of berries in the back of the car. She doesn't bother to run around the car and get in through the passenger seat. Instead she climbs right over my knee and into her seat. I help her with her seatbelt, hating that she doesn't have her car seat anymore, because they are so much safer for her. She's only small, smaller than she should be for her age, and the seatbelt is close to her ear instead of across her shoulder, making it dangerous if I have to brake suddenly. But then, I guess I should just be happy that we have a car that works.

"Where to?" I tease. "The fairground? School?" I reach down and push the shoe out of the doorway, and then slam the door closed.

"We should go find the safe place."

I turn to look at her, the idling engine the sound to our background. "What safe place?" I ask.

Lilly looks away, her smile faltering. "The one Sarah told you about."

I clamp my mouth shut, keeping my immediate reaction to the name Sarah trapped inside me. Those are not words for a child to hear. I count to ten in my head before I reply.

"There is no safe place, Lilly. You know that."

"But Sarah said—"

"Stop. Don't do this to yourself, or me. There is no safe place. Sarah was wrong, and she was a bad person." I reach out and turn her face to look at me. I need her to see me, not just to hear me. This is important. "Lilly, we know not to trust bad people, don't we?"

She nods. "Yes."

"And Sarah was bad, wasn't she?"

Lilly looks uncertain, so I carry on.

"She left you behind. You could have died."

She frowns and purses her lips, and then nods in agreement that Sarah was a bad person. I feel bad as her chin trembles beneath my fingertips. I don't want to upset her or make her feel bad, but she has to know who to trust if I go before her. I don't want her last days to be filled with fear, or pain, and that's all bad people will ever give her.

"Okay," I say, and I let go of her face.

Her eyes stay on me. I feel her stare as I pull the car out of its position and around the next bend.

"Don't be sad," I say.

"I'm not."

"You are. I know you are." I chance a glance at her, but she's not looking at me now and I feel even worse. The day was going so well and I've ruined it. "What do you think is around this next bend?" I ask.

"I'm tired," Lilly replies. She pulls her feet up onto the seat and turns slightly so that she is faced away from me. So she doesn't have to look at me.

"Okay," I say.

The car lapses into silence as Lilly pretends to sleep, and then eventually she does fall asleep. I drive for miles, listening to her soft snores and the roar of the engine. The day is coming to an end. There is not much daylight left, and I begin to worry that we won't find somewhere to sleep by nightfall. My body is exhausted now, and my eyelids drop every now and then until I jerk myself awake.

I finally pull over at the side of the road and turn the engine off before climbing out. I need a break from driving, and then I need a drink, or perhaps some more berries that will both hydrate and give me a little energy.

We are on a long and lonely stretch of highway with only dust for miles around. There is nothing here. We haven't even passed any abandoned cars in a long time, and this is beginning to stress me out. I pace back and forth at the side of the highway, trying to gather my thoughts on what to do and where to go as anger and resentment burn a wicked path through my body.

I put my hand in my pocket, finding my cigarettes, my lighter, and a folded piece of paper. I light my cigarette and put the pack and lighter back into my pocket. With the cigarette between my lips and one eye closed to stop any smoke from getting in it, I unfold the piece of paper, confusion furrowing my brow for a moment as I try to work out what it is.

It is a piece of map with blue crayon marks

scribbled on it, and I stare at it dumbfounded for several minutes, recognizing it, but also not. This was the map from the house, from mine and Lilly's safe haven, our place in the sun. It shows all the places that we have been, the hard journey that we have taken so far, across savage landscapes and ruined towns, running and hiding from everyone and everything. But there are marks on the map that I didn't put there, and I don't remember how the map got to be in my pocket. I scrunch the bit of paper up and throw it to the ground because none of it matters. Not where we've been, or where we go.

I finish my cigarette and stub it out under my shoe but I'm still no closer to making a decision on where to go, so I light up another one in the hopes that it will bring me some clarity. The minutes tick by, and I decide to get back in the car and just keep on driving. That really is the only solution. Keep on driving and see where we get to. I feel more alert now, and less likely to crash the car.

I climb in and shut the door, looking across at Lilly. I see that she is still sleeping soundly, and I'm glad. She is more peaceful when she sleeps, and I smile and hope that she's dreaming of something nice. I look out my window and see the scrunched-up piece of paper rolling in the breeze, and for some reason that I cannot explain, I open the door, get out, and go and get it. I unfold the paper and look at it more closely, finally seeing what is different about it.

There is a line of green through the middle. I

follow the line all the way down the page until I reach a small green crayon circle. In the green circle is a large field and the name of a town. I can't read the town name because there is a word crayoned over the top of it, but I see the other word, crudely written.

The word is *SAFE*.

I scowl down at the piece of paper, at its false promise, at the hopefulness it alights in me, at the death that it will more than likely bring upon us. The last time we went to one of these supposed safe zones, we were almost killed—not by monsters, but by men. Yet seeing the word circled in the crude green crayon, I can't help the small flutter in my stomach, the surge of something invigorating inside of me.

Hope. That's what the word *SAFE* gives me: hope. But it's false hope. It's always false hope. Yet like a moth to the light, fluttering out of the blackness, I have seen that word and I know that we must go. Because really, what other choice do we have? What choice do *I* have? I promised to protect her at all costs, even if that means losing my sanity to the possibility of hope. Even if that possibility is only so very slim.

I find us on the map and estimate the journey to be three days, as long as we don't hit any problems along the way. I fold the piece of paper back up, deciding not to tell Lilly. I might have false hope, but I can handle it. However, I don't want her fragile heart to be broken when we find that this place isn't actually safe. So I'll take us there, but I won't tell her where we are going.

I look at the horizon, at the sun so low in the sky now that it burns a brilliant orange. I don't need to squint my eyes anymore. It's muted by the shadows that are encroaching upon the landscape. I take a deep breath as I start to drive again, heading for... some place that may be safe. Yes, we have somewhere to head to now, somewhere to aim, but now we need somewhere safe for tonight. And quickly. Because the night is chasing the sun away, and with the black of night comes the screech of monsters.

Chapter Twenty-One.

#21. Sleep is for the wicked.

"Lilly, wake up!" I hiss quietly—too quietly, since she doesn't wake up.

I reach over and shake her, noticing the black veins on her neck are darker, but not quite as dark as the ones that have now traveled over my wrists and across my knuckles towards my fingers. I flinch, drawing my hand back abruptly because I'm shocked. It all seems to be happening too quickly—everything seems to be happening too quickly—and I'm scared. But more importantly, Lilly will be scared when she sees my hands, and I don't want her to be. I don't want her to look at me in fear. Just like I do not want to look at her in fear.

A screech resonates in the distance and a shudder wracks my body. I grip Lilly's shoulder gently yet urgently as I shake her again.

"Lilly!" I look out the windows on all sides as another screech echoes from somewhere, but I don't see anything yet.

Lilly is finally starting to wake—slowly at first, and then as if a switch has been flipped, she jumps and sits upright.

"You're awake," I say to her, in case she was worried that she was still sleeping.

"Okay," she replies, and then recoils when yet

another scream breaks out. She blinks and looks at me sharply. "They're here. The monsters." It's not a question, but a statement. And unfortunately, she's right. "They're here," she repeats, and I nod.

Yes, they are here, and they've been chasing us for several miles, and I don't know what to do. I should have let her sleep, blissfully unaware of the peril outside of this car, but I couldn't. I finally understand the term "metal coffin." I had always rolled my eyes at the statement, thinking that only people that were simultaneously trying to save icebergs, the ozone layer, polar bears, and—hey, what the hell—let's throw in some strange jellyfish that lives at the bottom of the ocean that no one will ever see. We can give it a name that doesn't make any sense too, with too many syllables and a silent *g*. Yes, I've turned into one of those hug-a-tree hippie-type people, because I finally understand the term "metal coffin."

This car is just that: a metal coffin, a one-way trip to hell. We're trapped in it. We'll die in it. We can't get out of it. It's a metal coffin and we are its willing occupants, because if we stop and get out of this car, we are just as trapped. So we'll stay inside, driving for as long as we can, and dying with each passing mile.

"What are we going to do?" Lilly whispers. She slides further down in her seat in an attempt to hide herself from view, and I'd worry more about the seatbelt cutting into her neck if I have to brake suddenly but I'm looking out the window, seeing the monsters dashing in front of my headlights, smoke and steam coming from any of their flesh that touches the light. The image is transfixing. I am transfixed by the sight of their bodies burning upon contact with the light. The smoke, the screams, the burning flesh—it all penetrates my body in so many ways that it shouldn't. Ways that make me feel inhuman and sick. Because I am gleeful at each and every burn they receive, and that's terrible and wrong, because they were human once, just like me and Lilly. And we shall be like them one day, if they do not kill us first. Watching them burn and scream is like watching my own mortality burn away.

"Mama?" Lilly whispers my name, and I blink and glance at her quickly.

"I don't know," I say truthfully, my voice calm even though I am anything but. And once again, I am witness to her nodding at the acceptance of our deaths—her death—and I feel guilt, failure, and hatred for myself running through my veins. I have let her down. This is all my fault. Why couldn't I keep her safe? She deserves safety. She's just a little girl.

"We can just drive," she says matter-of-factly.

I nod frantically. "Yes, and we will, but I don't know these roads and there isn't much gas left. I don't know how far we will get." I look at her again, seeing her looking determinedly at me. "But we can try," I add on, because I think she needs to hear that—that we will try—that I will try, until the very bitter end.

"We shouldn't give up," she says firmly, her mouth

a full pout.

"No, we shouldn't, and we won't."

"Promise?"

"I promise," I say. Though my promise isn't worth much, because I know that we really won't get very far at all and then the promise won't mean anything. But I promise her, because it's all I can give her: a rough promise to try and save her and to not give up.

So we drive. I tell her to close her eyes and put her hands over her ears, because I don't want her to hear their screams anymore. I feel their screams in my head, bouncing around and resonating inside my skull with such ferocity that I feel sick. I don't want that for her. I have my knife at my side, and I know that I will slit Lilly's throat before I let these monsters take her. Because they can have me, but they cannot have her. She deserves more than this, more than a violent death by them. She deserves more than this life gives her. But I can't give her more, I can only give her a swift end.

We drive and we drive, chasing the night away, and there is little I can do but pray that we don't meet any obstructions in the road. Pray that the sun rises soon and I can outdrive them. I see Lilly's lips moving, and know that she is doing the same too—praying, or perhaps singing. Either way, she knows that the end could be around the next bend. All it will take is us having to stop.

My muscles are tight, wound up like coils ready to spring. My jaw is locked like steel and cement, unable to open to utter a word, my teeth grinding so hard that I might snap one of them. I grip the steering wheel tightly, my eyes seeing everything and also nothing—the blackness that cloaks our car, the monsters running alongside us, behind us, and darting across our path.

The screams.

The noises.

The burning.

The smoke.

Keep alert, keep watching, keep a firm grip, and don't get distracted. Death is chasing us down, and I can't let it win. Where is the sun when you need it? Where is the sun and its burning orange glow? The only thing that can save us from this nightmare is so far away, sleeping, unaware that we need it so desperately. The sun sleeps and the monsters come alive, stalking and chasing us through the night. Sickness swishes in my gut. I don't want to die.

I look over at Lilly for a fraction of a second, seeing her curls hanging limply around her shadowed face. The black veins are almost at her cheeks, I notice, and I look in the mirror and see my own cheeks are beginning to darken with the blackness inside of me. I am a day or so ahead of her. Neither of us have much longer before it takes us fully, and then this is us chasing some other poor family through the night. We are all dead anyway, so I shouldn't worry so much, but I do not want to go out by teeth and nails. There can be no worse way to go.

I need distraction, I need concentration, I need something to stop me from panicking. I want to sing, I want to beg and pray and plead for longer. For more time with my Lilly—my sweet Honeybee—but it's all futile, and only the rising of the sun can protect us. There are shadows everywhere, no place to hide, until…

The car breaks free of the trees, the shadows vanishing, and I can see high and clear. The moon shines down brightly on us. It doesn't have the same power of the sun, but with a clear sky and no place for them to hide, it can work. It has to work. I see them now, at the sides of the road, hiding in the low hedgeways, skirting around broken-down, rusted cars—a slash of nails, the glow of red eyes, the screech and cry and hunger for our blood.

"Don't look," I whisper. And even to me, my voice sounds ghostly.

"I'm scared," she whispers back.

I reach over and clasp her small hand in mine. "So am I. But I'm here, I'll protect you." I swallow down the vile, bitter taste the words leave behind in my mouth, because I know that I can't protect her. I can't even protect myself.

There are empty fields on either side of us—dirty, dusty, barren fields with no life or vegetation growing in them. The beautiful scorching sun has, in a twist of bitter irony, decimated everything, and whatever else was left behind has been destroyed by *them*. This place is dead, every last part of it. There is a fragment of me, a deep, dark, subconscious fragment that wants to turn around and drive back to those shady green trees. A dark part of me that craves those cool shadows. I shiver and try to escape the feelings, knowing that this isn't me, that this is them—the evil in my veins darkening, spreading and killing me, slowly turning me into the very monster that I fear. I crave the shadows because the sun is becoming my enemy. Because the soft caress of darkness on my skin is soothing and less frightening than the thought of burning up in the light.

"Mama?"

I turn to look at Lilly, and I see her flinch back from me. I see the haze of red surrounding her, a cloud of blood and anger, yet I know that it is me and not her that is wrong here. And that if I could see my face now, I would see horrifying red eyes staring back at me.

"Mama," Lilly whimpers, her bottom lip trembling, silent tears spilling down hollow, dirty cheeks. "Mama, please."

She pleads for me to come back, but I'm lost in the sea of red and black. It froths in my veins, churning and eager, hot and desperate for me to let go. She pleads and I am sucked under, into the hateful monster that I truly am.

The car bumps and crashes over the broken road before smashing into a small wooden fence. The car chokes out the last of its energy just as the orange sun begins to slowly rise in the distance. I squint at its glare, at the heat that it emits, and I hiss, my mouth filling with warm blood…

And then it's gone. Like the snapping of a twig, I am back.

Lilly is crying, and I can see clearly: no blood, no haze, and no anger for her—for the life flowing through her veins. I reach for Lilly and she screams, and then I am crying and begging for forgiveness.

"I'm sorry, Lilly. I'm sorry," I plead.

She peeks at me from between her trembling fingers and must see that I am me again, because she dives from her seat and into my lap before I can say another word. I don't stop and think, I grip the handle on the door and throw it wide open. I get out of the car with one hand firmly beneath her butt to steady her, to protect her, and then I run on weak and unsteady legs.

I see the old electric tower in the center of the dusty field, and I aim for it. I can hear them so close behind me, but with every step forward I take, the sun rises higher and they slow down. By the time we reach the electric tower I am exhausted and out of breath. I chance a glance behind us, seeing them prowling, slowly, their skin bubbling and steaming from the soft glow of the sun that hits it.

"Hold onto me," I say to Lilly, and she scrambles around to my back and I begin to climb the tower.

Higher and higher I go, the sun slowly warming my skin, stretching forth until it touches all of me—all of us. It covers us like a blanket or protection, and I know that we are safe, that they can't get us now. I peer down at them and see them retreating, backing away in pain. But the way they stare, the hate in their red eyes, is almost too much. My arms are weak, and I know that we can't go on much longer.

The closest monster stares at me, its mouth opening wide and revealing its pointed teeth. What were its hands slowly clench and unclench in a very human gesture. I shudder, and feel Lilly squeeze me tighter, her face buried in my neck. I watch the monster backing away from us, feeling as though it is almost familiar to me. Like I have seen it somewhere, like perhaps it even knows me. But that is impossible. These monsters have a one-track mind, and they have no memories of their previous life. If they did, they wouldn't have killed their families. So no, I do not know this monster, and it does not know me, and yet still, there is something about it that stops me from looking away until it is gone. It is absorbed back into the shadows with one final scream of anger, and then we are truly safe.

Chapter Twenty-Two.

#22. We'll dig a hole and bury the world…

We stay up on the electric tower until the ache in my arms becomes too much for me to bear. I slowly climb back down, almost slipping and falling the last part because my legs are like jelly. But finally we're safe, on the ground, with the sun warming our faces and the darkness held at bay for another day.

We trudge slowly back over to the car, and though I crashed it into the fence earlier, and there is broken wood across the hood and underneath the front wheels, when I turn the key, it starts. The engine doesn't sound good, and I don't think that it will get us far, but we have to go…right now.

I help Lilly into the car and pull her seatbelt across her, noticing once again the deep black veins in her neck. She stares up at me, blinking sadly. She knows, I realize. She knows that neither of us have much longer. I stroke my fingertips down her soft cheeks and force a smile on my lips.

"We'll be okay," I say, the words sounding false even to my ears. I lean forward and press a kiss to her smooth forehead. "We'll be okay," I whisper again, though this time it's for me and not her.

"Okay," she replies, almost numbly.

I stare at her for a second or two, my muted gray eyes examining her big brown ones before I close her door with a soft click. I jog around to my side of the car, open the door, and then stop when a noise pulls my attention away. I turn to look behind us, my eyes grazing the horizon, the dusty, barren fields, the cracked and broken roads, but there is nothing there. At least nothing that I can see.

I climb in the car, shut the door, and I begin to drive, checking my rearview mirror continuously. Unease sits in my gut like rotten fish. Of course it does most days, but today feels different—worse somehow. Perhaps it was the closeness of death breathing down our backs, or the proximity of the monsters last night; how close we had come to being caught by them. Truly, at this stage, I do not know which would be the worse option. I saw how Lilly looked at me last night, I felt the monster in me take over, saw the red haze that descended upon me. And with that knowledge, I know now that once we get to the supposed safe spot, it will be too late. But I don't know what else to do anymore. We're just driving around and waiting to die.

I open my window and light a cigarette. I shouldn't, really; it's not good for Lilly—the whole passive smoking thing. I feel guilty as soon as I light it, but she doesn't say anything. I glance sideways at her and see that she's staring into her lap, her bottom lip sucked into her mouth and trapped between her teeth. I take a long drag on my cigarette, feeling the hunger pangs subside a little.

"Lilly?" I say her name but she doesn't even look

up. "Honeybee? Are you okay?" I watch her nod, yet still she doesn't look up. I leave her to her thoughts. She's a child; this is a lot for her to process on a daily basis, and I'm surprised that she hasn't crumpled in on herself. That's how most children were lost at the beginning. They checked out and their parents left them for dead. I hope those parents died a horrible and painful death for that sin.

"Open your window," I say to Lilly, and she does. The smoke isn't in the car, but I still don't like it. Her soft curls whip around her face, but she makes no move to brush them away. I finish my cigarette and throw the butt out of the window, and then I reach in the back of the car and grab the carrier bag of berries we had collected yesterday. I offer them to Lilly but she refuses them, and I frown at her.

"You need to eat," I say. But I don't press the issue when she doesn't reply. She'll know when she wants to eat. I'll only make her sick by forcing her. So I place the bag between our two seats and grab a handful of them to try and entice her. It doesn't work, and I give up after a small mouthful. The berries taste both bitter and bland, not like yesterday where they were juicy and ripe. No, today it feels like something in me has possibly changed, of course I am changing and adapting as the virus takes over, but it's in these strange qualities that I'm taken by surprise. Today I don't like the taste of the berries at all, and I want to spit them out of my window, but for Lilly's sake, I don't. Because then she would know, and then she would be even more scared, so I chew and swallow down the wretched berries for Lilly's sake.

The highway is long. It feels, at times, never-ending, with the barren fields of dust on either side of us. A small town eventually comes into view, and I'm filled with both deep relief and deep worry. I pull the car to a stop on the outskirts, feeling for some reason that we are not safe here, that we are being watched, and perhaps shouldn't stop at all. But we need fuel, and water, and food, and there might not be another town for miles.

I open my door and get out, listening intently for any signs of life, but there's nothing, not even the sounds of birds calling to one another to put me at ease and stop the dread in my gut. I check the windows of each building in the distance, squinting my eyes until they hurt, hoping to see...something. But there's nothing, just this deep sense of dread. I get back in the car and look over to Lilly. She's watching me attentively.

"Are you okay?" I ask, and it comes out irritable, but I really don't mean it to. I just want her to talk, to show something, an emotion. Anything. But all she does is nod. "Lilly..." I start to talk again, to say something, but then I lose the will to. The effort seems too much. I think I've lost her already, and I feel such sorrow for the loss that I can't seem to think or breathe for the moment. My chest feels tight, my heart speeding up. I think I'm having a panic attack, and then...

"I peed," she replies quietly. "I'm sorry."

Through the blur of panic I look to her lap and see that she has in fact peed herself. I look back to her face, and everything clears and rights itself almost immediately. A weary smile flits to my mouth, replacing the grimace from only moments ago. "That's okay. I should have stopped before now. It's my fault."

I will my heart to slow down, for my chest to loosen, and when I feel properly back in control, I start the engine and continue to drive into the town. I wonder why she didn't tell me that she needed to go, but when I glance sideways at her, she seems so small and lost that I think that may be the very reason why: she's lost, wandering frightened in a dark world inside her own mind, hiding from monsters and nightmares.

"We'll just drive through and see. We can get out in a minute and I'll help you clean up. Okay?" I say, and I feel almost elated that I haven't lost her yet.

"Okay," she mumbles.

I have no intention of stopping and looting anything in this town, but my curiosity is piqued so I at least want to drive through and see for myself. Sometimes you take chances—you have to if you want to survive—but other times you have to trust your instincts. My instincts are telling me to go and get far away from here. Much like my instincts are telling me that I don't have much longer left. And neither does Lilly.

But there is nothing to see in this barren town. It looks much the same as all the other towns we have passed through: empty streets, empty windows, and empty storefronts. Broken cars, broken windows, broken bones…

"I don't like it here," Lilly says.

"Me neither," I reply. "We'll leave now."

"Good."

The stores are all dark inside, and I know they are there. I can feel *them,* I can almost hear them. They're trapped inside, in the dark, listening to us drive past, their red eyes watching us from the shadows. Fear tickles my spine, tracing its deathly cold fingers down my throat and across my stomach and making me feel sick. This place is heaving with them, just one giant nest full of monsters. I reach my arm outside the car, feeling the heat of the sun on it and the warm air flowing between my fingers, a stark reminder that we're safe for now. I place my palm against the metal of the car. It makes me feel better, almost grounding me here in this moment, because I can hear them, calling to us, prowling back and forth in the dark, angry at us for driving away, and I feel lost in that knowledge.

I look across at Lilly and see her leaning against her door and staring out her open window, her hair still whipping around her face. And I know that she feels them too.

We exit the other side of the town and I feel better almost immediately—but again, I cannot say why.

Perhaps the distance between them and us, the proximity, makes me feel more like myself and less like them. I drive until we're a mile or two on the outskirts of this strange, nameless town, and then I pull the car over next to a small stream that runs behind an old bus stop. Lilly needs cleaning. The car is beginning to smell terribly and I know that she's embarrassed. She's a big girl now, so she always used to tell me, and barring this accident she hasn't peed herself in a long time.

I climb out and go around to Lilly's side. I open her door and unbuckle her and help her out. She may be dehydrated but she is still soaked through, and the smell of pee is strong. I help her over to the stream and I undress her, pulling her sodden panties and pants down her legs. I get our plastic bottle from the car and we both drink what water is left in it before I fill it up again and we drink some more. When I think that we have drunk all that we can, I fill the bottle up and put it to one side, and then I begin scrubbing her clothes in the water until I think the pee is all gone.

The clothes will take a little while to dry and so I spread them out on the embankment—all but her panties which I help her put back on. Wet or not, they'll dry eventually just from her body heat alone. Because I realized, as I helped her undress, that her temperature matches mine, and I am burning with a fever. Though other than being hot, I don't feel sick from it like I know I should. Her body is riddled with black lines, almost like the lines on a map. I don't dare take my clothes off to see my own body. I do not want to see the horror etched into my skin, branded into my blood. And I don't want her to see it either.

I get the berries from the car and Lilly eats, but I can tell she doesn't really have an appetite anymore. And neither do I. Which is worrying. We walk along the stream, splashing in the water. I try to coax a smile or a laugh from Lilly, but she has retreated into herself. Only this time I worry that maybe she'll never come back. The stream goes on for quite some time, and we follow it until it enters a bend in the road. Scattered plants are along the edge of the stream, but at the bend, trees are starting to grow tall and proud.

"Look, Lilly. Trees," I say and point, but she only shrugs sadly. "There could be food, something we can eat in there," I continue, but this time, she doesn't even shrug. "Do you like nuts?" I ask. "Because I think that tree has nuts on it."

She doesn't say anything, or even look up from her feet—though I do see her wiggling her pink toes in the water, which I think is a good sign. I take off my shirt and put it on her. It's dirty and sweaty, but I can see little goose bumps on her skin and I worry she might be cold. I take her hand and pull her toward the trees. She doesn't resist, and I don't worry about the shade from the trees because there isn't any—certainly not enough for the monsters to hide in. So we walk through the small trees, looking for nuts (that I know won't be there), looking for some small, innocent animal that has inexplicably survived after all this time, and perhaps we can catch and kill it (though deep down I know I couldn't really do that). And Lilly, the entire time, stares at her feet solemnly.

I'm about to turn back when I see something on the ground, so I clutch Lilly's hand tighter and walk closer to it. It looks like a hole, a wide hole that is very deep. I feel nervous—apprehensive, almost—as I almost reach the edge. A strange smell lingers in the air, a smell I can't place. Not tree sap, or earth, nor pine needles or dust. A smell that I both instinctually know, and yet equally shouldn't know. I let go of Lilly's hand and turn to her.

"Wait here, Honeybee," I say to her on bended knee, trying to catch her eye. But she doesn't acknowledge me in any way. It's as if she were here alone, and I were not even a figment of her imagination.

I sigh heavily and stand back up before taking those final slow steps toward the brink of the hole. My steps seem to take an age, but slowly, I find myself standing on the threshold of the hole, looking down into the darkness within. I blink, not quite sure what I am seeing at first, and then I understand.

Pit.

The word sounds dirty in my head as soon as I think it, and yet I cannot think of another word that is more suitable. This was supposed to be a mass grave, yet "grave" does not sound right in my mind. A grave is somewhere that you take your final rest. A singular, solitary hole for one, perhaps two bodies. A place where family and friends can visit from time to time, leave flowers next to a headstone, and speak to the spirits of their dead loved ones.

But this? This is a pit. A pit full of bodies. Bodies that are long rotted. Bodies that have been torn apart by monsters. Monsters that have become trapped in the pit after feeding upon the flesh of the dead, and have since been burned up by the sun. So in the pit, there are hundreds of rotting carcasses, both human and not, that are now burnt to a crisp.

Crisp.

What a stupid statement. Bodies don't burn to a crisp. They go black and melt into one giant form, and then they become indiscernible to the human eye, blackened and rotted until they are no longer one body or hundreds of bodies, but one giant blob of burnt flesh and blackened bone.

Lilly gasps from next to me, her hand squeezing mine tightly. I look down at her, my mouth open as it forms a silent *O*. She tugs on my hand, pulling me away from the gory sight, and I follow her numbly. Child leading mother.

It is all so wrong. This picture, this story, it's all wrong. Things shouldn't be like this. But they are.

We make our way back along the stream, back to Lilly's clothes on the embankment. She silently takes off my shirt and hands it back to me, and then she dresses in her own still-damp clothes. She immediately climbs back into the car, puts on her seatbelt, and waits for me. I stare at her, watching, scared, frightened to my core, because I am horrified by the mass grave of monsters and humans alike, yet Lilly—she seems untouched by any of it.

Chapter Twenty-Three.

#23. Once there was a little girl, and she used to smile.

Sometimes when I am lost in my own misery, I try to recall mundane things. Nothing of consequence, just something simple like the sound of a clock ticking, or how people used to mow their lawns in the summer. They are lonely yet familiar things. They remind me of home, of a life lost, without being too painful for me to recall. If I keep them abstract and un-personal, they calm me. They remind me that I am still human, because if I were not, I wouldn't remember them.

Tonight as I pull the barricade across the basement door of the dilapidated house we are hiding in, I decide which things I will think about. Perhaps the sound of a refrigerator clicking on and off, or the image of someone putting up a poster about a lost tabby cat. All of them are simple, non-threatening things that mean nothing to me, but will soothe me.

I pull the bar firmly in place, staring at it for several minutes with a hard frown. I think it will hold firm. No monsters have been here recently, and why would they? The place is all but demolished, no windows, no doors left, there are barely any walls left standing. But beneath the rubble we find the small trapdoor. It used to be a bomb shelter, I'm sure, and then was possibly converted to a storm shelter sometime after the war ended. Now it is a place to hide from the monsters. A new shelter for a new war.

I finally turn and make my way down the steps, slowly and surefooted. I find Lilly standing in the middle of the room, exactly where I had left her. The small candle I gave her is still burning in her hand, creating shadows and distorting her features. I place a hand on her shoulder and I expect her to flinch, or turn to look at me, to suck in a breath of fright, but she doesn't. She doesn't move. She isn't concerned, or worried of what I am or who I might become overnight. She is still and silent, like she has been for most of the day. My fingers pull her knotted hair to one side and I gently trace the black lines down the back of her neck. Still she doesn't flinch, and I know that she doesn't like me to touch the lines. I think that's why I do it. So that she will speak, ask me to stop, to pull away in anger or fright, or both, but still…nothing. She gives me nothing.

There is very little down here, but at least it's somewhere below ground, away from them, I think as I survey the small space. It's better than last night, at least. I leave Lilly in the center of the room and I take my own candle, cupping a hand around it so as not to blow out the small flame as I walk around. There was a bag of candles on a shelf—dusty, unused, long-forgotten. No one uses candles anymore. They attract monsters, the light piercing the blackness like a beacon, letting them know that humans are nearby.

But there is nowhere for the light to escape to down here, and so I enjoy the light that the simple candles provide, the smell of their wicks and wax burning.

The room is reinforced. Of course it is—it's supposed to withstand bombs and tornadoes. There is a small toilet that doesn't work, a unit that works as a kitchen but there is no food or water in it, and a small bed with no covers on it. The shelves are bare of belongings—no ornaments, no picture frames, nothing to tell the story of the people this place once belonged to. And I think I like it that way.

I make my way back to Lilly, wrapping my hand around hers, and I guide her to the toilet. I help pull her cotton briefs down and she pees, though of course I can't flush it. The old Lilly would have found it funny, to be using a real toilet again, but not this Lilly—not this child. I guide her over to the kitchen, coaxing her into a chair, and then I pick through the bag of berries, placing some in front of her. She looks down at them. Her belly is growling hungrily, yet I have to tell her several times that she needs to eat before she will. Eventually I think she has eaten enough, or perhaps I am tired myself. So I once more take her hand and guide her over to the small bed. I take the candle from her and help her to lie down, and she does, curling up on her side, and then she closes her eyes without hesitation.

I sit down next to her, running my fingers over her. Stroking her hair, her side, ignoring the sinking feeling in my heart, and trying to keep a hold on her for a little longer. My Lilly—my Honeybee—she's going. She's drifting along on a cloud of black poison and I can't bring her back. Every mile forward is sinking her further. *It's almost over* is all I can think. *It's almost over, finally.*

I sit on the floor up near her head, the light from my candle flickering over us, and I watch her for a little while, seeing how her features twitch every now and then as she dreams. Her skin is smooth and perfect, barring the black in her veins, her eyelashes still healthy and thick, but her hair…her hair is thinning. I run my fingers through her knots, and come away with hair trapped between my fingers. I stroke the loose strands from my hands and then do the same to my own hair, morbidly curious to see how bad I am becoming. Chunks come away with my touch, and I repress the whimper of fear which crawls up my neck.

"I don't want to die," I whisper into the darkness, a teardrop sliding down my face.

I had to say it out loud at least once. I know that I have no choice in the matter, and it's something that I have thought on many occasions, but I've never said it out loud. Not even once. Except for now. Because now it's near the end, and the final pieces are moving into place. I stroke Lilly's hair, and wonder if it would be more humane to put my hand over her nose and mouth right now. To cut off her air supply and let her stay asleep forever. No more changing, no more monsters, no more fear. But of course I won't, because I'm a coward. I love her too much to do that, but not enough to end it for her. Not today anyway, but maybe tomorrow.

A scream resonates from somewhere outside, and I recoil and then slowly climb to my feet. I'm surprised that they are here, though I really shouldn't be. But there had been no indication that they had been here recently, no scratching in the ground, no piles of bones of long-dead humans, no telltale nests—nothing. And there isn't anything here, nothing for them and nowhere for them to hide. I make my way back to the door, slowly climbing the steps, making sure to be quiet, silent as a mouse. The door fits perfectly within its frame, leaving no space for shadows to pass. I may not see them—the monsters—but I can hear them, loud and clear. The sniffing and clawing, the screaming and growling, their nails dragging over the door. But they can't get in. I'm almost certain that they can't get in.

I pull my pathetically small knife from my pocket and clutch it tightly, holding it out in front of me. Waiting, always waiting for them to find us, to catch us, to kill us. Waiting. It's a cruel torture.

The night goes on, the blackness suffocating. The noises are all around us, overhead and on each side—not just at the door, but everywhere. They are slowly closing in on me. On us. Lilly starts to whimper from somewhere in the dark and I go to her immediately, half driven insane from the worry of losing her and of the monsters scratching at the door.

She's sitting up in bed, crying. She's trying to be silent, to be hushed and soundless, but every noise seems to echo. She runs to me when she sees me, and then I am crying. Clutching her small bony body against mine, and crying against her neck and hair, so happy that she is showing some sort of emotion, but so sad that the emotion is fear again.

She clings to me, and I hold her fiercely. I sit on the bed with her. I don't like it because I want to be closer to the door, but it would frighten her more—and I don't want her to be more frightened than she is. I don't want her to feel scared. So I stay with her wrapped around me tightly, sitting on the edge of the uncomfortable little bed, as we wait for either morning or death.

I know when the sun awakens, because the world goes silent. The monsters bolt away, running somewhere to hide from their foe, and I carry Lilly gently across the dark room, toward the door. She won't let me put her down, so I let her cling to me while I slowly pull the barricade free and push open the door.

The daylight is bright—glaringly so—and I yelp in pain as the sun startles me, burning my corneas and making me see a glow wrapped tightly around everything. Lilly is still buried against my neck, so the impact isn't quite as strong for her, but I feel her flinch under the warm rays of the sun just as I do, and I know that it cannot mean anything good for either of us.

I lean against the doorframe, letting my eyes adjust and my senses become alert to the new day. Finally, I can catch my breath and feel steady enough to walk. I close the door to the shelter, trying not to worry too much when I see the claw marks on the outside of the door, and I push some rubble on top of it, though really, I know that it doesn't matter. They have found this place, and they will return tonight. They will be able to get inside and they will either destroy it or nest in it.

I shake my head, half angry and half sad, and then I make my way over to our car. It's in pieces—literal pieces: doors torn off, wheels punctured, the seats pulled out. The hood is open and the engine is quiet, long since finished ticking and hissing at its own destruction.

"We'll have to walk again," I say to Lilly, but she makes no move to get down. "Let's eat some breakfast first," I suggest, and I think she moves her head in a small nod because her hair tickles my earlobe.

I carry Lilly over to a small grassy area at the side of the road, away from the decrepit house and destroyed car, and I set her down and then sit next to her. I have to pry her small fingers free from me, and untangle her legs from around my waist, and when I do, she just sits there pouting at me. Her eyes stare sad holes into my soul, clearly unhappy with me setting her down.

I want to apologize, but I think it will make no

difference to how she is feeling, so instead I reach for the plastic carrier bag. Lilly abruptly reaches across me and snatches it from my grasp before throwing it as far as her little arms can manage, her lips letting loose a defiant scream. The bag doesn't go very far but the berries still scatter everywhere, little red lumps strewn across the dirty ground. I want to snap at her, to scold her and tell her that was a naughty thing to do and a waste of valuable food, but I don't, because all things being what they are, I can't blame her for throwing the rapidly rotting berries away. What tasted sweet and succulent several days ago now tastes vile and bitter. And not just because they are rotting, but because of what they represent: life. Our lives are slowly rotting away, turning black and disgusting. Enough to make someone sick? Enough to kill, perhaps?

So instead of yelling at her, I pull out my cigarettes and I light one, and then I lie back on the grass, staring up at the blue sky, and the yellow disc burning down on us. I smoke one cigarette and then another. They don't help my hunger pains today, and a headache starts low in the base of my skull. I think that I am dying, that this may be the final stages of the infection, but I can't be certain.

I look over at Lilly, who is still sitting up, and see that she has her hands covering her eyes. I think she may be crying and I ask her if she is, and tell her that it's okay to cry, that everyone cries when they are tired and frustrated, or sad and hungry. But all she does is shake her head at me and refuse to uncover her eyes. I sit back up, flicking away the end of my current cigarette and stuffing the near-empty pack back in my pocket, and then I turn to her and ask if she is okay again. I place a hand on her back, and I rub it in small soothing circles.

She finally removes her hands, and I see that on her palms are faint black lines, and her nails are growing long and are blackening from the cuticle up toward the tips. I try not to gasp or flinch. I don't want her to be any more frightened. Instead, I examine my own hands, and see the very same phenomenon. I shudder involuntarily. It runs down my spine, wracking my body with a tremble of worry and fear, which—strangely—makes Lilly laugh. I smile at her, my lips pulling back to reveal my dirty teeth, the dry and filthy skin on my face stretching as I let my smile widen, and the action feels odd on my face and lips. Lilly pretends to shudder too, and then I pretend, and before I know it, we're both standing up pretending to shudder and shake, jumping around on the spot and shaking our arms and legs out as if we have ants crawling all over our bodies.

And then Lilly stamps down angrily on one of the rotten berries, taking great satisfaction as the juices squirt out from under her shoe. She huffs out her indignation, frowning at the destroyed fruit before looking up at me, as if waiting for me to shout at her.

But I don't. Instead I stand on one that is near me, and her face lights up like a thousand spotlights are shining on it and she giggles, and so I find another berry and I do the same. Then we both run around stamping and squashing the vile berries, letting the red juice cover the ground and our shoes until there are no more, and I have a small cough from laughing so much. Lilly looks up at me with a small smile, and then I think I might cry when she offers me her small hand to hold. Right now, it is the most precious gift she could give me.

I take her hand in mine, and then I smile at her again and tell her that I love her deeply, more than anything else in the whole wide world. Lilly asks if I really mean it, and I tell her I do.

"I'll love you until the end of time, my little Honeybee." I smile. "You are mine, and I am yours, and that's the way it will always be. No matter what." My words come out a whisper at the end because I'm trying not to cry, but she doesn't seem to notice.

She smiles broadly, and then asks which way we are going. I say north, and she doesn't ask why north, or even ask which way is north, she just nods and says okay. We gather our very meager belongings and then we set off walking again.

Chapter Twenty-Four.

#24. I am not a failure, and yet I will fail.

We walk in silence again, but there is something light in our steps. The destruction of the berries was silly, and it troubles me, but Lilly is smiling again, her laughter is still ringing in my ears and making my heart feel full even though my stomach remains empty.

We still have a little water in a plastic bottle, but I will let Lilly have it all since it's not much. I try not to become too depressed again. Things are bad, and there is nothing I can do about that. But I have Lilly back, at least for now, and we are close to where the safe place was supposed to be. I feel both uneasy and happy about that. It won't matter, though; we are too far infected for them to allow us in, even if this place existed. But it would be nice, I think, to sit outside whatever walls they have constructed, and to know that I got us somewhere safe eventually. Even if it was too late. Yes, it will be sad too, but we're all going to die soon anyway, because there is no escaping the infection, so it doesn't really matter. We're all just trying to put off the inevitable, to extend what little time we have left. But at least I won't feel like I have failed Lilly completely if I can get us there. Maybe they will even give us some food while we wait for death.

"Mama?"

I look down at Lilly, catching a glimpse of her deep brown eyes before she looks away.

"Yes?" I say, still watching her.

"How did everyone get sick?"

I have never lied to her, and I choose not to lie now, though instead of answering her, I ask a question of my own. "Why do you ask?" I say, because she has never asked before, and I wonder what brought her to ask me now, after all this time.

She goes silent for a moment before looking up to me, her eyes meeting mine and she shrugs. "I don't know." She licks her lips, but it does little to take away the dryness of them, so I hand her the plastic bottle and tell her to drink some water. When she has taken a small mouthful, she gives it back to me.

We continue to walk, though both of our steps are slower as we get lost in our thoughts. I didn't answer her question, I only avoided it, and I feel bad for that.

"Who was the first?" she asks, breaking the silence again with more curiosity than I have ever known in her.

I think over her question, trying to decide why she is asking, and then I know the answer to my own thoughts, and I honestly can't blame her for asking. Everyone wants to know the answers to their own mortality, I guess. Even a child will grow curious to her own destruction eventually, and so I decide that the truth, once again, is the fairest route with her.

"It was a man named Edgar P. Jerrard. He was from somewhere in South America, I think. He was the first," I say. I try to recall what he looked like, but it was so long ago, and I hadn't paid much attention to the articles at the time—not until it was too late. I know that his face was all over the television and newspapers though, and I think he had blond hair once, before he lost it all. Before he changed into something less human, and more monster than the world cared to admit. I vaguely recall the articles, a bat, a virus that already existed, but somewhere, deep within the caverns where the bats had nested, it had changed to something even more dangerous than it had started as, and poor Edgar P. Jerrard had stumbled upon this very nest. It was improbable, and yet it happened all the same.

Lilly is still quiet, and I wonder what she is thinking, but I leave her with her thoughts, because we are all entitled to our own thoughts at some point. She doesn't speak again for a long time, and when she does, her words surprise me. Because out of all the questions that she could ask, the one she does, is the least expected.

"Do you think he is dead now?"

I stop walking and look down at her, a small crease forming between my brows, because I know that she is asking if I think he is a monster somewhere, afraid of the daylight, or if he is dead like the dead should be, and buried beneath the ground, slowly rotting away. "I don't know," I answer honestly. "Possibly." My voice sounds sad, depressed.

"He was a bad man," she replies, her expression

turning angry.

"No, no." I say and I kneel down, feeling the gravel of the road press into my knees. It hurts, but I don't mind, because I would rather feel something than nothing, and I know that soon enough I will feel nothing but hunger. The sickness infected everyone, it started with just one man, but like any disease, it mutated once it was released and given a new host body. The pathogens began evolving as they infected more and more people. And as they mutated and evolved, they infected the world, until no one was safe.

No one, was safe.

The disease became airborne, turning people violent and uncontrollable, until a new strain developed infecting people through water, then through animals, then through blood and fluids, until there was no escaping it, no hiding from it, and no defeating it. It was a global epidemic that destroyed everyone that it touched.

I cup her cheeks in my hands, and she stares innocently into my face.

"He didn't mean to hurt anyone," I say softly.

"But he did."

"If he could have chosen, he wouldn't have hurt anyone."

"But everyone is dead." She says, her eyes wide and pleading. And the way she says it is so tragic, and yet so beautifully simple that it pains me to even reply to her. "He killed everyone!"

"It's not his fault. It's no one's fault." I stroke my thumb gently across her cheek. "Lilly, he didn't want this, we can't blame someone for the things that they can't control. Not ever."

She gnaws on her lower lip. "And he couldn't help it," she says. Not a question.

"No, he couldn't."

"I won't be able to help it either, will I?" she says, her eyes glistening.

"No, you won't. And neither will I," I reply, my heart feeling as cold as my words.

"But you'll still love me, won't you, Mama?"

"I'll always love you," I say. "Until the end of time. Until the stars fade away forever. Until there is nothing left of anything and anyone, and even then I will still love you, Honeybee," I say with a tentative smile.

Lilly smiles back. "I'll love you forever too," she says, and then my smile grows wider.

"Good." I lean forwards and kiss her soft cheek, feeling the warmth of her under my dry lips. I inhale her; her scent, her goodness, her life, needing her to keep me strong through the dark days ahead.

"Why are we not dead yet?" Her words are sudden, abrupt and they halt me. I pull out of the kiss that I did not finish giving her. The pain of the answer is almost unbearable.

"Diseases affect every one differently. Some people can fight it easier than others, some people's bodies—their immune systems are stronger than others." I reply, looking into her face once more. She thinks this over for a moment, before speaking again.

"Like the flu?" I nod and she continues. "But you don't die from the flu," I shake my head no, "and you can get medicine for the flu." I nod again, and her shoulders sag with defeat because without even asking, she knows her next answer. There is no medicine, no shot, to make this illness better.

We will all die eventually.

She looks past me, down to her shoes, no tears are present in her beautiful eyes now, but she looks broken, sad and empty. I take a deep breath and then I scoop her up in my arms suddenly and I swing her around and around until we are both dizzy, and I tell her I love her so much I could burst, and she tells me not to burst because it would be messy. And then I laugh, and my heart warms up again.

When we stop being silly and continue to walk, I wonder if the secret to immortality—to keeping us alive—is love. Or maybe happiness. But then, perhaps they are one and the same thing. When I am happy, I can't feel the sickness anymore. I can't feel the poison running hot through my veins. So maybe if we just stay happy and love each other, it will be enough. I know it won't be, but I still think it's nice to think like that.

"Mama?"

"Yes, Lilly?"

"I'm tired," she says.

So I pull out her teddy—with its one eye—from

her backpack, and then I scoop her up in my arms. She rests her head on my shoulder, and soon I hear her soft snores and I feel her breath against my neck. I feel happy and reassured with her in my arms, even though I am tired as well.

It is easy to imagine the world being alive again, the way it had once been. With people and cars, and dogs that chased cats through their yards and barked when you walked past their gates. I can remember, quite vividly, the way my bedsheets had felt on my skin, and the way my husband's body had felt next to mine—the hairs on his legs tickling me, his kisses and his breath, hot against my mouth…

I can easily remember those things, and I can imagine the world and what it used to be, but most days I try not to. Because those days are long gone, and they won't ever come back, so what's the point? What's the point in memories if they only make you sad? What's the point in recalling the past if it only makes the present worse? If the happiness you once had breaks you a little bit more.

We are coming to another town, I can tell because I can see the beginnings of civilization instead of just the long, empty stretches of roads. I cross through a field, with its dry, cracked earth, in search of food. I go around groups of trees, even though I want to go into them. There could be animals that we could kill for food, there is shade from the scorching sun, but I can't go into them, because there could also be monsters. So I walk on instead, feeling the light breeze on my dry and dirty skin, my steps made slower by the hole in the bottom of my shoe that has allowed in some grit and stones. They stab into the bottom of my foot and make me limp, but I walk on regardless.

There are dry rabbit droppings on the ground, and they give me hope that there could be a rabbit burrow somewhere around here, but as I turn in one big circle, seeing nothing but dead, gray earth in every direction, I doubt that I will ever find the rabbits.

The fields must end somewhere, I muse, yet they feel like they will go on forever. I walk for several hours in silence, with just Lilly's frail body wrapped around me for company. My arms ache, even though she weighs very little, and my feet begin to really hurt, but I don't wake her up. She needs to sleep. Children need lots of sleep, I tell myself. It has nothing to do with the infection, I lie.

In the distance I see a building, and I head toward it. I worry, of course I do, but I try to push the worry aside and be excited, hopeful even. I try to imagine all the things that could be inside the building; food, drinks, clothes, cigarettes. My steps speed up, just a little, but enough to wake Lilly.

"I'm sorry, I didn't mean to wake you up," I say.

She yawns and blinks sleepily, and then she wriggles free from my arms.

"I'm still sleepy," she says wearily.

"Are you hungry?" I ask, and she nods. I look around us and then back to her. "We'll find something to eat soon," I say.

She nods and then takes my hand, and we begin to walk again. Lilly doesn't complain, she just walks beside me, her warm hand in mine, kicking some of the dry earth.

"Look," I say, and point to the building up ahead.

"What is it?"

"I don't know, but it could have things inside," I say.

"Like what?"

I shrug. "Anything."

We're nearly there now, and I want to run I'm so excited. My stomach feels hungry again, and I'm thirsty, and I know that these are all good signs. I think back to earlier, when I wondered if love and happiness could keep us human for longer, and I'm almost positive that it could be true. Because for the first time in a long time, I feel good—healthy, even.

We cross the last part of the barren field, and we come to the back of some small buildings. I still can't work out what this place used to be, though. There are small rows of things along the ground, covered in polyethylene tunnels, and I have a vague memory about what this place might be, but I can't grasp onto the thought. I'm surprised because this place doesn't seem destroyed like everywhere else. I lift Lilly over the small fence, and then I climb over and take her hand as we walk warily along the rows. Someone could see us and shoot us, I know this, but we have no choice other than to keep going, because there is nothing around. At least, not the way we just came. So forward it must be.

We check each of the rows of the small polyethylene tunnels, but they are all empty. Yet I realize that this place used to grow food. I think it was a small farm.

There is a small barn to the left, but I don't really want to go in there because it will be dark and I don't have much in the way of weapons to defend us with. We round the corner of the main building and I see a small greenhouse. There could be food inside, but I doubt it very much, and I don't say anything to Lilly because it would be cruel to lift her hopes only to dash them a moment later.

The windows are very dirty so I can't see inside until we get very close to it. When we are standing right outside it I pull Lilly behind me, and I press my face to the window and look in.

At first I don't see very much, but then as my eyes adjust, I gaze upon the many colors, and I realize that inside the greenhouse is food. Lots and lots of food.

I swallow, my mouth filling with water at the idea of eating all of this food, and I turn to Lilly with the biggest smile. She sees my smile and quickly comes from behind me and presses her own face against the glass.

"What are they?" she mumbles.

"Vegetables," I say to her, "lots of vegetables."

"Can we eat them?"

"Yes, Lilly," I say. And I find it silly, because

children are supposed to hate vegetables, but here is Lilly eager to eat them all. It's funny, but it's not. Yet I still smile.

I take a long look around us, squinting against each window on each building and listening carefully for any sound that is out of place. Making sure that we are truly alone. I can't see anyone or anything, and my stomach aches with hunger, so after a long moment in the hot sun, I take Lilly's hand and lead her to the door. I push down on the silver handle and pull the door open. The heat explodes from within and I choke on the warmth, the dampness following next. Small flies buzz out, and I swat them away distractedly.

There are pots and pots filled with plants. Greens, purples, oranges, reds—all things that we can eat. Some I know need cooking, but most can be eaten just as they are: raw, dug out from the earth, and I tell this to Lilly. We step inside and walk around slowly, my fingers grazing the tips of crisp leaves and my hand cupping a ripe tomato. I pull it, plucking it from its green stem, and then I sniff it, taking a deep lungful of the smell that only a tomato can make. I had forgotten this smell, but now the memory of it is back, flooding my head with a thousand images of things long forgotten. My mother used to make tomato soup, and it was delicious with basil. I would slurp it from a spoon, feeling it burning a hot path down my throat, feeling the sensation of it filling my stomach and nourishing me. She taught me the recipe too, and I would make it for my family to eat. I had basil growing on my kitchen windowsill, the smell used to fill my kitchen on hot days. I look down at Lilly, seeing her staring up at me expectantly, and I hand the tomato to her.

"What is it?" she asks curiously, her eyes flitting from the tomato to me and back again.

"A tomato."

She holds it in her hand, closing her eyes and sniffing it the way I had only a moment ago, giving it a gentle squeeze. "Can I eat it?" she asks, opening her eyes. "I'm really hungry now."

I nod and smile. "Yes, Lilly, you can eat it."

And I feel proud as she bites down on her first ever tomato, and the juices explode over her chin and lips, the little tomato seeds finding their way onto her stained T-shirt. She is caught by surprise by the sudden explosion, but then she hums her appreciation and takes another bite of it, sucking at the juices inside it. I feel proud, and happy—because I fed her, and I kept her alive for another day. It's just one day, but when every day is your last, one day is everything. So today, I have given her everything.

"What else can we eat?" she asks when she is finished, and I smile wider.

I pluck another tomato and hand it to her, and then I pluck one for me, and together we eat them. I feel euphoric as the food both feeds me and quenches my thirst. I have barely finished it before I am pulling Lilly along with me to some other food. I grab the green leaves sticking out of the earth and I pull. It comes easily, at first the hint of orange and then the rest: long, crunchy, covered in earth but the color still vivid.

"This is a carrot," I say to her. I wipe some of the earth off the skin and hand it to Lilly and she looks at it hesitantly.

"I can eat it?"

"Yes," I say, and pull one out for me.

We bite down on the carrots, and both groan at the same time as the flavor hits our taste buds and then we look at each other and laugh. The taste of dirt and carrots is in my mouth, and it's amazing.

"I like carrots," Lilly says, her mouth around the end of the carrot as she takes another bite.

"Me too," I say. "I think they used to be my favorite."

"I wish we could have carrots and tomatoes every day," she says, chewing loudly. The sound echoes around the little greenhouse, and a chill inexplicably runs down my spine.

Hunger makes us careless. But desperation is the real killer. When you're desperate you don't think things through. You take too many risks and you don't think about things properly. All you can think about is filling the hole in your stomach, making the thirst go away, finding somewhere safe to sleep. Making the child at your side smile again.

You don't think about who might have planted the food, or when they might be back. Not until it's too late.

Chapter Twenty-Five.

#25. Who are you anymore?

"I think we need to go," I say, my heart beginning to beat furiously.

Lilly looks up at me, carrot and tomato across her lips and chin. She doesn't whine or cry or argue, like children should. She nods, stuffing the half-eaten carrot into her pocket, and takes my hand.

I guide us back along the rows toward the door, sweat glistening off both of our foreheads. The days are always hot, but inside here it is hotter still—stiflingly so. I push the door open, stepping out, and I take a great lungful of clean air, and I hear Lilly do the same.

"Are we safe?" Lilly asks me.

"I don't know," I reply. Because I don't.

Bad people don't generally grow vegetables and fruit. They don't have the capacity to care for something and make it grow healthy and strong. They take life, not give it. The sound of a truck startles me, voices coming from the front of the building, and I panic. I turn in circles looking for somewhere to hide, somewhere to go, but there is nowhere within distance. Nowhere to hide before whoever it is comes around the side of the building.

I can hear the feet crunching across the gravel, the voices carrying in the wind to us. Lilly is squeezing my hand tightly but she doesn't cry, and I am amazed at her bravery in the face of all this world has to offer. I start to turn, pulling Lilly with me, when they see us and call out.

"Hey! Hey you!" A male voice, thick with an accent, older-sounding.

I decide all of this in a split second, but I don't turn to look. Instead I run, tugging Lilly along with me.

"A child!"

I hear the gasp of a woman as fear bursts out of me. I reach down and scoop up Lilly, pulling her into my arms as I run, trampling over the polystyrene tunnels and mud, destroying flowers with my heavy footedness, until I reach the small fence. I drop Lilly onto the other side of the fence, and I am halfway over when something hits the back of my head.

Lights brighter than the sun blind me, and I feel my grip loosening on the fence, my footing being lost as I tumble backwards, and I stare up at the brilliant blue sky and the yellow glow of the sun.

Why didn't you save us today, sun? I wonder, right before the world goes black.

*

I remember watching my mother cook tomato soup in our kitchen as a child. The way she would take me to the market with her and we would choose the ripest and biggest tomatoes together. We put crosses on the bottom of each tomato and then dunked them in hot water and then into cold to help remove their skins, and then we would blend them all up with the noisy handheld blender. My mother used to grow herbs in her garden, and she would send me out to pick some basil leaves for the soup. It was always my favorite meal, because I had helped make it. Me and my mom. I always wanted to nurture when I was younger. I would grow plants and help sick animals, and I remember wanting to be a vet or a farmer.

The smell of tomatoes are strong—strong enough to bring me back from the edge of blackness. I lick my lips, feeling them dry and cracked under my tongue. My mouth is filled with water and the rich copper taste of blood. I swallow it all down, my stomach giving a grumble of protest. I open my eyes but everything is a blur, so I rub my eyes and try again.

I'm in a kitchen, of sorts. It's dark, the flickering of shadows and lights are all around me, and when I try to sit up, the world spins and makes me feel sick. I'm on a table. The wood hurts my back, and I think that I am going to be cut up for food. Cannibalism is common these days and I am not quite infected yet. There is plenty of uninfected meat on my bones. I flex my fingers, swallowing back nausea.

"Lilly?" I cry, my words coming out thick and broken. "Lilly!" I scream, panic building and exploding out of me.

"She's sleeping."

I turn to the soft voice of a woman. She's sitting in a chair by my side, *knitting*, of all things. She's not old, though she's older than I am. I see her knitting and I expect her to be old, like a grandmother. Funny how I think of knitting as an older person's pastime. I frown at the woman with the soft smile and the knitting needles in her hands. The woman who is older than me and yet not old at all, and my lips pull back in a snarl. She eyes me warily before gesturing to the other side of me. I look across and see Lilly sleeping on a small, lumpy sofa bed, her breaths coming out relaxed and even. I sit up properly and swing my legs over the side of the table, my feet touching the ground but my legs not feeling strong enough to hold my weight—though I can weigh no more than ninety pounds anymore.

I stumble to my knees, and my breaths are coming so short and shallow I don't even hear the woman come over to me, nor the man she is with. They each take an arm and pull me to my feet, and I fight them, struggling to free myself from their iron grip.

"Calm down or you'll wake the child," the woman hisses in my ear.

Something in her voice makes me stop fighting, but it also zaps me of everything and I turn to a leaden weight in their arms. I hear the man groan and the woman huff, but I can't seem to make my body respond. They let me go, gently releasing my arms until I am kneeling by Lilly's side. I stroke the hair away from her face, seeing the spoils of food all over her.

I turn to look at the people—properly look at them this time. They are watching me as I am watching them. There is a moment of hesitation—of anger, of worry, of defeat—and I start to cry. The woman comes to my side and tries to hold me, but I push her away and she stumbles backwards. The man takes a step forward, his eyes alight with anger and menace, and he is everything that I have been protecting Lilly from, he is whom I fear.

"It's okay," she says to him, holding a hand up to pause him. "It's okay," she says again, this time to me. "We're not going to hurt you," she says. "Or the child. And we're not sick." She glances at her husband and then back to me. "But you are?" She voices her statement as a question, but she knows the answer already. "What about the child?"

And then I laugh, wretched sobs coming out between my laughs. The woman looks up at the man with concern. I can almost hear their unspoken words. They think I have gone quite mad, and perhaps I have.

"She is sick," the man says, his voice hard and rough.

"We fed her," the woman says, dismissing the man. She has silver hair, which is strange because she doesn't seem old enough to have gray hair, yet her hair is long and silver, the light from the candles reflecting off the strands as she moves. "Your little girl. We fed her," she says, her eyes staying on mine.

I look away, breaking her stare, and I look at Lilly. She seems content, food on her chin and shirt, her chest rising and falling steadily. Her head is on a pillow, and a blanket is over her shoulders. Both things seem clean.

"We didn't mean to hurt you," the woman says.

The man grumbles something and my gaze travels to him. He's older, but he's broad and strong, wide-set eyes and short hair. His hand is on a gun at his hip, and I realize that he thinks I'm dangerous.

"But you did," I say, my voice hoarse.

"Some water, Peter. Fetch some water," she says dismissively to the man, who I presume to be Peter.

He scowls down at me and storms off, his footsteps resounding around the space.

"He doesn't think sometimes, he just does. We have to be careful." She looks away, shame written across her pale face. "You understand that, don't you?"

Peter comes back and hands the woman a glass of water, and she, in turn, hands it to me. I take it, drinking it eagerly because my throat is bone dry and feels almost sticky, and I can't actually remember the last time I had a drink. I also think I bit my tongue at some point, and it feels swollen and sore.

"Was she frightened?" I finally ask when I've finished the water.

"A little," the woman says. "She, she tried to hurt herself," she adds on.

And I understand, because that is what I told her she must do if she were ever caught again and I couldn't help her. Because it would be better for her to die at her own hand than to endure the tortures that would inevitably follow her capture.

"We had to prove to her that you weren't dead

before she put down the knife." She looks severely concerned, and I want to laugh in her face. If she understands that you have to be careful because people can be bad, then surely she should understand why I told Lilly to…

"She was very worried about you. Wouldn't leave your side." The woman keeps on talking. "How…how is she still alive?" she asks, and I hear the familiar pang in her voice that I had heard from Sarah so many nights ago. Sarah—who left me for dead, who tried to take Lilly from me and then abandoned her also.

"She is mine," I say fiercely, and the woman holds up her hands defensively. "I won't let you take her."

"No, no, I wouldn't—"

"I am hers. I'll kill you if you try and separate us," I spit out.

The man—Peter—huffs out his annoyance and glares at me.

"You don't frighten me," I say to him.

"I should," he says back.

"Well you don't. Nothing frightens me." And I know I am lying, and they know I am lying, but I say it anyway.

"Mama?"

I turn abruptly and see Lilly waking up. She's smiling at the sight of me, and we both reach for each other at the same time, wrapping our arms around the other until somehow I am on the small sofa with her little body wrapped around mine. The woman is watching us, a soft smile on her face, and I see how truly pretty she is, even with her silver hair that glistens. The man is rough and hard, but even his features soften when they see us hugging.

He scratches his chin, and I can hear his nails grating over coarse hairs. "I'm going to lock up," he says, deciding I'm not a threat. He storms off, his footsteps ascending up the stairs.

The woman's eyes follow him before looking back at me and Lilly. "Don't mind Peter. He saw your lines." She points to my hands and I look down, seeing that the lines have darkened across the backs of my hands. "He's just worried."

"Rightfully so," I reply dryly. "But I'm okay."

She nods and her chin pinches in as she bites the inside of it. "I'm Mary."

"I like her," Lilly whispers into my ear. "She's nice. She smells like tomatoes."

"Some people are nice but they try to trick you, Lilly," I say back, and I don't bother to whisper it. I want Mary to know that I don't trust her, or Peter.

Mary's cheeks flame pink. But I'm not sure if it's anger or embarrassment. "I wouldn't hurt a child," she says defiantly, but I only arch an eyebrow at her.

"That's what they all used to say."

"Well I wouldn't."

"Then let us go," I say.

"It's almost nightfall," she replies, biting down on her lip. "We can't let you go tonight, but tomorrow you can go. I promise."

I don't say anything to that. Because it makes sense. And I don't want to leave at night—we'd be dead in minutes—but I also don't like not knowing where we are hiding, not knowing where the exits and entrances are. I fumble for the weapon at my waist and find it gone, and my eyes dart to Mary.

"The little girl took it from you," she says in a hurry, "that's what she was going to hurt herself with…" Her words trail off, sounding broken.

"Did I do good, Mama?" Lilly whispers against my neck.

"You did great," I say and I kiss her hair. She doesn't smell like Lilly. She smells like another person—another woman. She smells like tomatoes and bread, and another woman's arms. It's strange and I don't like it.

"You can have it back now," Mary says, and she stands up and turns to where she was knitting earlier. She brings my small knife over and hands it to me, her eyes wary and cautious. I want to snatch it from her grasp. My nerves are on edge, waiting to tumble over into the abyss. But I don't snatch it, I take it carefully and nod a thanks, and Mary seems pleased with that. And so does Lilly.

"Do you want something to eat? Some tea maybe?" she says, her hands wringing in front of her.

I nod a yes, too afraid of what will come out of my mouth if I try to speak. Mary wanders over to a small cabinet that has been laid out like a kitchen: a small bowl for the sink, a single gas burner for the cooker, cups and saucers, plates and silverware. All so very normal. She scoops up some food with a large ladle, pouring it into deep round bowls that have a blue pattern down the side. I see her every once in a while looking at the stairs to where Peter had gone out of earlier. She's nervous, but I'm not sure if it because of me, or for him.

She comes back and hands me a bowl of food. It's broth with potatoes and carrots and onions in it. I stare at the bowl in wonder, the heat rising from it, the smells making me feel dizzy with hunger and wanting, all of it enticing me, luring me in. I see dark meat in it, and I am so shocked to see meat, because I thought I would never get to taste meat ever again, and yet here it is, floating in a small bowl of broth.

Mary watches me blankly, and then after a moment she takes the silver spoon that sits in the bowl, and she eats a mouthful before handing the spoon back to me. This time I take it with a grunt of 'thanks.' Lilly clambers from my knee but stays at my side, hugging her teddy bear tightly and sucking her thumb. It's something she hasn't done since we left our streetlight at the top of the cliff—suck her thumb. Between greedy mouthfuls, I notice that her teddy now has two eyes, though they are odd. One is a large green button and the other is the black bead that was there previously.

I eat the broth, and then Mary hands me a steaming cup of tea. There's no milk, of course, but it tastes delicious all the same. It's not normal tea, and Mary tells me that it is made from nettles. Lilly has a cup too and she slurps it noisily and then gives a little burp. A small smile quirks the side of my mouth. I feel the pull of it inside of me before it even happens externally. I look at Lilly, and then at Mary, and we are all sitting around drinking nettle tea, like it isn't the end of the world and this is all perfectly normal. And it's nice, I realize. It's nice to share this burden with someone. I can tell that Mary is nice, not like Sarah, and I am about to tell Mary about the safe place I have heard about, and say thank you for stopping Lilly from killing herself, and for helping us, and feeding us, and all the wonderful things that she has done that she didn't need to do. I feel so much better after eating, my head so much calmer, so much clearer.

I'm about to say so many things, but then I hear it: the screeching of the monsters somewhere in the distance.

Mary looks sharply toward the stairs, her entire being trembling with fright, and I follow her gaze to the empty stairway, knowing from her look that he should be back by now.

"Peter," she whispers, fear vibrating through her words. "Oh God, Peter!"

"Are we secure?" I ask, not caring about Peter at all. And it's heartless and selfish, I know it is. But I don't care. "Can they get to us?" I say and stand, the half-full cup of nettle tea still in my hand. Only now the liquid is moving, quaking in its container as my hand struggles to stay steady.

Mary looks up at me, dread filling her pretty eyes, because she knows that it's not secure—that we are not secure, not until Peter is back. And she knows that I will lock Peter outside to protect Lilly. I will sacrifice him for my Honeybee without a second thought.

"Please." She stands and follows me as I make my way across the small room. "Please, just one more minute. He'll be back. I swear he'll be back."

Lilly is whimpering, Mary is crying, but all I can worry about is that there are monsters on their way and we are not secure. I reach the foot of the stairs, the screams of monsters far in the distance—but getting closer with every second, no doubt. There's several blades on a box at the bottom of the stairs, and I put down my half-empty cup of nettle tea and take the largest one, grabbing it fiercely in my grip, and I begin to climb the stairs. Mary is still begging me, and I wonder briefly why she doesn't try to stop me in any way other than to beg me. Perhaps she is so afraid that a part of her wants me to lock the door. Perhaps she would rather sacrifice Peter so that she lived.

"Please!" She whispers after me.

But her words mean nothing to me. I look down at her and I know in that split second why, I know that I was right: she needs me to be the monster so that her heart remains innocent. She wants me to lock the door, to protect us all—protect herself, certainly sentencing Peter to death—but it won't be her fault, because she asked me not to. It's a cruel thing to do, to make me the scapegoat, but I'll be the villain in this scenario if I must. If it means my Lilly living another day.

I reach the top of the stairs and look out. The daylight is waning, a musky sort of dull light still glowing in the sky, but the shadows are beginning to bloom from every corner. And with each new shadow, there is new fear to behold.

Chapter Twenty-Six.

#26. Who wants to be the bad guy?

"Please don't," Mary calls to me again, but there is no conviction in her words, no real plead for her husband's life.

I ignore her, because that's all I can really do. I come up into a kitchen—a real kitchen. Everything is oak and ceramic, a large white sink, wooden units and counter tops, pots and pans dangling from a hanger above the stove. *A country kitchen for a country man and wife*, I think. There are large tubs piled everywhere, and I can see the colors of food within them. Store for the winter—or just for life, no doubt.

I walk up the last step of the stairs, reluctant to go any further in case Mary does finally grow a backbone and lock me out. I glance back down to her, seeing her muttering, whispering, and pleading, but her eyes are wide with terror.

"Stay there," I say, and she nods.

"Mama?" Lilly calls.

"I won't be a moment," I whisper down to her. "I promise."

I don't know why I do it, why I put myself in the situation. It's part self-preservation and part humanity—especially when I've promised so many times not to leave her. But I need to know where we are, how unsecure a place it is, and if I find the man—Peter—along the way, great. If not, no trouble, no mind, no bother for me. But to keep Lilly safe, I need to go find out.

I walk around the piled-up tubs of food and out the arched doorway that leads to a dining room. In the center is a great big wooden table with a lacy sheet over the top. The table is set for supper, and I shake my head in wonder. A table set for supper like it isn't the end of the world. Part of me believes that these people would be better off dead if this was how they were living.

I reach a large brown front door. The small hallway surrounding it is dark, and I worry about going into that darkness. But I do, and when I reach the door I press down on the handle and step outside into the waning daylight. Screeches sound in the distance, and I breathe out heavily, the air catching in my throat.

I don't dare call his name, but when I take ten steps from the front door and my legs begin to shake I decide that it is his loss, his error to not return in time, and I head back inside. I lock the door, for what it is worth, and I make my way back through the house, shutting doors as I go, being as quiet as I can. I go back into the kitchen, past the stove, and to the space where the stairs descend.

I stare for a long second at the closed door, blinking back tears, already knowing my own judgment was wrong again. They have tricked me. They have locked me out, sentenced me to death. They have taken Lilly and sent me on a fool's errand.

I swallow down the lump in my throat, because at

least she is safe. That should be all that matters. They could have left us both for dead, but they didn't. Just me.

I put my hand on the handle, dread curdling in my gut…but the handle turns under my palm and the door opens rapidly, almost throwing me off balance. Peter is in front of me, and Mary right behind, and I can hear Lilly crying somewhere down below.

"Get inside," he grumbles, his expression a hard scowl somewhere beneath his beard, no doubt.

He grips my arm and pulls me inside, pushing me past him as he locks the door and then swings another door in front of the existing one. The second door is a thin sheet of metal with at least three locks. I stumble down the stairs and Lilly runs to me, crashing into my arms and sending us both to our knees. Her tears are hot and wet on my face and neck, and she burrows her small body against mine. She sobs relentlessly until Peter stomps down the stairs and stands over us, and I look up at him, barely holding onto my emotions.

"Shut her up." His cold eyes blink emotionlessly, an unspoken truce going between us. "They're coming," he says gruffly.

I press my mouth against Lilly's curls and hush her, whispering my most calming words, and she quiets immediately, almost as if I have changed the channel on the television. She blinks up at me, her eyes red and puffy from crying.

"I thought you had left me," she whispers.

I frown. "I will never leave you." I push the hair

back from her cheeks, cupping her face in my hands. "Not ever," I say with as much conviction as I can muster.

She rubs at her tears and continues to cling to me, and I stumble up to my feet and carry her across the room. I sit down on the small sofa, with Lilly still wrapped around my waist, and I think how childlike she is today. I both hate it and love it. I love that she is young and acting her age; it is, after all, what I strive for on a daily basis—to keep her young and innocent. But I hate it because I need her to be older right now, stronger both mentally and physically. She fumbles around for her teddy bear, finds it, and snuggles it into her side, all without moving from my lap. Mary is hugging Peter, but there's no love lost between them. He seems cold, and much like an empty canvas.

He glances my way every time the scream of monsters sounds out, and I know what he is thinking. I can hear it without him putting voice to those thoughts. Mary is unaware, trapped in her bubble of fear and terror, but not Peter. He is astute and he knows what I have been thinking for days now. They have been happily growing vegetables and fruit, living a simple life without the monsters for a while now—that much is obvious and it doesn't need to be said. It is clear by the panic on Mary's face, in the way the doors were left unlocked, and that nothing had been destroyed. I don't know how or why, but they haven't seen monsters in a while. I hate them for this fact. Hate them with all of my being. Jealousy runs rampant through my heart and soul at their freedom, their obnoxious way of life.

While Lilly and I have been running and hiding, Mary and Peter have been casually living off the land and adjusting to this new way of life. I wonder if this was how Sarah had felt about me and Lilly. If she had been jealous and full of spite for us. Perhaps that was why she left me behind and abandoned Lilly at the roadside: she thought it was deserved, since we had been living in quiet peace.

Nevertheless, life is what it is, and the simple fact remains. The fact and truth that Peter knows and I now know for certain.

The monsters are following me.

I don't know how or why, but they are. A familiarity has been growing within me at every nightfall. Perhaps it is my eventual turning that is bringing me closer to their nature, making me more perceptive to this knowledge. Because, no doubt, I can feel them when they arrive. It feels like they are chasing me—trying to catch both me and Lilly before we change. We are food to them, and if they can hunt us down before it is too late, we will be a tasty meal. I know this, almost like I can taste the succulent flesh caught between my teeth, the blood flowing down my throat, hot and thirst-quenching. And if they don't reach us in time, that's not a problem; we will become a part of their colony. Two more monsters to enter into the fold.

I look away from Peter's angry glare, hating the accusations in it. Another loud chorus of screeching overhead and we all know that they are here. The sound is so loud I can hardly think, but I do, I must. I force myself to control my breathing, to think steady thoughts and to truly acknowledge the danger we are in.

"Do you have lights down here?" I ask. Because right now the small cellar we are in is lit by only a handful of candles. And by the looks of them, they will not last long.

"We have flashlights. But we don't use them unless it's an emergency," Mary says, turning herself away from Peter to face us.

"This is an emergency," I say calmly, thinking that she is stupid for not realizing this already.

Peter is still staring, but he nods sharply and stalks off somewhere into the shadows. I don't like that I can't see him, and I realize that I still don't trust him in any way—certainly not now that he knows my truth. Would he sacrifice me and Lilly to save himself and Mary? Yes, I believe he would, and after the way Mary had been earlier, allowing me to climb the stairs and possibly lock Peter out, I know that she would too. Despite how much she clearly cares for Lilly.

Self-preservation is one of the strongest things there can be. It is why there are no more children, no more old people, no more sick. If it's a choice between saving you or saving someone else, it will always be to save yourself. Especially if the other person is infected, like I am. No matter the cost to your soul. I should know, I think, as I think back to the night spent in the car with the dying person.

I clutch my knife tighter as Peter stalks back into view. In his hands is another plastic tub, much like the ones filled with food upstairs. He slides it onto the table where I had been lying earlier and pulls the lid off. The sound is sharp in our silence and we all look toward the stairs. When nothing happens, he puts his hands inside and begins pulling out candles and flashlights—both large and small. He flicks the switches, testing and checking their use. Several have batteries that are long since dead, but there are three that still work, and lots of candles.

Peter also pulls out several knives and one small pistol, which looks old enough that my grandfather could have used it in the war. But he has the one at his waist also.

"So these are—" Mary begins.

"A last defense," I finish for her.

If the monsters find us, which they are sure to do, if they break through the door, which is more than likely, we use the light to protect us for as long as possible. And if we cannot keep them back long enough for the morning to come, then we take down as many as we can.

"The child," Peter says, nodding his head toward Lilly, who flinches instinctively.

"What about her?" I say, my eyes narrowing.

"There's a space for her to hide. She'll be safer."

He frowns and I frown back.

My mistrust of him is strong, but Lilly's life is the most important thing. If there's somewhere safe for her, then I have to listen, I have to try.

"Where?" I ask.

Mary looks at her husband and then back to me, her eyes shining with wetness. It makes me trust her less, and I stand, holding my knife out in front of me, a snarl already on my lips.

"It's okay, it's okay," she says. "It's where…it's where…" She stumbles on her words, chokes on memories and tears and then almost jumps out of her skin when a loud crash sounds from up above us. Possibly the door caving in, but I can't be certain.

What I can be certain of is the many clawed feet scrambling around the house, the screaming and screeching as they search us out. Running upstairs and downstairs, around and over furniture, crashing through windows and doors as they flood the house in an attempt to find us.

"It's where we hid our grandson," Peter finishes for us, seemingly unfazed by the noises in the house.

"And yet he's not here," I retort, knowing it's both cruel and unlike me to be so. And also surprised that they say 'grandson' and not 'son,' because I didn't think they were old enough for grandchildren.

"He…he died, of the sickness," Mary says sadly, her eyes flitting to Lilly still wrapped in my arms. Her gaze traces across Lilly's light curly hair and then down her neck. Her hair has pushed to one side, showing the crude black evil visibly running through her veins. Yes, Lilly is dying of the sickness too. Yes, it will kill me when it takes her—unless it takes me first, that is.

"I'm sorry," I mumble, feeling shameful. Feeling cruel.

"No matter," Peter says, his voice gruff and harsh. "Come with me."

He stalks off and I stand and follow him, carrying Lilly with me. To the left of the main room is a smaller room. It is a storeroom of sorts and there are cardboard boxes and tubs piled high, shelves stacked with glass jars filled with food, and I stare wide-eyed at how much they have here. They have been preparing for a long time, I realize, but then, what do you do at the end of time when you have nothing left to do with your days but survive? You plan. You store. And you wait.

I was jealous previously; insanely so, I realize—my second realization in as many minutes—but it was unjust of me to be so. They have less than I do. Even with their shelves stacked high with food, they still have little. They have each other, but just barely.

Peter quickly pulls some metal shelving away from the far wall. It screeches on the hard ground and I wince at the noise, but we all know it doesn't matter anymore. It's only going to be minutes, if not less, before they find us anyway. He pulls the shelving away, and several tubs fall, toppling over, and Peter kicks them to one side and points to a small metal door that was previously hidden behind the shelving.

I look at it and then him, and he reaches down and pulls the heavy little door open. Inside are quilts and several small jars of food, what looks like a flare gun, and a knife. Lilly peeks around to look inside, her eyes going wide.

"What do you think, Lilly? Do you think you could hide in there?"

She has no choice, really—I will be insistent that she does—but children like to feel at least a little in charge of their lives, so I pretend that there is an option when really there is not.

"Will you come in with me?" she asks in a very small voice.

"No, there isn't enough room for me," I say. "But if you are hidden in here I will be able to concentrate better. I won't worry so much."

"You'll be safer?" she asks.

"I will. We all will," I say.

"Okay," she replies, and then buries her face against my neck.

A long, drawn-out screeching sound is accompanied by a short series of animalistic screams, and both Lilly and I flinch. Peter, though, stays as solid as stone, calmly waiting for us. I put Lilly down after kissing her on the head and taking a deep lungful of her in, and then I help her into the small space. She fits in comfortably, gulping almost comically loudly.

Peter points to further in the space. "Lantern," he

says simply.

Lilly scurries around in the hole before coming back to the entrance with a small lantern. She flips a switch and the lantern glows brightly. Both Lilly and I let out small breaths of relief, both of us glad that she won't be trapped in the dark.

"I need to shut it," Peter says behind his beard, and I nod.

"See you soon," I say to Lilly, not sure if I'm lying to her not.

"Promise?"

"Promise," I say.

Peter swings the metal door shut, locking it with a large lever, and then he drags the shelving back in place. He turns to look at me afterwards, but I can't tell what he's thinking or feeling. He's an empty mask, a blank canvas, emotionless, devoid of anything.

"Don't let anything happen to my Mary," he says, startling me. I thought he didn't care for her, but apparently I was wrong.

"Look after Lilly," I retort, and he nods his head.

I realize that we are giving each other orders in case the other dies, and though I don't trust people, at all, I believe that he would look after Lilly. At least until the time came that she wasn't Lilly anymore. And so I nod firmly, making my vow to him. Agreeing to protect his Mary, should anything happen to him. We have our pact, and I promise to keep it.

Mary sticks her head around the door, her eyes

wide and her breathing erratic.

"They've found us," she says simply, her eyes wide and frightened.

Chapter Twenty-Seven.
#27. Jigsaw pieces.

Mary stares at Peter, her chin trembling. He nods and moves toward her, and they both move back into the main room. I turn and stare at the little door behind the shelving, where Lilly is hiding. Of course I can't see it, but I know it is there. I only hope that if the monsters get in, that *they* won't know it is there.

I follow after Peter and Mary, finding them both moving around the room, lighting candles everywhere, attempting to make the room as brightly lit as possible. He hands me a bag of one hundred small candles—the pathetically tiny tea lights that only burn for half an hour or so. This isn't going to work—not with these. We need bright lights, streetlamps, the glow of the sun. Not these simple things. They won't burn for long enough. They'll buy us some time, but not enough, of that I am certain.

Yet still we light them, placing them all around the room. Peter drags a tub over to us and pops the lid open. My eyes go wide, seeing two more flare guns and plenty of flares inside. These will help, I decide. These will definitely help. He moves off again, dragging a tall metal bin to the bottom of the stairs. The sound of claws on metal is beginning to drown out every other sound around us—even the sound of furniture being overturned and torn apart above our heads. Peter looks up nervously toward the door, and then quickly begins throwing in paper and books, bits of wood—anything that will burn. Mary and I grab things and throw them in, too, and then we step back, arming ourselves with flashlights and knives, ready to wait it out.

We stand in a small line, waiting for them to break through the door. I look across at Peter, seeing his face still hard and unchanged, and then I look at Mary. She is frightened but calm, her breathing steady and even. Her hands are her only real giveaway—the slight tremble of the light.

"How do we get out?" I ask, feeling panicked. "In the morning, if we make it to morning. How do we get out?"

"We'll cross that bridge when we come to it," Peter says.

The door seems to bow under the pressure from the monsters behind it. The metal groans, the sound almost lost behind a frenzied scream of anger. The hinges snap simultaneously, finally giving way, and the door explodes inwards, sliding down the concrete stairs. Mary gasps but stays firm, her flashlight still turned off and hanging by her side.

Two monsters tumble down the stairs, falling into the small flickering flames of the tea lights, effectively snuffing several of them out. They scream in agony, their red eyes bulging in their skulls as the light caresses their skin. They try to back up, but another two burst through the open door straight after them and charge down the stairs. They can't slow their descent in time to stop themselves from barreling straight into the bin at the bottom. One sits shaking its head in surprise before standing back up. Peter raises his flare gun and fires it directly into the bin, and it immediately erupts into flames of red light. The two monsters screech and back away, moving up the stairs and away from the light. They look half blinded, rubbing at their eyes as if there were grit in them. The two that fell down have finally made it to the top, licking their open wounds and glaring down at us with hatred.

A large shadow passes behind the small group, and the four of them part, allowing space for another of their brethren to slip between.

My throat squeezes shut, the air refusing to make its descent into my lungs. I am suffocating from the lack of air, but more so from the truth that now stares down at me with venomous eyes. This is the same one I have seen several times now. Its clothes are tattered and worn, its head free from hair, and in many ways it looks just like the others do: nondescript, simple, deadly. But this one stands out to me like no other has, the simple pearl necklace that hangs from its neck almost like its calling card. There is no doubt in my mind: this abomination has been tracking us. And now here we are, trapped and at its mercy.

Why me? Why Lilly? But I know why if I think about it: I had let her suffer, and now she wanted that same suffering for me. This was all my fault. It has its demonic red eyes fixed on us, and it is unrelenting in its cause. It snaps its jaws at us three, scouring the room for what I think is a way down to us, a way to get to us without touching the light that was our protection, but then it hits me that it's looking for Lilly. Rage fills my belly, anger coursing through my veins as strong as the infection.

"You can't have her," I murmur. "You can't have her!" The words explode from my lips just as the air finally gushes in and allows me to breathe.

It snaps its jaws again, letting me see its rows of razor sharp teeth. The others look up at it with obvious respect in their gazes. It doesn't want me; it wanted Lilly. It had wanted her all along. Mary places a hand on my forearm and I flinch and pull away, my knife slicing into the soft, fleshy part of her arm minutely. But it is enough.

Enough for her to cry out, enough for a single drop of blood to escape, and enough to send them into a frenzy. She pulls away from me in shock as Peter steps forward and the monsters scream for our blood. He raises his knife up, and I wonder if he will try to sacrifice me for the sakes of him and Mary. I know I would if the roles were reversed. He couldn't possibly know that they are after Lilly—my Honeybee.

He glowers down at me, and resentment burns from him in waves. He blames me for this, for bringing the monsters here, and I can't blame him. I *am* to blame—both me and Lilly. The monsters were tracking us, and we have come here and brought death down on everyone's heads.

"The candles won't burn for long," Peter says beneath his bristles. "We need to keep them lit for as long as we can."

I nod, not sure what else to say.

"She must live," he says, and I nod again. Because in that I am in total agreement: she must live. I demanded it.

Only I'm not sure if he is talking about Lilly or Mary.

Our eyes meet, connecting like no others have before, and I nod again, understanding. We turn back to the monsters, waiting, patiently waiting for the lights to wane and our blood to flow.

Time passes quite quickly when you're waiting for death. I had heard otherwise, read in books how time should slow down and you could see the most important moments of your life flash before your eyes in a blur of memories and happiness. How each second was a minute and each hour a lifetime. But that does not happen. At least, not for me.

The night passes quickly. The monsters sacrifice many in an attempt to reach us, and the screams of them will be forever burned into my memory. The stench of their burning flesh makes my stomach curdle. The entire time, the pearl-necklaced monster stands at the top of the stairs, waiting, watching, and biding its time. Morning will be coming soon, and time is running out. The candles are gone; only the light from the flares now remains. The room is becoming thick with smoke, practically debilitating now as the room fills with it, making us choke and cough, desperate for fresh clean air. Most of the smoke is billowing upward toward them—toward the world outside—yet still enough remains to make my lungs burn.

I light my last flare, firing it into the bin at the base of the stairs again as the current one flickers and then extinguishes. The monsters take two steps forward as the light dies out, and then scream in pain when the new one bursts to life. We are tired, frightened, exhausted beyond anything. Adrenaline long worn off. The monsters are halfway down the stairs when it happens: when they put their pieces in place, and an idea forming for them. The cogs almost visibly turn when they work out what they can do—how they can get to us.

I had realized it about an hour before. Another monster had slipped down the stairs, the hard stone steps made slippy by their putrid flesh melting and burning where the light had licked them. It slipped, dragging another with it. As it hit the bin at the bottom, its body received the full force of the light and began melting across the face and chest. The monster behind cowered for several moments, untouched and unharmed by the light, before quickly scampering back up the stairs with a high-pitched scream of what was quite possibly gratefulness.

Peter and I had exchanged a look, both of us realizing what they hadn't and both of us praying that they wouldn't.

The small tea lights have long ago burned away and there are no more left to light. The only thing between the monsters and us are the metal bin full of flares and our three flashlights, which we have kept as our last resort—our final line of defense. I just used my last flare, but Peter still has one remaining. It's enough to get us through until daylight, I think, which surely can't be much longer. And I'm glad that I calculated so wrong when I assumed it wouldn't be enough. We just need to keep them at bay for a little longer, until daylight comes to be our savior once again and we can push our way out of this house and into freedom. The monsters can follow and burn or stay and hide.

But now it's too late as they slowly creep down the stairs, their tiny brains figuring out what we had known all along. One of the monsters clutches, with clumsy, clawed hands, the sheet of metal that Peter had sealed across the door earlier. The dull metal slips from its fingers and another monster comes to help it. Between them, they come down the stairs, the light blocked from their path. Their bodies stay unharmed while their fingers, rounded over the edge of the metal and clutching it tightly, begin to sizzle and pop as the light licks away at their sensitive flesh.

They reach the bin, the monsters at the top of the stairs watching warily, and then they place the metal over the top of the bin, snuffing out the light and plunging us into an almost pitch black nightmare.

"No!" Mary cries out.

I suck in a sharp breath as the sounds of clawed feet scamper down the stairs. Peter fires his gun into the center of the room, the flare hitting one of them directly in the chest and exploding the room back into an eerie red light. Mary cries next to me, frozen in fear, her sobs obnoxiously loud even with the backdrop of monster screams.

I pull out my flashlight and shine it directly in front of me, catching the full face of one of them. It squeals and scrambles backwards, its hands clawing at its eyes, scraping at the skin that sizzles and burns. In those few seconds I see more pain and anguish than I may have ever seen before. The light hits its eyes and I see its humanness for a split second before its head bursts into flames.

"Your flashlight!" I yell at Mary, who was still yet to move.

Somewhere within her fear she must hear me, because her light joins mine and the room grows brighter still. Beneath the chorus of screams and squeals I know Peter is inserting another flare, and then his own flashlight comes on, creating one block of solid light in front of us—a wall of light to protect us all. The monsters back up another step, their skin bubbling in pain. In their panic and frenzy they have forgotten the trick of blocking the light, but they will remember it soon enough, of that I have no doubt.

"I need to get Lilly. We need to get out of here," I yell over to Peter. I hate saying her name out loud, knowing that they are so close—that the one that has been hunting us is so close and will hear me say her name. It shouldn't matter; they don't understand us. Yet it feels dirty, saying Lilly's name in front of these beasts that want to harm her—kill her.

I see his head move, but can't see his expression. I'm not sure if it was a shake of the head or a nod. However, seconds later his shape moves in the smoke and I can't make him out anymore. I trust that he has gone to get her for me. I have to trust her life with his.

I cough and wheeze, the smoke becoming unbearable and making me gag and want to vomit. Flares weren't designed for small spaces like this, and it's only a matter of time now before we suffocate in it. The smoke is no longer escaping up the stairs, but is trapped down here with us. I lift my shirt up, trying to pull it over my mouth and nose to stop some of the smoke getting to my lungs before I suffocate. My eyes burn and stream with painful hot tears as the red smoke continues to billow around us.

A muffled cry to my left makes me turn, and I see shadows moving amongst my tears and choking. But I would know her cry anywhere.

"Lilly!" I cry out, coughing and choking on the thick smoke.

"Mama!" she screams back.

We shine our flashlights as a collective, making one block of light as we force our way toward where the stairs should be.

My foot hits the metal bin and I push the sheet of

metal off the top of it. Light and smoke begin escaping once more, and I turn and drag the bin in place behind us, blocking the path behind us so they can't follow us out. I keep my flashlight aimed down at them, my burning eyes searching the smoke-filled room, seeing only the flash of teeth and the glow of red eyes.

Somewhere above me I hear things banging, and I stumble blindly up and out into the kitchen. The door is gone, torn off the hinges completely and lying across the kitchen floor in pieces. I look around for Peter, for Mary, but mostly for Lilly, and I see the shape of a body moving across the kitchen. I stumble half blind after them, the screaming echoing around me, the crashing of tables and cupboards as monsters fling themselves against things in a bid to rid their bodies of the light and flames that we'd cast upon them with our flashlights.

I catch up to Peter and Mary, seeing the small shape of Lilly clinging onto his back. She never looks up, but keeps her face buried into his shirt, her arms tight around him like she does with me, and I hope with everything I am that I can trust him. We move through the house, looking for a way to escape but finding almost every exit blocked with monsters. Our flashlights only do so much. Most of them are willing to sacrifice themselves for each other. Finally we make it to a downstairs bathroom, and Peter swings the door open and steps inside, dragging Mary in with him. They wait for me, and I step backwards into the small space, pulling the door shut behind me.

There is one small window, and through it I see the light of morning, the early caress of the sun on the world. I outwardly sob as Peter smashes his elbow through the window, letting in the fresh air. There isn't enough time to wait; the monsters are too desperate and angry now, and they will sacrifice themselves just to take us down with them.

Peter lifts Lilly from his back, pushing her through the window and dropping her gently outside. Mary is next, and when she lands on the ground, Lilly scrambled into her lap, her bloodshot eyes staring up at me. Peter helps me up to the window and I lower my legs outside, and then he looks at me.

Somewhere beneath his beard, I think he may have smiled.

"Protect her." His voice is rough and broken from the flare smoke—or perhaps emotion—and he chokes on the words.

Mary stands up, still clutching Lilly to her. "Peter, come on, get out." She pushes me to one side, thrusting Lilly into my eager and waiting arms.

Peter shakes his head. "No way I'm getting through this window." He hits the frame to prove a point that it couldn't be broken and made wide enough either.

"No, no, you have to," Mary wails, reaching through into the hole and clutching at it.

Peter pries her arms away from him and I know that he definitely smiles this time. His eyes flit to behind us, to the sun slowly rising in the sky, casting a protective blanket over the three of us. Banging and screaming echoes out to us, and he looks toward the door, his eyes never once showing any fear.

He aims his flashlight at the door, not looking at us anymore. "Go on now, get going. Get away from here. I don't want you seeing this."

I turn and walk away, definitely not wanting Lilly to see it.

"You look after her," he calls after me, but I'm still unsure if he means Lilly or Mary.

The sound of wood cracking and splintering inwards follows seconds after his words, and then I hear Mary scream as a gun goes off. Her sobbing follows me as I round the corner, feeling Lilly's nails digging into my arms. And like an anchor, I hold onto the pain of her sharp nails, needing it to keep me here, keep me grounded. Because without it, without her, I would be lost in the insanity of it all.

Chapter Twenty-Eight.

#28. Misfortune lights my way.

We walk around the side of the house until we reach the front yard, and then I sit down heavily on the small porch swing, the wood already warming beneath me. Lilly clings to me, whimpering softly. I rest my head back, staving off a cough, though I can feel it tickling in my chest, burning in my throat. I close my eyes and let my skin absorb the sun, the heat, the brightness. I let it all soak into me, letting it burrow down deep and head straight to my heart.

The soft crunch of gravel makes me open my eyes, and a distraught-looking Mary comes from around the side of the old farmhouse. Her eyes stay down as she comes toward us, and I stop swinging long enough for her to sit down next to us. We stay in silence for several long minutes, all of us taking soothing lungful's of fresh, clean air, absorbing the sun, embracing the silence.

I break the silence first, my eyes still shut, my face still tipped toward the burning disc in the sky. I don't want to, but we don't have time to relax—not really. A handful of minutes, just grains of sand in the timer, really. The sun will pass, and night will fall, and then they will come again. I know it now. I am certain of it.

"What will you do?" I ask, my voice sounding

croaky and unsure.

I feel guilty. This is our fault—my fault, really. If we hadn't stumbled across this place, they would have been fine. Peter would still be alive and Mary would be with him. They would be weeding the vegetable patch, jarring food, preparing for the inevitable. An inevitable that hadn't touched them yet—at least, not like the rest of the world.

Mary meets my question with silence, and I set my head straight and open my eyes, staring at the side of the barn right ahead of us. I can see from my peripheral vision that she is looking straight ahead now too, both of us staring at everything and at nothing. She doesn't reply to me, instead keeping her secrets locked up tight inside her own head.

I stand up, ready to leave—needing to leave—but then I realize that, once again, we have lost everything. I sit back down, my heart feeling both full and empty, my soul tired—weary, almost. How many more times can we do this? I let out a heavy breath and the cough that has been tickling my chest expels itself. I cough until my lungs hurt even more, and then I hack up black phlegm. Lilly stays on my lap the entire time, restricting my coughs and stifling the air, which I needed to breathe, yet neither of us let go of the other. Neither of us are willing to relinquish our hold on the other.

"I have a truck," Mary finally says, gesturing toward the small barn. She turn to look at me, her eyes empty, soulless. "You can have it." She stands up and looks across at the house before sitting back down again with a heavy sigh like I had done only moments ago. "What's the point?" she mumbles under her breath. And then she begins to cry.

I sit there listening to her grief, letting my body soak up her pain like it's soaking up the sun's rays. I have to, because this is my fault. I am to blame for her pain, for bringing death to her door. The very least I can do is sit here with her while she cries for the loss of her partner, for the fear that she now feels for the future.

Lilly pries her face away from my chest, small creases down her face from the material on my T-shirt. A small sweat patch has gathered thickly between my breasts where she has been breathing and crying against me. She reaches a small hand over to Mary, placing it gently on her forearm. Mary looks down at it, a small smile tainting her grief. Her eyes meet Lilly's and fresh tears pour from them, a waterfall of tears cascading silently down her cheeks.

"You have to live," Lilly says, her voice so small and weak.

Mary sniffles and shrugs her shoulders.

"You have to," Lilly insists. "We can't let them win." She pouts.

Mary stares silently at Lilly, the tears still flowing. "They've already won, dear," she whispers back, and stands up. "Take whatever you need," she says, and walked away. "I won't need any of it."

We watch her walk to the edge of the property,

staring across the sunlit field that we had traveled across only yesterday. Just one day and their world has been destroyed. Just one day and the monsters had found us. Just one day until they would come back.

Mary stares across the fields, her arms wrapped around her middle, her shoulders shaking. Peter had asked me to look after her, but I was still unsure on if he meant Lilly or Mary. When the infection first hit, the children were the ones that were sacrificed. They were the weakest, the slowest, the most likely to get you killed. Parents turned against their own, grandparents forgoing grandchildren to save themselves. Most people shared in that view, but Peter and Mary didn't—they were willing to risk their lives for the sake of their child. It had been too late for him, but they had wanted to help Lilly. They had hope for Lilly.

I stand up, Lilly's arms tightening around me as I do. I hold her tight and move across to the barn, opening the door with a small creak. Inside is a truck. It was red and shiny. Lilly will like it—once she sees it in the light, anyway. I open the door, placing Lilly on the driver's seat while I search for the keys. I check under the seat and inside the glove box, but find nothing. Lilly kneels up on the seat and flips down the sun visor and the keys fall out.

"Well done," I say, my throat still tight and sore. I force a smile and hope for one back.

Her mouth doesn't move, not even a quirk, but her eyes flash with happiness.

I climb in the truck and scoot her over to the passenger side. "Time to buckle up, Honeybee," I say, and reach over to fasten her in.

I glance around the barn, wondering if there is anything else we can take—weapons or blankets. We have nothing now, though Lilly still clutches her teddy bear with its mismatched eyes. I can't see anything other than farm tools and dry straw, so I stick the key in the ignition. The truck revs to life and Lilly reaches across, placing her hand on top of mine. I look at her, the light from the sun shining in through the open doors and the cracks in the roof, and I smile again. This time she smiles back.

I pull the truck out of the barn and look across for Mary. But she is gone. Back inside the house or to somewhere else, I'm sure. I feel guilt eating away like cancer in my gut, but if it's a choice between them or Lilly, I will always choose Lilly. My choice to come to this farm had cost them their lives, but it had kept Lilly safe, at least for one more night. And that's all any of us can hope for anymore—to survive one more night. To make it through another day. And we had.

"Mama?"

I turn to Lilly's soft voice and wait for her to ask her question. She glances out the windshield toward the greenhouse. The windows are smashed, the small glass building toppled to one side, but the food is still there. She looks toward me in a silent question. I can't see Mary anywhere. I want to ask her if it's okay to take some food, but I know that I would take some even if she said no. I nod at Lilly and drive the truck over to the broken greenhouse. I help Lilly out of her seat, carrying her on my hip over to it because I don't want her walking through the shards of glass.

We don't have a bag to put anything in—not even a carrier bag this time—so our arms will have to do the carrying. I open the door of the greenhouse, the heat washing over us once again in a bizarre sense of déjà vu despite all the broken windows. We carry several pots of tomato plants and pull up armfuls of carrots and beans, piling them all onto the backseat of the truck in a tidy disarray. Carrots stay with carrots, beans with beans and so on, but earth and dirt cover them all, leaving stains on the interior carpet. There are two tubs of water, which had been used for watering the plants, standing just inside the doorway, and we fill as many containers as we can with it and stack them in the back of the truck also. I'm not convinced it will be safe to drink, but I'd rather take some than not. Besides, we can use it to water the tomato plants, if nothing else.

Finally ready, we both climb back into the truck. I strap Lilly back in her seat and turn the truck around, pulling out of the yard and away from the farmhouse. I look in the rearview mirror, still not seeing Mary anywhere, and I hope that she didn't go back inside the house to be with Peter. I suppose it doesn't really matter. Either way I have condemned her to death. I have taken away her home, her food, her husband, and her safety. I should be ashamed of myself.

I look over at Lilly. A large tomato is in her palm and she bites into it with gusto, the small yellow seeds mixing with the juices and dribbling down her little chin. She smiles across at me as she eats, showing me her teeth, and my conscience is eased, my guilt swallowed up by this small moment of happiness that she is having.

Look after her, Peter had asked. And I will. No matter what.

*

I drive until the sun is at its highest point, and then I know that I need to pull over—at least for an hour or so. I need to put distance between us and the farmhouse, but I haven't slept all night and I'm exhausted. Beyond that need, I'm hungry—famished, almost—and my chest is still burning from all the smoke that I inhaled. I need a drink of water, I need to bathe, I need to eat, and I need to sleep.

Life is made up of a series of needs. Of desires and wants. Of things we must have and things that we think we have the right to. Right now, I know that I need to sleep, but it's bathing that takes the highest priority. I pull us off the main highway and down a small country lane. I saw a sign an hour or so previous for a small lake, and I've been following the signs ever since. As we round a sharp bend, the bristles of the bushes dragging along the sides of the truck, I am nervous. There are too many things we need to do in such a short space of time.

The road opens up into what used to be a relatively

small parking lot and I shut the engine off, take a steadying breath, and step out of the truck. Lilly is asleep, the remnants of a carrot still firmly in her grasp. I don't wander far from the truck—not after the fright I gave Lilly the last time. I examine our immediate surroundings, always keeping the truck within view as I scout out the area, checking that there are no dark spaces for the monsters to hide.

There is a short path that leads to the lake—or at least so the little brown sign says. I stop walking and close my eyes, listening intently. The world is so silent that I can hear the water lapping at the edges of the lake. I open my eyes and pull out my cigarettes, noting that there are only two left, since three of them are broken. I light one and walk slowly back over to the truck. Lilly is still sleeping, the juices on her T-shirt staining the front. It makes me smile. I climb up onto the hood of the truck and watch the world while I smoke, allowing Lilly five more minutes of peace.

I like it when she sleeps like this—satisfied, content, unfazed by the horrors. This is how a child should be; this is how *she* should be consistently. Life should not be made up of finals and survival, it should be made up of forevers. My heart aches with grief, but like yesterday and the day before that, I bite the inside of my cheek until it brings tears to my eyes, I count to ten, and I let myself be grateful for the day in which I live.

I roll my filthy sleeves up, examining the depths into which the blackness has now sunk. I hold my cigarette loosely between my lips and squeeze a vein near my wrist, wondering for a second if I were to open up the vein if I could squeeze the evil back out. My nails dig in, the liquid so close to the surface that I can smell its stench of wickedness, but I don't have the courage to pry open my flesh and squeeze it out. It would be futile anyway, I know.

I finish my cigarette, not feeling any better for it, and then I go to the passenger side of the truck and gently open the door. Lilly's soft snores greet me, calming my wretched soul a little. I stroke her cheek, pushing tangled knots away from her face. She is so calm, so innocent, I think, my throat feeling tight with anxiety. I pull out the map from my pocket, the one Sarah left for me, and look at where we are on the map and where the safe place is. We could be there in under an hour, I realize. *Not even a day before we are safe,* I think. *That's all we need to get through together. Hours.*

I think back to Peter and Mary and wonder if it would be cruel to bring the monsters that are following us to the doorstep of a supposed safe place, but I quickly dismiss the thought. No matter what, I will take us there now. We are too close to possible safety, and though I still don't believe it to be true, I have to try—for Lilly, if not for me.

Chapter Twenty-Nine.

#29. Piles of bones should frighten us.

"Lilly," I whisper against her cherub cheek, placing a soft kiss where my breath touches.

Her mouth hangs open, her head flung back, but when I whisper her name she snorts a little and closes her mouth. Her eyes stay shut, though I think she is waking up, slowly.

"Honeybee," I whisper, and give her another kiss. I place this one on her forehead, and when I pull back she is smiling, eyes still closed.

Her skin is translucent almost, and I can see the darkness running in her veins along her throat and cheeks. My sweet Lilly. The blackness is spreading quickly. She opens her eyes, and for a moment we are both startled. I see red eyes staring back at me, but they vanish when I blink. I think I must have imagined them but then Lilly looks equally as frightened as I am, and it's then that I know that she saw the world through blood-tinted glasses like I have done many times.

"It's okay," I say, unclipping her belt and pulling her from the seat.

She snuggles against me. Her body is warm and sweaty. She doesn't let go of the tomato in her hand, but she doesn't eat it, either, and that's okay.

"There's water. We can go wash if you like," I say

against her neck, and I feel her bob her head in a *yes*.

I bang my hip against the door of the truck, closing it, and I start to walk us down to the water. I thread us through the broken path, with the strangled weeds on either side clawing and grasping for purchase at our ankles. We break free of them and I stumble, almost dropping Lilly when I see the piles of bones.

Piles and piles and piles of bones.

Both animal and human and monster. As if we are all one huge surrogate family. The air sticks in my throat and I try to swallow down the wedge that is blocking the air's passage to my lungs. I feel dizzy for lack of it. Dizzy with fear and dizzy with hunger. Ravenously so. I can smell Lilly, her blood fertile and alight to my taste buds. I pant, my mouth filling with water, barely able to see…

"Mama?"

The balloon snaps and I am me and she is she, and the world is filled with bones again, but I no longer want to add to the piles. I pant and choke on sobs that escape me, gripping Lilly with force.

"I'm okay, I'm okay," I say to her and to me. "I'm okay." But I don't know if I believe myself anymore. I am not okay, I do not have long left. The thought is soul-destroying, heart-breaking, and I feel the depths of who I am shattering inside of me.

I don't want to die.

We stumble onwards, toward the shore and to the water, ignoring the mounds of bones as if they were merely mounds of sand. Inconsequential, inconvenient, invisible…

I put Lilly down on the muddy earth, her back facing away from the piles of nothing, and her feet sinking ever so slightly into the thick goop of the shore. Then we both sit, feeling the goop sink around our bottoms. It is cold, but I don't mind. I begin to take off my shoes. Lilly's laces are knotted too tightly, so I have to help her untie hers. I pull off her worn shoes and see that her socks have a large hole in near the big toe and I say sorry that I don't have nice socks for her to wear but she only shrugs, unconcerned. I feel bad, though. It's another stab to my heart. Like I have failed her again because she has holes in her socks.

We slide off our pants and then shrug our T-shirts over our heads. We avoid looking at each other's bodies, though. There's no point in seeing that destruction. Not on each other, and not on ourselves.

I stand and take Lilly's hand, and then she stands, too, and I guide us into the water. It's cold, chillingly so, and we shiver as the water laps lazily against our broken bodies. I help to wash Lilly, letting the water turn brown with the filth that comes away. I rinse her hair, trying to pull my fingers through her knots. She has lice, and I feel even worse. What kind of mother lets her child get lice? After I have washed her face, I see that her lips have turned a little blue because she is cold, and I tell her to splash around to warm up. I don't want her to leave the water yet—I think it's good for her body to be exposed to air and water. We might not ever have this chance again, I think. Because as I scrubbed at Lilly's back with my hands, I did look at her veins, and in turn, my own.

We don't have much time left. It's almost over.

Lilly stands looking confused while I wash myself. Her body trembles from the cool water and the air that licks her. Her fingers flick over the top of the water, unsure as to what to do, and I realize that she doesn't know how to splash and play in water, not deep water like this, because she never has before, and my stomach hurts with the realization that she has never swum in the ocean.

I finish washing, rinsing my own hair in the water, and then I turn to Lilly. Her wide brown eyes stare back at me blankly, her lips a soft blue, her skin pale but for the black lines criss-crossing over her skin. I smile. It's hard and hurts my cheeks to do it, but I do it regardless. Then I flick some water at her and she gasps, her mouth opening in a large *O*. I flick her again, making sure the water splashes her face this time. She gasps again and looks down at the water, at her hands grazing the tops of it, and then she flicks me back.

The water hits me in a series of cold drops, and I raise my hands up to block them. I look between my fingers and see that she is smiling too. Her eyes have a little life back in them, and I can see her teeth because her smile is wide. She flicks me again and giggles, and then I flick her back, and before I know it we are both throwing water at one another and laughing and smiling until our bellies hurt.

Lilly comes forward and throws her little body at mine, her chest still rising and falling with laughter.

"I don't want to die, mama," she whispers against my cold skin.

I hug her tighter. "I know, neither do I," I kiss the top of her head, her hair damp against my lips, "we can sleep soon and forget this all happened."

"Promise?"

"I promise," I reply.

I don't know how I should feel about that. Happy that this will all be over soon, or sad that this will all be over soon. I wonder, for a moment, if we will be together when this is over, or if we will each be with our respective families. Up until now, I did not believe in heaven, or anything else after this life, but right now, as my arms are tight around Lilly's frail body, I hope and wish and pray that there is something afterwards.

I want to see my family again.

And Lilly, because she is a part of me now. Forever.

Her hands are cold so I pluck her out of the water and kiss the top of her damp head again, and then I carry us from the water back to the shore.

I help Lilly dress first, forgoing my own needs for hers, like I always do. Like a mother should. When she is dry, huddled with her knees to her chest and a smile still on her face, I finally get dressed, sliding my dirty clothes back on my semi-clean body. I kneel behind her and thread my fingers through her curls, separating each one until there are no more knots. We keep our backs to the piles of bones and move further down the shore, and we take long drinks of the water until we are both sated.

"My belly feels swishy," Lilly says, her voice a whisper.

"Mine too," I say and smile.

She doesn't smile, but she does take my hand, and I feel her warmth thread through her fingertips and wrap around me. Her cheeks have a little rosiness back to them, her curls are drying and they bounce lightly when she walks, her lips are no longer blue but a soft pink, and her eyes have their spark back in them. I feel happy that she looks like my Lilly again. Like a little girl. Right now, in this moment, we are mother and daughter walking along the beach.

We walk back along the overgrown path, back toward the truck, and when we get there I help Lilly inside it, buckling her back into her seat. I grab some of the fruit and vegetables from the plants in the back, and then I sit next to her and we eat with the windows open, the sound of the water hanging all around us and the fresh air cleaning out our smoke-damaged lungs.

The tomatoes are incredibly juicy and I moan when I bite into one, my mouth salivating, desperate for more. I swallow it down, almost certain that I can hear the fruit hit my stomach with a resounding *splat*. I look over at Lilly every now and then, watching her eat with gusto, biting carrots and tomatoes, eating beans and lettuce. Her eyes begin to get heavy again, and I smile and tell her to go to sleep.

When she's snoring softly I get back out of the truck and slide myself up onto the hood, and I smoke my very last cigarette. It seems fitting to smoke the last one now. We are clean, and fed and watered, she is happy—she even laughed today. I feel something that might be happiness. So yes, I smoke my last cigarette to finish off the brilliance of this day. I do not think about Peter or Mary, or the monsters that are chasing us. I decide that if today can be this good, then tomorrow could be even better. That tomorrow we could find the safe spot on the map and they would open their doors to us, and we wouldn't need to run and hide any longer. I decide that the people there will be good and true, that I can trust them. I pretend that I don't have a haze of red blanketing my vision right now, and that it isn't nearly time for me to die. That the tomatoes were really good, and that I didn't crave Lilly's blood the entire time I was eating, and that I can't hear her little heart thumping in her chest, slow and melodic. The sound soothes me; it reminds me that she is still alive and there is still a reason to keeping on living myself, to keep on fighting.

I pretend, and I force myself to hold on. Because I have to. Because that's what mothers do. I am Lilly's mother and I will protect her until I can't.

I fall asleep on the hood of the truck, the sun warm on my face and body, my blood pumping languidly through my dying veins. I sleep, but I don't dream of anything. I feel content in my sleep, I know this, even with the lack of dreams.

*

When I wake, I see that the sun is beginning to fall and the sky is becoming darker. Rain is coming, making the daylight fade faster than it should. My heart stills for a fraction, my ears pricking and searching the world for the first wicked screams of the monsters. It's still quiet though, barring the crack of the storm brewing somewhere in the distance. I am panicked, frozen in fear because I fell asleep and I have slept for far too long.

The first screams pierce the sky like a balloon exploding. It is sudden and loud, startling me enough that my body jumps and I slide a little off the hood. I sit up, finally free of my terror-filled stupor, and I jump down from the truck, glancing in to see Lilly's brown eyes staring back at me. Her face is blank, her eyes a bloodshot pink like I know mine are. She is frightened, and that forces me to move, to conquer and move past my own fear.

"It's okay," I say as the first drops of rain begin to fall.

I tip my face up to the sky, letting the drips splat on my hot skin. I dart my tongue out, flicking it across my parched lips, and then I look back in at Lilly. She is still watching me, her eyebrows pinched together. Another scream echoes out to us, and I know she feels it too, though possibly not as strongly as me…the pull. The pull of the scream. My heart constricts, wanting more of the scream, my body feeling the tug of the call.

I swallow, knowing that they are coming, that they are searching for us right now. They can feel us like we can feel them. I can almost hear their panting thoughts as they hunt us down. And they are close because I didn't drive us far enough away. I didn't put enough distance between us and them. Instead I slept, in the sun, letting my happiness kill us both.

The next scream is so loud it chills my blood. The rain is coming down harder and plastering my hair to my face, and I sob because I'm stupid and they are here. My breaths are coming too quickly for me to keep up with, and I feel dizzy and sick from it.

"Mama!" Lilly screams.

Her face is panicked, and I know—as my mouth fills with blood, as I feel the pinch of too-long nails and deformed toes in my boots—that I am almost gone. I shake my head, as if dazed and needing to escape from the cage in which I am trapped, and I run around to my side of the truck just as the first monster charges out of the trees. I drag the driver's door open and jump in, slamming the door shut behind me. With a scream of agonizing pain I force the door back open and release my now broken hand, and then I slam the door closed again, clutching my crushed and bloody fingers to my chest as I cry loudly.

"Mama, Mama, Mama!" Lilly calls my name over and over as we are surrounded by red, glowing eyes and angry screeches. "Please Mama!" She begs and begs, but I can't stop shaking, can't stop the red and black blood from dripping from my crushed fingers.

A monster slaps my window with its own deformed hand, and I look at it and see the pearl necklace hanging at its throat. It snaps its teeth at me, looking almost gleeful, which is peculiar as I've never seen any expression other than anger and hate on their twisted and bony faces. I reach across my own body and turn the key with my unbroken hand, and try to grip the wheel with my damaged one while I change gears, but it hurts so much.

"Lilly, I need you to help me," I say, my voice sounding far away, like I've been swallowed under water. I am almost not me.

She nods, her chin trembling, her eyes bleeding frightened tears.

"I need you to do the gears. I can steer with my other hand if you do that."

She scoots closer to me, putting both hands on the gearstick, and nods quickly. I flick on the headlights and see the many monsters surrounding us back away with yelps and screams of pain. Smoke from their singed flesh flying into the sky. The sound of tearing metal makes me flinch, and I tell Lilly to put it in first gear but she stares at me blankly, so I tell her first looks like a line and then she does as I ask and I press down on the accelerator and steer us around in a large circle. The monsters jump out of the way of the light, and then they throw their hard bodies against the side of the truck to get us to stop.

"Second," I yell to her. "It looks like a duck," I say, and she uses all of her strength to change gears as quickly as she can. I press all the way down on the accelerator and yell at her to change to third and then fourth and then we are speeding away, the monsters chasing closely behind us.

Lilly is sobbing, her hands still clutching the gearstick, ready to change when I need her to. I am breathing hard. The infection has hit my lungs now; I can hear it crackling through the small pockets that should be filled with air and not poison. The world is red and vibrant, alive and dead all at once, but I am pushing my way through it. It won't end like this. It can't.

I glance at Lilly, seeing her tear-stained face, and I grit my teeth, swallowing down the blood that has filled my mouth. It won't end like this. I will protect her.

I will protect her until I can't.

Chapter Thirty.

#30. The end is only the beginning.

I once had a goldfish. I was around six at the time, and my father won it when we spent the day at the fair. My mother said that it wouldn't last a day, and my father agreed. "Those fish never last more than a day," he had said to me, but he won it fair and square and I promised I would look after it until it died, no matter how long or short that may be. I carefully carried it all the way home and I found a bowl for it to live in. I filled it with water, dropped some pebbles along the bottom of the bowl, and fed it breadcrumbs. I called it Henry. The funny thing was, it wasn't even gold; it was white and black, with speckles of yellow. Not a goldfish at all, really.

I stared at Henry, with his speckled gills, swimming around and around his little bowl for over an hour, his bulging eyes staring back at me blankly. I was waiting for him to die, like my mother and father had told me he would.

My parents eventually told me that I had to go to sleep because I had school in the morning and I wouldn't be able to concentrate if I were tired from having watched my goldfish all night. I cried myself to sleep that night, knowing that it would possibly be the last time I saw Henry alive. I knew he would die, and I felt like I must have done a terrible job of looking after him for him to die so soon.

Sure enough, when I woke in the morning, Henry was floating on his side at the top of the bowl, his eye staring unblinking toward the ceiling of my bedroom. I cried all day, and I refused to eat my dinner. My mother bathed me and washed my hair, and then she gave me some warm milk before bed, and still I cried. Father came in and sat on the edge of my bed, wiping away the tears that still trailed down my cheeks. He spoke to me in his deep voice, his hand stroking my hair as it splayed out across my pillow.

"Death is inevitable, my darling," he said. "It comes for us all in the end."

I cried even harder at that, because I didn't want to die and I certainly didn't want my mother or father to die either. "Why can't we live forever?" I asked him.

"Because life would not be life if we did not die," he soothed.

I still cried, unhappy with his answer, because who could ever be happy with that answer?

"To love means to sacrifice. I would sacrifice myself for you, my darling, just as your mother would, too. When you love someone, you never truly die. You live on in them, a part of your soul forever touching the earth and gracing people's lives."

I didn't understand. It made no sense to me. I vowed from that day on to never love anyone, not if it meant saying goodbye to them eventually. I was scared to die—of death and saying goodbye—and I was scared for people to leave me. So I grew up lonely. Until the day I met my husband.

He was handsome and caring and he wouldn't take no for an answer. He begged me over and over to go on a date with him, and then one date led to another and another and then one day he asked me to marry him. I said yes, because I knew that it was too late then, I knew that I had fallen in love with him and to lose him at that point would be like dying. We had a child not long after that, and I was happy. Until the world died and everyone I had ever loved died right along with it. And then I was alone again, and I was glad it was quick for the people I loved, only I wished I had gotten to go with them.

Then I found Lilly. She was in the field of sunflowers, surrounded by the yellow glow of their petals. By the buzzing of the honeybees, which were unaware that life had ended and no one needed their sweet honey anymore. And then we had each other, and I was glad I hadn't died with my family, because I got to be with Lilly, and I loved Lilly as much as anything else I had ever loved before her.

I glance over at her. "Don't cry, Lilly."

"But I'm scared, Mama," she sobs. "I'm scared to die."

My heart aches for her, for her pain. For the goodbyes we must share. She has never shared with me her fears. Not like this—so fresh and vulnerable, like an open wound waiting to be healed. Only there's nothing to heal her wounds with. "Don't be scared. There's nothing to fear," I say, my words a gasp of pain on my cracked lips. "I'll always be with you. Forever."

"Promise?"

"I promise." I say, almost choking on the word.

Lilly meets my aching gaze and then abruptly tears her stare away and continues to cry. She looks out of the window, ignorant to my words. I don't blame her; I understand how scared she must be. I am too.

"Mama," she whispers. "Mama, look!" She points into the distance, diving up to her knees and pressing her face against the glass, staring toward the bright glow of light across the field. "What is it?"

"A safe place," I whisper in shock, daring to believe. I had gotten us here? It was true…

"Can we make it?" she asks quietly—as if by whispering it, we wouldn't somehow jinx it.

I swallow down the blood that fills my mouth "I think so," I breathe out. "God, I hope so."

The bright glow of lights is in the center of a field—a large circle of light in an otherwise dark world. Around that great circle the monsters are swarming. The earth is thick with them. They have been called by the lights, by the humans just beyond their reach, but they can't go any further toward the food source. Some of them turn their gnarled bodies toward our truck as I drive over the soft slope of the embankment. I crash over a collapsed fence and straight into the sea of writhing bodies. They part abruptly away from our headlights, but their nails claw and slice down the sides of our truck as we pass them.

"Lilly, the flashlight," I say. We will need to run, I decide. At some point we will need to run, and we will need the light to do that if there is any hope of safety.

She leans over, but her seatbelt restricts her small body from reaching down. "I can't get it," she whimpers. She looks up at me, determination gritted across her small features, and then she reaches over and unclips herself, and I don't scold her for it, because I need her to do this. I need her to be brave, just this one last time with me.

She tumbles to the floor in a heap and then scrambles through the small space between our seats until she is in the back. She fumbles around. The noise from the monsters is overwhelming, but her small mutters as she hunts through the toppled over plants and soil are louder, her resolve and strength a high-pitched call to my primal instincts.

I glance back and forth between Lilly and the field of monsters, the truck rocking from side to side as they attack it from every angle. We are close now, close enough that the lights of the safe place are brighter and they—whoever is behind those walls of steel and stone—can see us. More lights turn toward us, glaring in our direction, but they don't penetrate far enough across the field of darkness to touch us. To protect us. We are so close and yet there is a world between this one and that.

A monster throws itself at our truck, ignoring the glare of our headlights and slamming itself against the hood. The force rocks us, unbalancing us, and the truck jerks to the side and slows its momentum. Another monster slams against my window, and I feel rather than see the glass shatter inwards at me, small fragments sticking in my arms and face. It reaches a bony hand in to me, scratching long nails down the side of my face and arm until I elbow it away with a scream of pain and fright. Claws tear at my door, finally ripping it free from its hinges, and then bodies are pulling at me, and pulling at the truck and then we are as one, toppling over and over, the world a spinning top, the lights and darkness colliding into one confusing blur. A mish-mash of metal and monster and human.

Screams assault my ears, both monster and child, until the spinning top stops and the monsters converge. The truck is upside down and I am folded into the footwell of it. I choke on bile and blood and the taste of hunger in my throat, the gasping pants of death dragging me under, begging for my change. My eyes glare into the darkness, searching for Lilly, finding her trapped in my arms, beneath me. I am hanging upside down, my seatbelt holding me in place. Lilly was flung forward when we crashed but I have caught her, still protecting her. Always.

I look down at her, her eyes squeezed shut, her sobs ceased, and my heart stutters. "Lilly?" I whisper against the onslaught of senses. So many new things I now see and hear. The sights, the smells, the tastes, the mind that is cracking, splintering into something else, someone else. "Lilly?" I say again, my voice a long moan.

She opens her eyes, and all I see is her. Her sweet face, her cheeks tear-stained and scarred from this life, her curls a tangle around her ears. My body is protecting hers, curved over her like a cage of arms and legs, and crooked spine. My senses are tumbling, my body breaking, sweating, and transforming. But I can hear the call of humans, the people behind the wall. They are calling to us, yelling at us to get up.

"You need to run," I whisper, the truck rocking sideways as the monsters scramble to get to us. We are blissfully trapped in our little bubble of life and death, and I know that this moment is our last, but it can't stay this way, we both know that. Goodbyes have come and gone, the rest is all irrelevant now.

She lifts her arm, proudly showing me the flashlight still firmly in her grip, showing me what a good girl she was for finding it among the carnage. "Are they good people?" she asks, fear lacing her words, her brown eyes glinting up at me. The truck rocks and rocks, the scratching of nails on metal, of monsters screams, of hunger and anger and the promise of pain to come…

"I think so," I say, but I can only hope and pray that they are. Pray that they are not all like Sarah. Sarah, who abandoned my Lilly by the side of the road but left me with a map to this place.

I cry out loudly as the poison burns away at my blood, absorbing itself into my body, and I feel myself lose my grip on this life. The world immediately goes silent outside the truck—in the other world that we didn't want to explore—barring the rain and the thunder and the cry of men in the distance. The monsters have stopped attacking us, as if waiting for something to happen. Brighter and brighter the red glows inside of me, the rich black poison pouring through every one of my diseased organs and suffocating them. "You need to go now, Lilly," I whisper, my throat constricting, my voice breaking into something else. A voice so deep, that it can't ever be truly mine. "I need you to go."

She blinks once, twice, staring up at me innocently, and then she nods firmly, because she knows it to be true. Because I would never send her away if I had a choice. She reaches up and places a kiss against my lips, and when my tears fall, dripping onto her cheeks, they are black, stained with the poison that is killing me.

"I love you, Mama," she whispers. "I'll see you soon."

"I love you too, Honeybee." But I can't say anything else because it hurts too much, and I don't want to see her soon. That's the worst thing that could ever happen. Because I want her to live. I want her to be free. I want her to be safe, in the bright lights of life.

I scoop her up, ignoring the fact that my limbs feel longer and that my nails are able to cut away at the metal of the door. My fingers are hooked and bony, and my feet have torn right through my old boots. I stretch out of the hole I have made in the side of the truck, holding Lilly's fragile body in my arms, protecting her from the sharp slivers of metal and glass. The monsters hiss and snap at me, and I hiss and snap right back, warning them to get away. I stride forward, the monsters always a single step behind me. They are confused, unsure of what is happening. I smell like them, I look like them, but I'm acting like a human. They stay back, wariness keeping them a step behind.

Their growls become more incessant, louder and louder the further toward the light I walk, away from the softened black that I yearn for. I look down at Lilly. My breathing hurts, my chest is burning as if it is on fire, and I set Lilly down on unsteady feet and shaky legs. A single trail of blood runs from the crown of her head to her jaw and I wipe a crippled finger along it, hungry. So, so hungry.

I press the flashlight to her chest and push her forward. She stumbles and then takes a single step away, and the monsters behind me scream in fury. With those screams my own words break free, and I turn and bare my sharpened teeth at the monsters that try to follow her. They back up a step, unsure. I am one of them, but not. I am their brethren, but not. They don't know, they don't understand. I see the monster with the pearl necklace. She cocks her head to one side, snarling at me, confused, unsure, angered that this is happening.

I look back to Lilly, seeing her steps uncertain, scared, sad…

I blink, feeling the rage inside of me burning my body up, my hands needing to tear and destroy. My breathing is ragged and I am drowning, choking on phlegm and hate, bile and death. My skull is moving, bones altering, and the feeling is agonizing. Lilly stands still, a steady stream of pee trickling down her legs as she watches me, her mother, disappear before her very eyes.

"Run, Lilly," I whisper with a snarl, hating myself.

She still stares, unsure, confused, frightened for me and for her.

Are they good people? She asked.

I hope so, I replied.

"Run!" I scream, as blinding pain ignites behind my eyes.

She turns, her flashlight flicking on, and the bodies behind me converge, surging forwards in a stampede. She is still in the shadows, trapped between the light and the dark. She isn't moving quick enough, she won't make it…

"Run, run into the light, Lilly!" I scream and beg and plead until the monsters charge me, my new brethren sending me into the ground.

Clawed feet and hands hack at my back, scraping my skin away from my bones, and I watch her, my Honeybee, running for her precious life. Her little feet pounding the earth. Running toward the light that can save her. People are yelling from the tops of the towers and walls, shining their lights toward her, willing their illumination to grow brighter, to shine further into the darkness.

"Run!" I scream in pain and agony that has more to do with my fear for her not making it than anything else. "Run!"

And then the cold blackness envelops me, sucking me under as it wraps me in its warm embrace and sets me free, even as I fight against the freedom it so willingly gives. I go toward that darkness kicking and screaming, fighting with every instinct that I have. Fighting them, fighting it, fighting death, and the life that it wants to take from me. Fighting for the soul it is sucking from my fragile, death-riddled body.

I fought for Lilly, and for me, and for us. Because I was hers, and she was mine, and it would be that way until it was not. It had been that way since I had found her, hiding between the flowers in that bright sunflower field.

I would protect her, I would always protect her, until I could not.

I would be with her, always, until I could not.

And I would love her forever, even when I was not.

I am lost.

I am alone.

But I have loved.

Epilogue.

Lilly.

The time of monsters was over. That's what they said to me.

The man with the green uniform carries me into a white room, with tiles on the floor and a table in the center. It smells funny in here and I wrinkle my nose at the smell. His voice echoes around the room even when he whispers.

"The time of monsters is over," he says again. "You're safe now."

I think he is nervous because he keeps looking at me and his eyes are wide. When they opened the big door outside, everyone stared at me. Mama used to say that there were no more children left in the world—that I was probably the only one left—and I think she was right, because they look at me like I am special. Like I am the only one.

He keeps repeating that. Saying it over and over again. *You're safe now. They can't hurt you here.* But I was a monster. We were all monsters—that's what Mama had said. It was inside of us all. It was inside of me, I could feel it. It made me feel strange. And it had taken mama away from me. I watched it change her. I watched her fear as she left me alone in the dark.

"I need you to drink this," he says, placing a small cup on the table between us. His voice is soft, kind. I think he's a good one, not bad like the rest. I want to trust him, but I'm scared.

"When you've drunk this, my friend is going to help you wash." He smiles, and I think his smile looks strange.

I swallow. My throat is sore from crying. I want to swallow whatever is in the small cup because I am thirsty and it might stop it from hurting. I reach for the cup, still watching the man across the table. He smiles again, but this time his smile makes my tummy tickle.

"I washed today," I say. But then I remember I peed myself and I would smell now. So I look down at the small cup again, feeling embarrassed.

"I need you to drink that, sweetheart. Then we can get you all cleaned up. You don't need to worry now, you're safe here."

I don't understand why he keeps saying that. It makes no sense to me. I pick up the cup and look at its contents. The drink is orange. It looks like pee. I feel bad again, so I swallow all of the drink, even though it tastes funny, so that I can wash and not feel sad because I peed myself. I'm a big girl now. Mama told me so.

I cry when I think of her. She saved me. She got me somewhere safe. But she couldn't come with me, because the poison got her. I will be like her soon, and that scares me. Because it looked like it really hurt her, and I don't want it to hurt me. I could see the pain in her pretty eyes that turned red, and in her lips that made a funny shape. Her pretty mouth that always made me smile. Her face had lots of lines on it, her eyebrows meeting in between her eyes. Those things all told me that it hurt her a lot, that it must have been the most painful thing ever to change.

A door opens and a lady and a man come in. They both have long white coats on. Everything here is very clean. Mama would have liked it a lot. She liked me to be clean, and to make my hair untangled. She said she would get me clean socks soon.

"Hello." The lady kneels next to me, and I look at her. She is pretty like mama was. Her face is clean and her hair goes all the way to her shoulders. I like it. "My name is Doctor Marie Stentson. You can call me Marie if you want. I'd like to put this around your arm and check your blood pressure, if that's okay. It won't hurt, I promise."

She asks me, and her voice is soft like Mama's used to be, so I nod okay and hold out my arm, watching as she wraps the thingy around it. She pumps something and the thingy goes tight, and then the room is silent while she concentrates. I look at the other people. They all smile when I look at them, but they seem very sad. Marie looks back up to me, and unwraps the thingy from my arm.

"That's very good, we still have time." She smiles, and looks at the man that came in with her. She nods to him, and I get scared and start to cry again. "No, no, no, don't cry. Hush, darling. Everything is going to be okay now." She leans up and wraps her arms around me, but I feel even sadder because she isn't

Mama. She's just a lady I don't know, and her hugs don't feel as warm as Mama's did. "What's your name?" she hums against my ear.

"Lilly," I whisper back.

"Do you miss your mother?" she asks me, and I nod. "I'm sorry that she didn't make it. But she would want you to get better. She would want you to trust me."

I pull out of her arms and look into her face. She seems nice so I decide to be truthful. "I'm scared."

She nods like she understands and her hair moves around her shoulders. It looks soft and I want to touch it, but I don't because I don't really know her.

"Don't be scared. You're going to be okay now. They can't get in here." Her voice is still soft and it makes me feel sleepy.

"Mama won't let them," I whisper, feeling angry.

"No, she won't." She smiles. "What was her name?"

I don't need to think about this. "I don't know," I whisper back. "She never told me."

Marie's face looks funny. Her eyebrows pull in like Mama's used to when she was worried, so I tell her some more things and hope that she understands.

"She found me in the bright place and kept me safe."

"She found you?" The lady's eyebrows scrunch up even more and she doesn't look as pretty, but I don't tell her that because it would be rude to. "She wasn't your real mother?"

I shake my head no. She wasn't my real mama, but she was because I can't really remember my real mama anymore. I just remember that my first mama made me really frightened and looked like she wanted to hurt me, so I ran away from her before Daddy came home from work, and then I couldn't find my way back. Then the world went dark, and I was scared and alone. Until my new mama found me. But I didn't know her name. Perhaps I should have asked. I worry about that and think I must be very bad not to know her name, and then I start to cry some more.

The lady hugs me again, but I don't stop crying for a long time. I feel tired and I yawn through my tears.

"I need to give you an injection and then we're going to wash you." The lady says. Her mouth smiles but it doesn't reach her eyes because she still looks sad. It makes me feel angry again. I don't want to wash. I want my mama and I want her arms and her smell and her kiss and her touch, and I want to sleep. And I want a tomato. I cry when the lady gives me an injection anyway. I cry because it hurts when she does it, and it hurts me all over afterwards like I am on fire, and I cry because she did it when I wasn't ready. And that's not fair; she should have waited until I was ready.

"I wasn't ready," I say and cry some more.

"We never are, Lilly," she says. But I don't know what she means. "It's okay. You can go to sleep soon, and when you wake up, you'll feel better." She stands back up and straightens her skirt. She holds out her hand to me and I take it, following her, feeling sad and tired and itchy all over. But my eyes don't hurt anymore and everything looks better than it did before everything started to turn pink.

My body feels strange. I don't like it. I want to go to sleep but they won't let me yet; they keep saying I have to wash. So I follow the lady and she helps me take off my clothes and she looks at my body and bites on her bottom lip like she is worried, and then she washes me with soap that smells funny and makes my skin sting. I cry again, and then I get angry because I don't want to cry anymore. I want to be brave.

After I am washed and I smell nice again, she wraps a big orange towel around me and makes me dry. I like the towel because it is soft and bright and makes me think of the yellowy orange flowers that me and Mama picked and ate. I like thinking about Mama, but it makes me sad because I miss her. The lady—Marie—helps me into some clean clothes, a long T-shirt that goes to my knees and some shorts, which she has to tie at the waist to stop them from falling down. I like the smell of these clothes. The lady gives me clean socks, and I think they are new. And even though I am tired and sad, new socks feel nice on my feet and I wriggle my toes and want to smile, but I don't—because even though I am clean and I have nice new socks, I still miss my mama and I wish she was here with me.

The lady takes my hand and walks with me to a small room. In it is a bed with pillows and a cover, and there's a small brown teddy bear on the pillow. It's not my teddy bear, not Mr. Bear or the one that smelled funny. But I don't mind too much because it has two matching eyes and is soft and white. She helps me into the bed and pulls the covers around me.

"You're going to be okay now, Lilly. Everything is going to be okay now," she says. And I believe her. I blink and then I start to feel sleepy, and she strokes my hair like Mama used to. "It's going to be okay. You're safe now. The time of monsters is over."

I close my eyes, listening to the distant sound of my mama's screams in the air, and I feel safe and sleepy.

"Goodnight, Lilly."

Into the Light

Book 2

Coming winter 2016

ABOUT THE AUTHOR

Claire C. Riley is a *USA Today* and International bestselling author. She is also a bestselling British horror writer and an Amazon top 100 bestseller.

Her work is best described as the modernization of classic, old-school horror. She fuses multi-genre elements to develop storylines that pay homage to cult classics while still feeling fresh and cutting edge. She writes characters that are realistic, and kills them without mercy. Claire lives in the United Kingdom with her husband, three daughters, and one scruffy dog.

AUTHOR OF:
ODIUM THE DEAD SAGA SERIES
ODIUM ORIGINS SERIES
LIMERENCE (THE OBSESSION SERIES)
THICKER THAN BLOOD SERIES
TWISTED MAGIC (RAVEN'S COVE SERIES)
SHUT UP & KISS ME,

CONTACT LINKS:

WWW.CLAIRECRILEY.COM
WWW.FACEBOOK.COM/CLAIRECRILEYAUTHOR
HTTP://AMZN.TO/1GDPF3I

'She writes characters that are realistic and then kills them without mercy' – Eli Constant author of Z-Children, Dead Trees, Mastic and much more.

Acknowledgments.

Huge thank you goes to A. Meredith Walters, Jessica Austin Gudmundson, Shelly Cave and my agent Michelle Johnson. Thank you for believing in me and this story.

Thanks goes to Eli Constant for not only the beautiful cover but your constant encouragement. To Amy Jackson for your editing and also your friendship.

But most importantly, to my children, who without having you in my life, I would never know the true depths of a mothers love. Being a mother is the bravest thing I have ever done.